Copyright © 2022 by Jesse D'Angelo

Edited by Mason Hargis

Cover art and design by Jesse D'Angelo

Additional graphic design by Jan Bratslavsky

All rights reserved.

No part of this book may be reproduced in any form or by any electronic or mechanical means, including information storage and retrieval systems, without written permission from the author, except for the use of brief quotations in a book review.

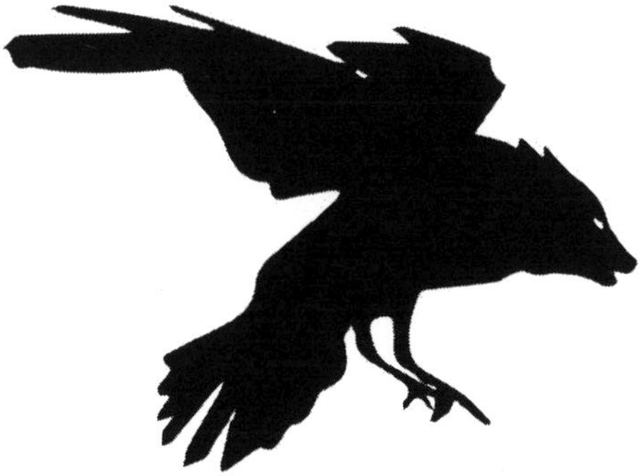

JESSE D'ANGELO
COMPOSITE

SPECIAL THANKS

Jordan Lummis
Lyndsey Smith
Rodney Brown
Aaron Davids
Joseph Garland
And my lovely wife, Lauren
For putting up with me
You rock

For Ann Howard.
You were always so good to us.
May your spirit live on, happy and free

CONTENTS

1. Everett Falls — 1
2. Stella — 9
3. Clarkson's — 17
4. A Simple Sketch — 25
5. The Volunteer — 31
6. Small Town Girl — 41
7. Crosshatching — 49
8. The Watcher — 55
9. The Deep End — 65
10. Composite — 73
11. Breaking News — 81
12. Gravity — 89
13. The Basher — 95
14. The Bald Man — 103
15. Gut Feeling — 109
16. Giving Thanks — 115
17. Database — 121
18. Not My Scumbag — 127
19. That's What People Do — 133
20. Stakeout — 139
21. Closing Time — 145
22. Show And Tell — 151
23. Lake Everett — 157
24. Space Man — 165
25. Red Christmas — 169
26. Jimbo — 177
27. Pursuit — 185
28. Pizza Dough — 191
29. Breaking And Entering — 197

30. Lair	205
31. Not a match	215
32. Draft	223
33. The Collector	233
34. Smash And Destroy	243
35. Fight For Your Life	251
36. Cliffhanger	261
37. Violator	273
38. Fall	285
Also by Jesse D'Angelo	291
About the Author	293

CHAPTER 1
EVERETT FALLS

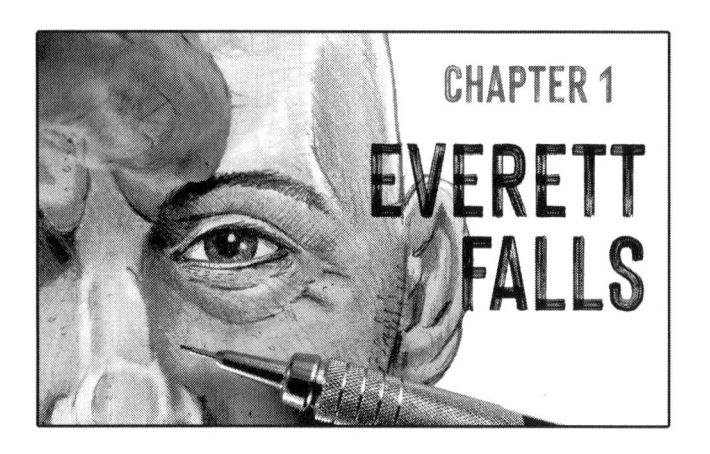

FREDDY LUCCIO WAS HAVING one of those dreams.

The little boy was him, his younger self, he was sure of that. Who the dark figure was, he had no idea. It was a man wearing what appeared to be a long, black slicker, a shadow in the night. The little boy was running, always running. His feet were bare, leaving footprints in the snow. His breath was a white mist swirling in front of him. The man was getting closer. Freddy was terrified.

"Freddy! Freddy!" His mother was out there in the woods too, lost and confused, trying to find him. Her blouse billowed in slow motion. She searched the frozen nightscape, diving into darkness. The dark figure also crunched through the snow. He gripped a hatchet in his gloved hand. Freddy continued to run, death on his heels.

It was always this dream, or a variation of it. Sometimes he was in a basement, sometimes a warehouse. Sometimes his mother wasn't there. But always it was the little boy and the shadow man. It came to him in times of stress, and he didn't know what to make of it. But it had carved a niche into his psyche and he didn't understand why it frightened him so much.

After all, it was only a dream.

FREDDY WOKE up on the Metro North as the train pulled into the station. His face was pressed against the glass, dried spittle on his lips and in his sparse beard. He stretched and ran his fingers through a head of disheveled, chestnut hair. His brown eyes blinked away the nap, looking through the scuffed windows to admire the New York afternoon. The conductor announced through the speakers:

"Next station stop, Everett Falls. Must be in the front four cars to exit Everett Falls. Everett Falls, next stop."

The town looked just as he remembered it. A hazy sky muted the colors and promised a chill September breeze. The courthouse was right where he remembered it. The Post Office, First National Bank, Gino's Pizza, all familiar. The axe throwing place was new, and the parking meters where now all credit card enabled, but it was the same old Everett Falls.

Townspeople ambled to and fro, going to their jobs, to the A&P to pick up their groceries, to drop their kids off at school. Brick and stone construction echoed a bygone era. Freddy sighed, his head full of fog. *Must have coffee.* The train's brakes shreiked as it slowed down.

EMMYLOU HARRIS PLAYED on the radio.

Penny DiGiordano tapped the steering wheel. Her

brown eyes were locked on the train platform. The doors of the train opened and commuters spilled out, buzzing and hustling like busy bees. Penny's eyes ticked over to the rear view mirror to make sure she looked okay. She'd done a good job with the eyebrows today, and she was of the belief that her makeup job made her look forty-five instead of sixty-five. Her hair was straight as linguini strips, and dyed as black as it was in her youth. She smashed out the fifth cigarette in the past fifteen minutes and continued tapping the wheel. Her eyes scanned the crowd.

His gait was unmistakable. There was a confidence in that strut, yet still a meekness. He was five foot six, wiry, and the spitting image of his father at that age. Penny smiled as she watched him descend the stairs. His well-worn jeans and jacket were fitted to his physique. His chiseled Italian features were focused as he struggled under the weight of too many bags. Penny beeped her horn and waved out the window.

"Freddy!"

He smiled as he saw her sitting in the 2016 Toyota Camry. She climbed out of the car to greet him as he shuffled forward. He pulled a large rolling suitcase, had a back-pack, an over-the-shoulder bag, a portable lap-desk, and another small suitcase.

"Hey, Aunt Penny."

"Look at you, beardie," Penny gushed. "C'mere."

She gave him a warm hug and began taking things off his hands.

"Oh, no no, it's okay," Freddy said. "I got it."

"Shh, cut it out." She had already taken the larger

suitcase from him and thrown it in the trunk. He chuckled and started loading up the rest of his things.

"I don't remember it getting this cold here in September. *Man.*"

Penny shot him a sinister grin. "Oh, you ain't in California no more, boy."

THEY DROVE.

Freddy's eyes watched the landscape pass outside the window. They breezed up I-22, through a stretch of road Freddy remembered very well. The interstate was flanked on either side by the dynamite-blasted rock faces of a hollowed-out mountain, stretching over one hundred feet high. He remembered admiring those vertical granite walls, the surrounding woods, the leaves in the fall, everything. It was a beautiful place to live. But still, there was pain in his eyes, guilt.

"Thanks for doing this, Aunt Penny," Freddy said, nearly as a whisper. He looked down at his feet like a man defeated.

"It's hard trying to make a living as an artist, kiddo. Always has been."

"I just hate to impose, y'know?"

"Oh, please."

"It's just... I was doing so well there for a while. Y'know? It's like... I was making good money, doing boards for movies, music videos, living on my own. And then it was like, I had no choice. I had to move back home with my parents. But then we were just at each other's throats... It was just not a good situation."

"It sounded pretty bad that last time I talked to you on the phone," she said. "Even last time I came to see you guys in LA for Christmas, I could sense the strain. You can't live like that, Freddy. You need a fresh start. And you're welcome to stay with me as long as you need to, okay?"

Freddy smiled, trying not to laugh. Her thick New York accent always amused him. When she said "as long as you need to," it sounded like "as *lawng* as ya need ta."

"You're the best, Aunt Penny. Thanks."

"Believe me, it's my pleasure. I've been all alone here since Bill died five years ago. I'm happy to have the company."

"Thanks."

"Now, whadda you say we go get some coffee? Huh? Get some groceries before we head back to the house?" Freddy chuckled at her accent. *Cawfey.*

"Yeah," he said. "Coffee sounds great."

THE FOG WAS CLEARING. The caffeine had done its job. Freddy pushed the shopping cart down the snack aisle at A&P as Aunt Penny excitedly tossed in goodies. The fluorescent lights brought everything into stark focus. Reality had set in. This was it. Freddy was really there, back in New York. The air felt different. People looked strange. Everything had a different texture, smell, feeling.

No more sunset strolls down the Venice boardwalk. No more hanging out with the guys in North Hollywood on Saturday nights. No more breakfast burritos at

Chuy's, hot dogs at Pink's, rides down the Pacific Coast Highway. No more working on movies and TV shows, hanging out with actors, seeing his name up on a screen, living like a big shot. The dream was dead. He had failed. Freddy swallowed hard.

"Oh yeah, baby. Tostitos." Penny happily snatched a family-size bag of chips from the shelf and tossed it into the cart. "Get whatever you want, please."

"Cool," Freddy said politely.

"You okay?"

"Yeah, sure. It's just been a long day. Long flight. Hell, this whole past month, forget about it."

"Freddy, you're back in New York now. We say *fuggetaboutit*. You got that?"

He laughed. "Eyyy, fuggetaboutit!"

"That's better. You're a New York Italian, remember that. God, how long's it been since you been back here?"

"Well, I've been back to New York a few times, but Everett Falls? Haven't been back here in, what, twenty years?" Freddy shook his head as he pushed the cart forward.

"Wow... So you say you think your agents can still get you work out here, right?"

"Well, that's what they say. Said there's plenty of storyboarding work in the city. But it's impossible to say for sure. That's the problem with this business. They get me a job for a couple days, then I don't hear anything from them for months. It's just like, so all over the place, you know? I need to find something else to do, 'cause this shit's getting old."

Freddy stopped to pick a box of extra-butter popcorn

off the shelf. He held it up to Penny as if asking if he could get it. She gestured for him to toss it in.

"Yeah yeah yeah, go ahead. Anything you want," she smiled and pulled playfully at his sleeve. "Gotta get some dog food too. Stella is just so excited to meet you."

Freddy swallowed hard. *Dogs.*

"Cool," he managed to politely spit out.

"Maybe pick up some razors while we're here?"

"What, you don't like my beard?"

"Mmmm, might take some getting used to. You look like you're the singer in a grunge band." She laughed, leading them around fellow shoppers and into the meat aisle.

"Yeah, laugh it up," he said. This made her laugh more.

"Ah, you'll be all right, kiddo. You're a smart, talented young guy. We'll get you back up on your feet. Just get some little shit job around town for now, start saving money. Like I said on the phone, you can use Bill's Volvo to drive around, long as you put gas in it. It's just sitting in the garage collecting dust."

"You really are spoiling me, Aunt Penny."

"Damn right. Gotta spoil somebody, and you, young man, are my guinea pig..." Penny's eyes went wide, drawn in by the lush red morsels sealed in plastic wrap. "Ooh, steaks! How 'bout some steaks? I'm gonna get some steaks."

Penny excitedly scooped up a package of tender meat, and Freddy couldn't help but smile. Her energy was infectious.

CHAPTER 2
STELLA

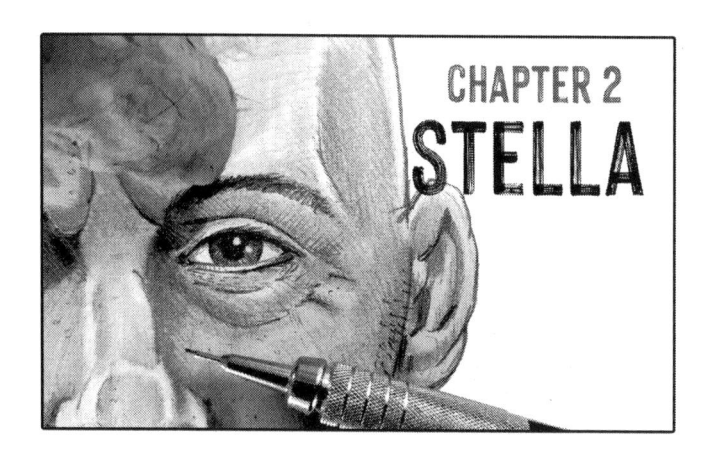

HE DIDN'T REMEMBER the house. Maybe it was the fresh coat of eggshell paint and the slate-gray trim. The lawn was expansive and could use a good mowing, and the rose bushes out front had begun to wither in the chill fall air. It was a modest two-story home, flanked by trees and bushes, the neighbors a good distance away. A two-car garage attached to the main house and a chain-link fence bordered the property. Down the street, a school bus dropped off two kids. Up the street, an elderly couple in matching track suits walked their Lhasa Apso. In the sky, birds. On the ground, ants.

Freddy put on a brave face as Penny eased the Toyota into the driveway. It was a warm and welcoming home on a picturesque street. Or was it a life sentence at a state penitentiary? Either way, there was no turning back now. He was out of money, out of options, his feet were sore, and he desperately needed a shower. This was it, the end of the line. Freddy sighed.

Penny hopped out of the car with a wide grin on her

face. Freddy could already hear the yapping of a small dog coming from within the house. His heart sank.

"That's my baby," Penny said, grabbing two bags of groceries from the back seat. "Come on, kiddo. Let's boogie."

"Okay..." Freddy whispered to himself and climbed out of the car.

Penny unlocked the front door and swung it open, her eyes lighting up with joy as they were greeted by what Freddy could only describe as a ball of lint with legs. Stella was a tiny little thing, of no discernible breed, with scruffy corn-husk hair that hung over her eyes. She wiggled and quivered and wagged her little tail, yipping and yapping excitedly as she scurried over to greet Penny.

"There she is! There's my girl! Hi, baby!"

Penny put her bags of groceries down and squatted down to pet the little ball of nervous energy. The high-pitched vocalizations of the tiny beast instantly reminded Freddy of a novice violinist making his instrument shriek. Freddy winced and forced a smile. Penny picked up the dog, who immediately began licking her face, and turned to Freddy with an earnest grin.

"Stella, this is Freddy. Say hi! Say hi!"

The dog yipped and yapped, the intense frequency slicing deep into Freddy's brain. He politely reached to pet the creature's head. She reacted with a tremble, guttural growling, and more yips and yaps.

"Hi, Stella," Freddy said in his best baby-talk voice.

"Awww, she likes you," Penny said.

Yip! Yip! Rrrrrrr! Yipyipyip!

Freddy made a conscious effort to not cringe.

"She seems scared," Freddy said.

"Oh, she's just excited is all. She'll get used to you. Come on, let's bring in the rest of the stuff." Penny put the dog down and scooted back outside. Freddy took a quick look around the foyer. It was warm, quaint, inviting. The diminutive canine buzzed and grumbled by his feet. *Fucking dogs.*

"God help me," Freddy muttered, and went outside to help.

DINNER WAS DELICIOUS. Penny had hit a home run with her 'famous lasagna.' Freddy finished the last stray morsels, even the string beans, reclining back into the couch's cushions, ready for a coma. Penny was curled up on her side of the couch with Stella in her lap and her third Stella Artois in her hand. She reached for the remote and switched on the news, waiting for the weather forecast.

The cozy home had been cleaned for Freddy's arrival, but there was hardly a square inch unoccupied. The wallpaper was an old floral pattern. There was barely any counter space, as every table and piece of furniture was adorned with framed family photos, collectible porcelain trinkets, pens and pencils, a jar of loose change, a bowl full of marbles, a bowl full of functionless balls of twine. Family photos continued up onto the walls, along with old art and the occasional curling at the edges of the ancient wallpaper. The carpet was older than Freddy. Fortunately, the TV was new.

Freddy grumbled in satisfaction and sipped at his

own beer. The sun had set. The neighborhood kids had stopped screaming. Everything in the world was warm, soft, fuzzy, and good. Everything except the news, of course. The news was there to remind you to lock your doors, learn martial arts, buy a gun, have regular doctor visits, and always tell your loved-ones that you love them, because you never know.

"Authorities in Maple Crest still have no leads in the investigation into the disappearance of twelve year-old Maurice Washington, who went missing last Tuesday," the anchorwoman reported. A posed school photo of the young boy appeared on the screen beside the anchor, which then dissolved into a recent candid photo of the child playing in a park. His eyes twinkled, his smile beamed, he was full of life. The next shot was a press conference at the family's home, with the bleary-eyed parents answering questions fired at them by hungry reporters.

Penny shook her head in disgust and muted the TV.

"What is wrong with this world?" Penny grunted as she peeled herself off the couch and placed Stella on the floor. "Never anything but bad news." She touched Freddy's shoulder and shuffled around the coffee table, approaching a wall of framed photos. She finished off her bottle of beer as she focused on one photo in particular. It was her, a million years ago, with an impossibly bright smile, arms wrapped around the neck of a handsome young man. Bill. His hair was a typical early 80's shag. His features were round and his eyes kind. They couldn't have looked happier together.

She reached up and touched the framed photo.

"This was Bill's birthday party, 1983. First time I ever met your Grandma Lynn. You never got to meet her, right?"

"No, I didn't."

"She was a character," Penny chuckled. "I got him a brand new camcorder. State of the art. Only weighed about fifty pounds!" She laughed and cleared her throat, trying to fight off the mist in her eyes. "I forget what we had for dinner that night... But it must have been amazing. Lynn was a great cook, if nothing else." She turned back to face Freddy, walking back to the table. "Don't watch the news too long, Freddy. It'll make you forget there's still good in this world."

Freddy nodded. "Where's Maple Crest?"

"It's a few counties over, maybe a forty-five minute drive... Well anyway, I think I'm gonna turn in. It's my bedtime."

"So early?"

"Yeah. Have to wake up at six, get to the high school by eight. Brand new school year. Ugh."

A ringtone sounded from Freddy's phone. It was the famous five-note chime from "Close Encounters of the Third Kind," *do-de-do-do-doo*. He looked at the screen to see —

One new text message: Rick.

Freddy shook his head and put the phone back down.

Penny bent down to start clearing off the table, but Freddy scooted to the edge of the couch, waving at her to stop.

"Oh, no no," he said. "I'll get this stuff."

"You sure?"

"Yeah, yeah. I got it." Freddy stood and crossed around the coffee table, giving his aunt a warm hug. "Thanks for dinner, Aunt Penny. Thanks for everything."

"No problem, kiddo. Love you."

"Love you too."

"Don't stay up too late."

"Okay," Freddy chuckled as she pulled away, heading for the staircase.

"Goodnight, Freddy."

"Night."

"Come on, Stell," she called to the dog, "let's go."

Penny ascended the stairs with a yawn and a stretch, Stella scurrying to join her. Freddy stood alone in the living room. He sighed, then remembered his phone. He scooped the device from the couch and checked the message from his friend Rick.

Traitor, it read.

Freddy laughed and typed his reply, *Suck a dick.*

IT DIDN'T TAKE him long to put away his things. His clothes fit into two drawers in the dresser of his new room, with his one light jacket and button-up nice shirt hanging in the closet. It was a small guest room, clean and sparsely decorated. A single-size bed, dresser, small desk and chair were the only furniture. A window looked out at the neighbor's house. Penny had left a few magazines on the counter that he would never read.

He took out the travel-size light box from his suitcase, along with his sketch pads, pencils, and other art supplies. He had a few adult DVD's stowed away that he'd probably never have the time or privacy to watch. He paced a little, looked around, paced some more. Good time for a shower. Freddy grabbed his bag of toiletries and a towel and headed to the bathroom.

The water was hot and the pressure strong. He came back to his room clean and refreshed. He changed into his sweats and a t-shirt. Sat on the bed. Looked around. Tapped his feet. *May as well try to do some drawing.* He scooped up his sketch pad and favorite Draft/Matic mechanical pencil, and snuck downstairs.

He turned on the TV and lowered the volume. Leaving his pad and pencil on the coffee table, he went to the kitchen seeking out the liquor cabinet. There were a lot of options, and he went with the Grey Goose. He searched the cupboards until he found the right glass, then went about preparing his favorite drink. One can of Lacroix lemon seltzer. Splash of cranberry. Splash of vodka. Two ice cubes. Freddy drank in the cool beverage, feeling that nice burn running down his throat. *Oh, yeah.*

He plopped onto the soft couch, comfortable but still alien, and began flipping through the channels. There was a bad Sci-Fi movie on, professional golf, political debates. Freddy took a sip of his drink and continued scanning for something to watch. He stopped on a true crime documentary. The show was just starting, and a gravel-throated, overly melodramatic voice-over artist began his narration.

"In the spring of 1982, Carolyn Mason, registered nurse and mother of two, mysteriously vanished from her home in Tulsa, Oklahoma," he growled. Freddy leaned forward. *"Although there were no witnesses and no signs*

of forced entry, authorities believed she had met with foul play..." Stylized images flashed across the screen. Photos of the victim, reenactments of the crime, all cut to a catchy musical score. *"But with no body and no evidence, the case remained cold for over fifteen years, until the day forensic science would catch up... WITH A KILLER!"*

The flashy animated logo of the show swooped and flickered onto the screen: *"Forensic Justice."* Freddy grunted and rested back into the couch, intrigued. He took another sip of his drink, then put it down. He opened up his sketch pad to the first blank page and got his pencil ready as the show began. His hand hovered over the paper. He could draw anything he wanted. Super-heroes, monsters, still-life portraits, cars, nature landscapes, Freddy could do it all.

His pencil did not move.

He looked down at the blank page and saw only emptiness. He sighed and put the pencil down. *Why even bother? I'm not an artist anymore. I'm a failure.* He took a big gulp of his drink and continued watching the show. Detectives and forensic technicians were interviewed, chilling crime scene photos shown, ominous music played. Freddy sunk deeper into the couch and let it all wash over him.

CHAPTER 3
CLARKSON'S

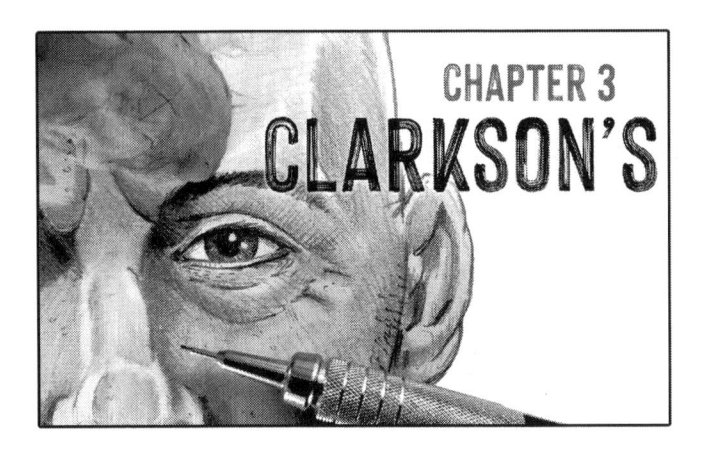

FREDDY'S EYES cracked open to peek through the haze. Morning light streamed into the bedroom. The blanket was warm and the bed cozy. *So comfortable. Maybe I'll just stay in bed all day.* He shifted to lay on his side, his toes poking out from under the sheets. Laying still, he tried to fall back asleep, but his bladder had other ideas. Freddy grumbled and finally gave in to the urge, tossing his blankets aside and swinging his feet off the edge of the bed.

After relieving himself and brushing his teeth, he slumped his way downstairs. His unkempt hair was like a bizarre modern art sculpture and crust was in his eyes. He scanned the empty house. All was quiet and still. He shuffled into the living room. Quiet and still. He went to the foyer, peeking out the front window. Quiet and still. His eye detected movement in the den, so he moseyed in to investigate.

Stella was in her doggie bed, gnawing on her favorite chew toy. She froze as she noticed Freddy standing over her. A low growl rumbled from her throat.

"Morning, Stella."

The little mutt continued to grumble, her body tense as if preparing to bolt. Freddy chuckled and shook his head as he turned back to the kitchen. *Must have coffee.* He scratched his balls and went about the task of preparing the hot elixir. He loaded up the machine with fresh grounds and water, then turned it on. The coffeemaker sputtered to life, steaming and hissing as the water heated and filtered through the grounds. Freddy paced and swung his arms, bored.

On the kitchen table, Aunt Penny had left something for him. It was the local morning newspaper, opened up to the classified section. Freddy looked down at the help wanted ads, shaking his head. He sighed and chose a mug from the cabinet, as well as sugar and creamer from the fridge. The coffee percolated as it filled the pot. Freddy poured himself a cup, loving the sound of that hot flowing liquid. He added in some sugar, then some creamer, stirred, then took a sip.

Ohhhh, yeah. Coffee good.

With every sip, Freddy came to life. He sat down, looking at the classified section presented before him. *Fuck.* He took a sip of coffee, sighed, then picked up the paper, diving in to see what career opportunities were waiting for him out there in the bustling metropolis of Everett Falls.

"I HOPE twelve-fifty is okay to start?" David Nelson asked as he led Freddy on a tour of Clarkson's Pharmacy. The ex-college football star was now a collection of old injuries and pains, stitched together into the shape of a man. His chest had shrunk and his belly had grown, and a bald spot was taking over real estate on the back of his head. His once rich ebony skin was now chalky and dry. Eyes that once burned with passion now drooped, and the basic mustache came standard on this model. His dreams had shattered long ago, their remnants blowing away like dead leaves.

Freddy nodded. "Yeah, that's fine, I guess."

"Good," David continued. "You do well after two months, you get a fifty cent raise. Then another fifty cent raise after six months." David gestured left and right as he led Freddy down aisle one. "So here we have all our dairy products, obviously. Your milks, your cheeses, yogurts, stuff like that. Up at the end you got your eggs and whatnot." The lumbering sales manager led Freddy around the next corner, continuing to show off the grandeur of the quaint shop.

It was the typical American Pharmacy/all the crap you could ever need store. Neglected, understaffed and overstocked, Clarkson's trailed right behind CVS and Rite Aid in the ranks of corporate pharmacy chains. Florescent lights cast the space in a uniform, sickly sheen. The same fifty songs played in a loop ad nauseam along with radio promos from sponsors like O'Reilly's Auto Parts and Big Al's Carpets. Elderly patrons waddled along, loading up their carts, and a feeble attempt to cover the stale musk with air freshener was apparent. Freddy held his poker face.

"What we really need right now is someone to work the stock room," David explained, rounding the next corner. "Y'know, organize things in the back, stock the shelves, help customers find what they need... All that good, fun stuff. That sound all right to you?"

Freddy nodded.

"Good. Now, aisle six is where all the feminine hygiene products and adult diapers are. You got your tampons, douches, maxi-pads, and whatnot..."

Freddy nodded again, scrunching his eyebrows to appear more interested. David rambled on, pointing out the delicate intricacies of how toiletries were to be placed on shelves. Freddy struggled with the urge to roll his eyes. He could walk out of there right now. He could keep looking, find another job. Something else, anything else. He looked past David and let another figure come into focus, a young woman crouched at the end of the aisle.

She was like a tall glass of lemonade, a slender blonde, the sun coming through the front windows to accent the outline of her hair. She wore the standard khaki pants and blue polo shirt that were the uniform at Clarkson's, and she dutifully priced boxes of AA batteries with a label gun. Wire frame glasses rested atop a small, pretty nose. Handmade, beaded bracelets and rings decorated her hands. Her ears were not pierced. She glanced over at Freddy as he and David approached, but then quickly looked away.

"...But don't worry about that too much, 'cause we only do that once a month anyway," David finished a long-winded explanation that Freddy hadn't been paying attention to. Freddy nodded as if he understood. "Now, at the end of this aisle here is where we have all the batteries, electronics, phone chargers, and whatnot. Oh, here. Meet Charlotte."

She stood to greet them, her shoulders slouched in a meek and timid posture. Her eyes were a pale, sky-blue behind her glasses, and her mostly perfect skin was marred with the odd pimple here and there. She was the same height as Freddy and slightly younger, and she struggled to make eye contact. She opened her thin lips and a tiny, polite voice came out.

"Hello," she said.

"Hey, how you doing?" Freddy smiled.

"Char, this is Freddy. He's gonna be joining our happy little family. Freddy, you have any questions, you ask Charlotte. She's the assistant manager, knows this store inside and out."

"Cool," Freddy said.

Charlotte blushed, bashfully looking away. David tapped Freddy's shoulder and continued around the next corner. "Now over this way is the breakfast cereal and our little market section," he continued his spiel.

"Nice to meet you," Freddy said, pulling away.

"You too," she replied.

David nodded and smiled at an old lady as he led Freddy past the front check-out area. There were six registers, but only one open. David lazily waved to the high school student stationed there, watching YouTube videos on his phone. "That there behind register one is Brian. Don't work too hard, B." Brian absently waved at the new guy without pulling his eyes away from the video screen. "Over there is Betty stocking the make-up aisle. Hi, Betty."

"Hi," the plump mother of three cheerfully chimed. Freddy smiled.

"There's Kevin in the pharmacy," David continued, pointed out the shaggy-headed kid in the white coat, doling out prescriptions. He and Freddy nodded politely to each other. David pushed through the back doors, leading his new hire into the stock room. "And this is where you'll be spending most of your time. I'm sure you can see now why we need help with it."

"Yyyyyyeah."

Lopsided aluminum shelves were overflowing with products and dust-covered boxes of all shapes and sizes. The piles filled every corner of the cinderblock space, and reached nearly to the cob-webbed rafters and swinging fluorescents. Two trash bins overflowed. Flattened cardboard boxes had been stacked years ago and forgotten, and the musky scent of mildew and garbage hung thick in the air. There were old shipping pallets and hand-trucks, a utility sink and an assortment of brooms, mops, and cleaning supplies. In some spots, there was too much trash and clutter to even walk through. Freddy stood with his mouth agape.

"Anyway, this is where I need your help," David said. "I need you to start organizing and cleaning this back room. Bring whatever you can to the front of the store, stock those shelves, and just... Y'know. Organize. And whatnot."

Freddy nodded.

"Okay, great," David smiled. "I'm gonna go get your Clarkson's shirt and employee name tag. Then we'll fill out the rest of the paperwork, get you set on a schedule, okay?"

"Okay," Freddy said and gave David a close-mouthed smile.

"Great," David said, slapping Freddy's shoulder. "Wait here, I'll be right back."

David strode through the swinging doors before Freddy could say anything else, leaving him standing alone in the clutter. At least it was cool in there, cool and dark. He looked around, shaking his head, resigned to this strange new twist of fate.

"Fuck me..."

CHAPTER 4
A SIMPLE SKETCH

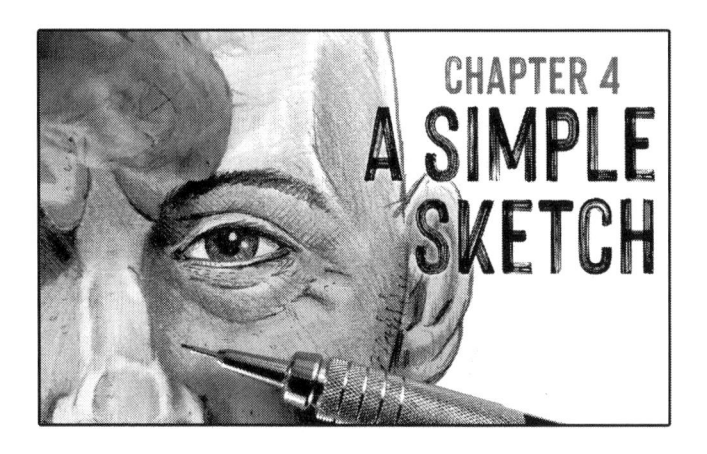

THE ALARM RANG at six a.m. Freddy stumbled out of bed, brushed his teeth, took a shit, and got dressed. He started his Uncle Bill's old Volvo 960 and drove down Interstate 22, past the supermarket and police station, and went to work. Slipping into his Clarkson's shirt and name tag, he clocked in, hauled boxes around, cleaned the store room. Charlotte showed him the ropes, how to stock the shelves, how to set up the daily newspapers, where everything went. She walked with a shuffle, spoke like a mouse, and slouched her shoulders in order to appear as small and invisible as she could.

He drove home, Stella barked at him, he had dinner with Penny, took a shower, took a shit, fixed himself a couple cocktails. He watched TV and ate snacks, sipped his way to a nice buzz, and had his sketch pad and pencil at the ready. But he did not draw. He went to bed late, dreamed about a little boy running from a shadow, then did it all over again.

Wake up at six. Drive to work. Follow Charlotte around. Go home. Eat dinner with Penny. Get drunk.

Watch TV. Go to sleep. Wake up at six. Drive to work. Follow Charlotte around. Go home. Eat dinner with Penny. Get drunk. Watch TV. Go to sleep.

Days became weeks.

Freddy had forgotten how beautiful New York was in October. Leaves were changing colors and falling, floating in the cool wind. There were frequent rainy days, and he soon bought himself a warmer jacket and a pair of waterproof boots. The air was crisp and clean, the people friendly. There was a nice lake he could walk to, put in his ear buds and listen to music. Always alone. He kept his sketch pad close by, even started to draw a couple of times, but never got far. Whatever he tried to draw would be left unfinished, and he'd pour another cocktail.

He felt a stab to his pride every time he looked at his weekly paycheck, trying not to compare it to the money he used to make. The store room was clearing up nicely thanks to him, and he had a special corner hidden between stacks of boxes where he could hide and sneak a break. Social media was just a touch away on his phone, and he would absently scroll through the faces and stories as he sipped at his Snapple in his favorite hiding spot. Close friends, family and strangers alike. All distant shadows. Nobody had a voice, nor a hug or handshake. They were just faces on a screen now, posting vapid memes and selfies and photos of themselves at upscale cafes.

Freddy saw Charlotte working around the store, helping customers, operating the cash register. *Little cutie must be ninety pounds soaking wet,* he thought. He could easily scoop her up and carry her around, or she could jump on his back for an old-fashioned piggyback ride. She was thin and delicate, but also soft and warm, he imagined. Sweet and shy and timid, an innocent, church-going little goodie-two-shoes. A good girl, not what he was used to at all.

Freddy sighed and went back to his work.

THE SKETCH PAD and mechanical pencil sat on the coffee table, untouched. Freddy shoveled a few Tostitos into his mouth and washed it down with a gulp of vodka-cran spritzer. It was night. He was nestled into his favorite corner on the couch, wearing the same unwashed pajama pants and shirt he'd worn the past week. It was ten o'clock, which meant it was time for a two-episode marathon of his favorite new show on Court TV.

"Julia Watkins had been shot three times in the chest, and was not expected to survive the night," the throaty narrator began his introduction. News footage flashed across the screen. Police investigating, inconsolable family members at the crime scene, a young woman rushed into the hospital on a gurney.

"I couldn't believe it, just couldn't believe it," the victim's mother said in an interview, her eyes full of tears. *"There she was on life support. My little girl... And I just... I... I went in and held her hand... And I had to say goodbye."*

Freddy couldn't help but get misty-eyed as he watched the tears of the grieving mother. More images cut together on screen to the beat of an ominous electronic score. A funeral procession, security footage of a man fleeing the scene of the crime, forensic scientists in a lab examining hair fibers under a microscope.

"Julia Watkins died later that night," the narrator said. *"The fifth in a string of brutal murders. She was buried in Park View Cemetery on August fifth, 1991."*

The next interview snippet shown was a detective, a heavy-set man in his sixties with an awkward bowl haircut and a lopsided mustache. *"By this point, frustration had really begun to set in,"* he said. *"We had five murders with no conclusive evidence and no suspect. The first real break we got was when one of Julia Watkins' neighbors came forward and said she saw a strange man running out of Julia's house that night."*

The narrator continued, *"The witness sat down with a police artist to create a composite sketch of the man she saw that night."*

Freddy leaned forward, intrigued as he watched a reenactment of the scene. An older woman described the man she saw as a police officer with a sketch pad did his best to draw the portrait. Freddy scratched the scruff he called a beard as he watched the sketch come together.

"Finally, the elusive killer had been given a face, and the police had their first break." The screen dissolved to reveal the finished drawing. It appeared to be a young black male with dreadlocks and eyeglasses, but the quality of the art was questionable at best. It was amateurish, with no regard for facial symmetry, lighting or perspective. The face looked flat rather than three dimensional. There were no highlights, no shadows, no personality or life to the face. Freddy scoffed. *"Now, a*

simple sketch heats up the hunt for a killer... On Forensic Justice!"

The show's logo swooped and flashed onto the screen as the electronic music reached its crescendo. Freddy let out a sigh. He reclined into the couch to watch the show, but now something else was calling to him. It was an old friend, one he hadn't seen in a long time. He looked over at his sketch pad, finally picking it up. He held it in his lap, debating as he stroked the cover. *Fuck it.*

Freddy opened the pad to the first blank page and began to draw.

THE SHADOW WALKED THE STREETS.

He was there in Everett Falls. Looking in shop windows, nodding at passersby. If he kept his mouth shut, he could pass for human. Nobody noticed. He loved that. This was his party. A hulking black blot in the night, he strolled across the street, free as the wind. He took in all the sights and sounds and smells of the quaint hamlet.

The Shadow laughed to himself and thought,

You people have no idea what you're in for.

CHAPTER 5
THE VOLUNTEER

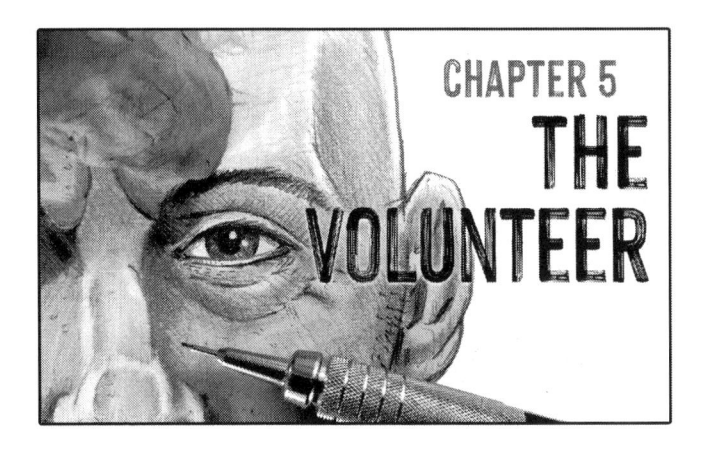

THIS MORNING WAS DIFFERENT. It was a Monday, one of his two days off from work, along with Sunday. Freddy stood at the mirror holding a BIC razor, hot water running into the sink. It had been a long time since he'd been clean shaven. He splashed water on his face and went to work, sliding the razor across his signature scruff. No shaving cream, hot water would do. The years peeled away, and when he finished he looked twenty instead of twenty-eight. He then took a comb to his usually tussled hair and did his best to look presentable.

He took a step back to admire his handiwork. His skinny physique could use some improvement, but that would require a bit more than a few minutes in the bathroom. Freddy sighed and shook his head, laughing at himself. *What the hell am I doing?*

Clothes came next. He slipped into his favorite jeans and sneakers, then buttoned up his one good shirt which he hadn't worn since he'd moved here. Keys, wallet, shades, cell phone—check. There was one last thing to grab before leaving the house. He pulled a black bound portfolio from his bag and flipped it open. The plastic sleeves protected a collection of Freddy's best art.

He flipped through the pages, a smile threatening to split across his face. The art was mostly commercial pieces: storyboards from movies and TV shows he'd worked on, video game character designs, comic book splash pages, and of course a healthy selection of monsters. There were, however, three very nice portraits, two in soft pencil, one in bold strokes of pen and ink. These would best suit his purpose for the mission ahead. He closed the book. *What the hell am I doing?*

Freddy clopped down the stairs, portfolio in one hand, car keys jingling in the other. Aunt Penny had already left for work, leaving him alone in the house.

Almost.

Stella scuttled to greet him with a snarl, shaking and trembling.

Yip! Yip! Rrrrrrrrrr! Yipyipyip! Rrrrrrr...

"Good morning, Stella. How are you, huh girl?"

Freddy reached a tentative hand to pet her, but the mutt jolted back.

Yip! Yipyipyipyip! Rrrrrrr...

"Alrighty. See you later then." He rolled his eyes at the minuscule beast and bolted out the front door.

HE STEERED the Volvo down I-22, his usual route to work, though Clarkson's was not his destination. The air was cool and thin, the sky mostly gray with promising patches of blue peeking out. He realized he was gripping the wheel too tight and relaxed, taking a deep breath. *What is this, prom night? Get a fucking grip, Freddy.* He turned on his favorite Ben Harper playlist on Spotify and cranked the volume up as he continued down the road.

The police station appeared on the left, but instead of passing it as he always did, Freddy pulled into the parking lot. He found a space, parked, and cut the engine. *What the hell am I doing?* Freddy shook his head, hesitating. *Something. That's what you're doing, bitch. You're doing something.* He looked into the mirror for the twelfth time, ran his fingers through his hair. Tapped on the wheel. *Fuck it.* Freddy grabbed his portfolio and slid out of the car.

He strode up to the front entrance of the three-story, modest gray building, adjusting his shirt. There were police cruisers as well as civilian cars, and security cameras dotted the premises. Well-trimmed hedges and trees lined the property, and large mirrored windows of the front wall gave him a snapshot of his own awkward gait. *Loosen up, fucker. Take that stick out of your ass.* Freddy shook out the tension, taking one last deep breath as he made it to the front door.

The lobby was small, dim and empty.

In front of him, a row of plastic chairs were bolted to the floor. Across the room to his left, a sliding window of bulletproof glass. To his right, another bulletproof pane. Beside each window was a door with a fingerprint reader for employee access. Freddy walked to the right side of the room, looking through the window. Nothing. Just an empty desk and computer, with other desks and office equipment further back. Not a soul.

Freddy shrugged and crossed over to the left window. He leaned in and peered around. All he could see was a similar vacant reception desk. All was quiet. *Is anyone here? Well, the lights are on...* Freddy waited a minute, contemplating rapping on the glass, but decided against it. He hesitated but finally called out.

"Hello?" Nothing. He waited again. "Hello?"

He heard the creak of a door opening, and then footsteps. After a moment a short, elderly woman limped into the room and regarded him from behind the protective glass. She did not look impressed.

"Yeah?" Her New York accent was almost comical.

"Uh, yes," Freddy cleared his throat. "Hi. Um, is there someone in charge that I can speak with? Like the chief, or captain... Someone?" Freddy stood politely at attention. The woman looked him up and down through thick glasses. Her hair was like a puff of cotton candy. She wore a badge, but no gun.

"And what's this regarding?"

"Well, um... I'm an artist. I brought in my portfolio, just y'know, to show what I can do. I-I thought I could like, volunteer my services in case you guys ever need a sketch artist. O-Or whatever."

She looked at him with unblinking eyes.

Finally, "Wait here a moment. I'll go get Detective Sergeant Harney to come speak with you." She turned and waddled out of sight.

"Okay," Freddy called back with a close-lipped smile. He swung his arms and began to stroll around the lobby. He paced around and took it all in, noticing more details than before. On the central wall was a painted badge and the words "Everett Falls Police Department." On a side wall, a glass case with dozens of mounted patches, each a police badge from a different precinct. They were a variety of shapes, colors, and designs. Some were stars, some ovals, some silver, some gold. They all hung proudly, representing the broad fraternity of New York's law enforcement agencies.

Also hanging from the walls were plaques and framed photos of several police officers in uniform. Plastic holders displaying pamphlets to rape crisis groups and suicide prevention hotlines. The floor was a laminate masquerading as Venetian tiles, and the edges were beginning to fray. Freddy finally went to the row of chairs to sit. He tapped his feet, drummed on his knees with his fingers.

Minutes passed.

The door on the left opened after what seemed like a year, and a large bulldog of a detective strolled in. His veins pumped with pure Irish blood, his head shaved clean as a cue ball. He appeared to be middle-aged, stocky and tough, with a blue buttoned shirt and brown slacks. A holstered Sig Sauer P320 rested on his right hip, and a gleaming badge was clipped prominently to the front of his belt. His face was handsome but intense, and his Caribbean-blue eyes scanned a document he held in his hand.

He walked towards Freddy.

The nervous young man rose to his feet, standing at attention. He put on his best professional, polite smile, and began to raise his hand, preparing for a shake. He opened his mouth, ready to introduce himself, when the officer spoke first.

"I'll be right with you." His eyes did not come away from the paper he was reading as he walked past Freddy without missing a beat.

"Oh, okay," Freddy stammered.

The detective reached the opposite door in the lobby, pressed his finger into the reader, and buzzed himself in. The door swung shut behind him, leaving Freddy standing alone once again. He ambled in a circle, kicking his feet lightly and adjusting his shirt one more time. He opened his portfolio, flipped through it briefly, then brought it back down to his side. This time he didn't wait long before the big man came back into the room, offering his hand.

"Detective Sergeant John Harney. Nice to meet you."

It was like shaking hands with a cement mixer. Freddy smiled amicably, trying to not let his face betray any signs of pain.

"Hi, I'm Freddy Luccio. Good to meet you too, sir."

"Right this way."

Harney gestured for Freddy to follow as he walked back through the first door. They walked through the first admin office, where the front desk lady was easing her way back down into her chair. Freddy nodded and smiled as he passed, "Hi, thanks," he said as they kept walking. They passed a break room where two uniformed beat cops sat at a table drinking coffee. Freddy smiled and waved to them as they passed. "Hi." They both looked up at the young stranger, befuddled.

Harney led Freddy into his office, taking a seat on the

corner of his desk. It was a small space, utilitarian and anything but glamorous. Papers were stacked on his desk, along with his computer and multi-line phone. A cork board hung from the wall adorned with wanted posters and missing persons flyers. Nothing flashy or Hollywood about it, a million miles from the neon-lit police station movie sets Freddy had worked on once upon a time.

"Have a seat," Harney said.

"Thanks." Freddy picked one of the two leather-bound chairs in front of the desk and sat down, trying to not appear antsy.

"So, what can I do for you?" Harney's voice was a deep, thick New York husk.

"Well, um, I'm an artist. Just moved here from California. Uh, I used to do a lot of comic book work, storyboards and video game designs, stuff like that... Anyway, I'm becoming interested in getting into forensic art. You know, doing composite sketches, age progressions, that kind of thing. Or like, when they take a human skull and digitally figure out what the person looked like when they were alive? I've been really getting into that kind of stuff."

Harney nodded, his face like stone.

"So, I just thought I'd come in and show you what I can do," Freddy continued. "Y'know, offer my services to you guys in case you ever need any art done. I mean, I wouldn't charge anything, I just mean like, volunteer. I... I just want to help, y'know?" Eloquent it was not, but Freddy was relieved he'd at least gotten it all out. Harney nodded and gestured to the portfolio.

"All right. Show me what you got."

Freddy passed the book over and Harney began to flip through it.

"I've been drawing monsters and super-heroes so long. Stupid shit like storyboards for cereal commercials and whatnot... I-I really want to use my skills to actually do some *good*, y'know?"

"Mm hm."

Harney looked at each piece of art, his face betraying no emotion. His eyes glittered like blue gemstones and Freddy couldn't help but be taken by their luminance. He flipped through each page, his poker face never faltering. Freddy nearly held his breath as he watched the detective scan through monsters, storyboards, and video game character designs. Each piece was an impressive work of art, and the three serious portraits denoted the youth's proficiency at drawing the human face. Harney nodded, impressed. He finally spoke.

"Well, this is very good work."

"Thank you." Freddy allowed himself to breathe.

"'Course you know, this is a very small town. Very little serious crime here. Maybe a small theft or assault from time to time. But we don't need an artist very often."

"Oh sure sure, I know. I'm just saying, like, if you guys ever need anything, no matter how big or small... I'd just like to help however I can." Freddy's eyes were earnest. Harney nodded, allowing a small smile.

DETECTIVE HARNEY LED Freddy back the way they came through the hallways of the station. They passed the woman at the reception desk and Freddy nodded politely. "Thanks again," he said. "I'm Freddy, by the way." The stone-faced matriarch studied him like a specimen in a lab, deciding whether or not to reply.

"Donna," she finally croaked.

"Cool, thanks. Have a good one."

"All right," Harney said, leading Freddy back into the lobby, holding the outside door open for him. "So, I got your number, and I appreciate the offer. We'll definitely let you know if something comes up. All right?"

"Sounds good. My pencil's yours if you need it."

Ugh, that sounded so lame!

Another detective strolled in through one of the side doors, catching the tail end of the conversation. He was an oafish young cop with ginger hair and a mustache. He watched as Detective Harney shook hands with the young stranger.

"Okay, Freddy," Harney said. "You have a good one, all right? Talk to you later."

"Okay, thanks. You too, sir."

Harney released Freddy's hand from his vice grip, letting him back out into the parking lot. He closed the door and turned to see the red-haired young detective eyeing him with a quizzical look.

"Hot date, boss?" the ginger cop quipped.

Harney snickered and ambled back inside.

"Shut up, Miller."

CHAPTER 6
SMALL TOWN GIRL

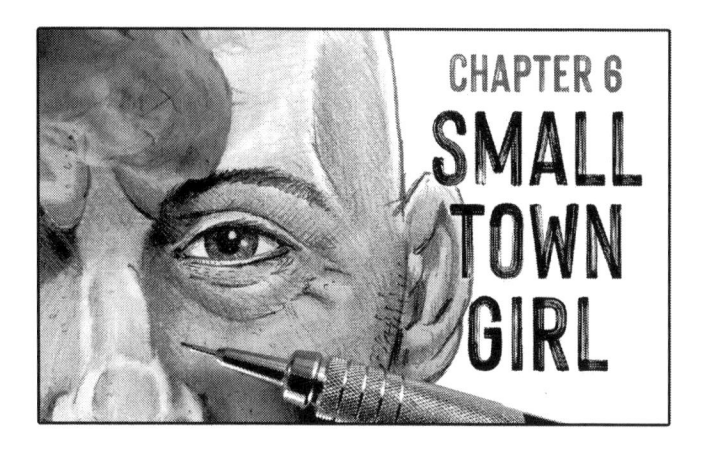

CHARLOTTE'S FINGERS were slim and delicate, yet strong. Working hands. She and Freddy unloaded boxes of shampoos and body washes, and he kept looking at her hands. He had a thing for hands. Hands were hard to draw. He could tell she was wearing no perfume or makeup except a little mascara, and she found it a struggle to hold eye contact. *If only she'd work on that posture,* Freddy thought. *What a cutie.* She looked up at him and made eye contact for a fleeting second before looking away.

"So, this is a lot of fun, huh?" he smirked.

"So much fun."

"Y'know, there is just nothing I enjoy more than loading up shelves with shampoo. Woo!"

She laughed again at his goofiness, afraid to show her teeth.

"You're weird," she said.

"Thank you. So what the hell do the 'cool kids' do around here, anyway? The most fun I've had is getting a couple slices at Gino's. Like, what do you do for fun around here?"

"Nothing, really," she shrugged. "Go to the mall, go to the movies, go to dinner?"

"So you're telling me you never have any fun?"

"I mean, sometimes. I don't know."

An exasperated David shuffled up the aisle towards them. He had the look of a man who just wanted to go home and get plastered. Or put a gun in his mouth. Or both. Each breath was a sigh.

"Char," he called out as he stepped up to them, "I'm sorry, sweetie, but I need you to work a double tomorrow."

Her heart sunk and her shoulders drooped even more as she turned to face him. She searched for the words.

"Oh, but... but..."

"Betty's sick and Patrick's out of town. It's always something with these people. I need you to fill in."

"I-I..."

"Think of it this way: Time and a half. Right?" David shrugged, turning to walk back the way he came. "Thanks, Char. I can always count on you." And he was gone.

Charlotte deflated, looking at her feet.

"That sucks," Freddy said.

"Tomorrow is my uncle's birthday," she sighed. "Me and my dad have plans to go over there for dinner. My cousins are in from out of town and I haven't seen them in a year..."

Freddy put down the box of conditioner and circled

around to face her. "You should tell him that. Tell him you have plans and you're busy."

"I can't. Somebody needs to be here."

"Well, then let David pull the double. He *is* the manager, after all. Why does he have to push it off on you?"

Charlotte shrugged.

"Y'know, you should really stand up for yourself."

"Yeah... Not too good at that, I guess. I just can't, I don't know..." she held up her fists in a mock fighting pose, then let her arms slap down to her sides again. She sighed and went back to work stocking the shelves. "It's okay. I'm just a scaredy-cat, I guess."

"Now now," Freddy said, returning to work himself. "You are a strong, independent woman."

"Ha! No, I'm not. I'm weak."

"Stop that! You are a lioness! C'mon, let me hear you roar!"

She giggled. "Oh, sure. Rawr."

They laughed and continued working. A moment of silence passed, and Freddy tried to break the awkward tension.

"So what's this I hear you don't like sushi?" he asked, loading up rows of dandruff-free shampoos. Charlotte cringed and scrunched up her little nose.

"Uch, no way."

"Oh my God, it's so good."

"Are you crazy? It's raw fish. That's gross."

She tossed an empty box aside and hauled over a new one.

"You're the one who's crazy," Freddy swaggered.

"You've been living in this little town too long. Never tried sushi, never tried shrimp. Never saw *Star Wars*, for the love of heavenly *God!*"

Charlotte giggled like a chipmunk and playfully pushed him away.

"Okay, fine. So I'm sheltered. I don't see a lot of movies, I still live with my dad, and I don't like seafood. So sue me."

Freddy laughed, admiring her corn-yellow straight hair. He shelved the last bottle of conditioner and tore open another box.

"You okay? You look like you're in pain."

"Oh, my neck has been bothering me," she said, rubbing it. "It does that sometimes. It's okay."

"I think you just need to loosen up," Freddy nudged. "Have some fun once in a while. You're too tense."

She shrugged. "I guess so."

Freddy rocked from his heels to his toes, hesitating.

Do it, chickenshit!

"So, uh..." *Don't be a pussy!* "Would you like to do something sometime?"

She shrugged. "Oh... Uh, O-Okay."

"Cool. What would you want to do?"

"Go to the mall? Go to the movies? Go to dinner?"

"Sounds good to me," Freddy smiled. "It's starting to get *cold* here. I need a new pair of gloves and a hat."

The melody from *Close Encounters* chimed from his pocket. Freddy pulled out his phone to see one new text message from Rick:

Putting some ice in the BO-O-OWL!!

Freddy shook his head and humored his friend,

giving him the answer he knew Rick wanted. Freddy typed and sent his message:

Tryin to replenish my SO-O-OUL!!!

Freddy laughed at his own stupidity and slid the phone back in his pocket.

"So, we'll go to the mall," Charlotte chirped. "I have a few things I need to get."

"Cool." His phone beeped again and Freddy rolled his eyes, feeling the need to check it although he already knew exactly what it would say. It was always the same lyrics from the same sophomoric songs they wrote together when they were twelve.

My fingers are mighty COLD!!

"Awesome," Freddy said to her, trying to not make her feel ignored as he returned the text. "Sounds like a plan, ma'am. Maybe this weekend?"

"Sure. Okay," she shrugged and smiled.

Freddy sent the text. *Dude I'm working right now. Fuck off lol*

He put the phone back down on the shelf as he continued to work, and just as he expected, three seconds later there was another reply from Rick:

SAY IT!!!

Freddy sighed and clacked his response, shaking his head.

Because I'm putting some ice, I said a-putting some ice in THE BOWL! Now fuck off I'm working!

Freddy silenced the phone and stuck it back in his pocket. He smiled at Charlotte, who looked at him quizzically.

"Sorry," he chuckled. "Just my asshole friend."

. . .

THE LAST REMAINING leaves clung to their branches as the temperature steadily dropped. After midnight in Everett Falls was a quiet time, no big parties on the residential streets, no drag racing, no inconsiderate neighbors. A few bars remained open on the main strip but every other business was closed save for the all-night diner. Few lights flickered in the ticky-tacky houses.

A man came home from work all bundled up, steam coming from his mouth as he hustled to get inside. An old couple watched TV in their living room, perfectly comfortable with their curtains being open. A woman walked her golden retriever. The brisk wind whistled and a tabby cat watched squirrels play from the comfort of his windowsill. There was no moon in the sky.

Katie White steered her silver Accord onto Hazelnut Lane and found a parking space. She held her cell phone up to her ear as she eased the car to a halt and cut the engine. With practiced movements, she scooped up her purse from the passenger seat, slid out of the car and locked the door behind her, saying "Uh huh... Uh huh..." every few seconds as she began to walk.

She was an All-American beauty queen if there ever was one. With wavy brown hair and sculpted porcelain features, she was twenty-two and the not-so-secret crush of every boy she came across. Her teeth were perfectly straight and gleaming white. She could be in movies, commercials, print ads, a news anchor, anything she wanted. Not that she knew what she wanted yet. At the moment she still wore the red vest and name tag from

AMC theaters beneath a coat and scarf, and simple jeans and Converse sneakers.

"Uh huh... Yeah, I know," Katie chuckled. "I know, I know, he was totally giving me the eye... Yeah... Oh, whatever. I don't think so... Oh, please! Get over yourself, Chelsea!" She laughed, trying to keep her voice down. Wouldn't want to disturb the sleeping neighbors. She shivered and held her coat closed with one hand and her phone in the other. Her house was just up ahead.

A shiver ran through her body. But it wasn't the cold.

She looked left, then right, and kept on walking.

"Listen, I gotta go, Chelse... 'Cause I just got off work, I'm almost home, and my feet are killing me... Give me a break, okay?"

Katie couldn't shake the feeling. She looked again but saw nothing. But then, footsteps, soft and distant. She stopped for a moment and turned to look back. A block behind her, a large, dark shape strolled up the sidewalk. A chill ran through Katie's bones and a shot of peppermint through her veins. She walked faster.

"What?" She lowered her voice to a whisper. "Oh, shut up. I'm not doing that... 'Cause I'm not, that's why! Ew, that's gross!" She kept her eyes forward, not daring to turn around. The footsteps were still there behind her, soft and steady. Her heart was throbbing, her shoulders tensed. She walked faster.

"Look, Chelse... I gotta go. I'm almost at my house. I'll call you tomorrow, okay? ...I'm hanging up now! Okay, talk soon. Bye, bitch." She hung up and pocketed her phone. The feeling of cold and dread sank deeper into her core. The street seemed imperceptibly darker. The footsteps sounded closer now. Katie reached into her coat pocket and grabbed her house keys. Her heart was pounding like a bass drum now, and she couldn't help but look behind one more time.

The dark figure was still behind her, closer now.

He wasn't walking a dog. He wasn't smoking a cigarette. He was just walking slowly on a dark street late at night. Katie walked faster, pulling out her keys and getting ready to fly into her house. The lights were on inside; her father was still awake. She reached the front steps and ran up onto the porch, jingling to find the front door key. She dared not turn to look behind her, but she knew. The man was still there, strolling in the dark. She could feel his presence.

Her hands shook as she found the key and tried to insert it into the lock. She fumbled and swore under her breath, missing on the first try. The presence was right behind her now. Katie focused, steadied her hand and slid the key into the lock. The door opened and she bolted inside, closing and locking it instantly. She stood with her back against the door, catching her breath.

Her father sat in the living room, watching The Raiders vs. The Chiefs game. He turned with a smile to greet his little girl.

"Hey, sweetie. How was work?"

CHAPTER 7
CROSS HATCHING

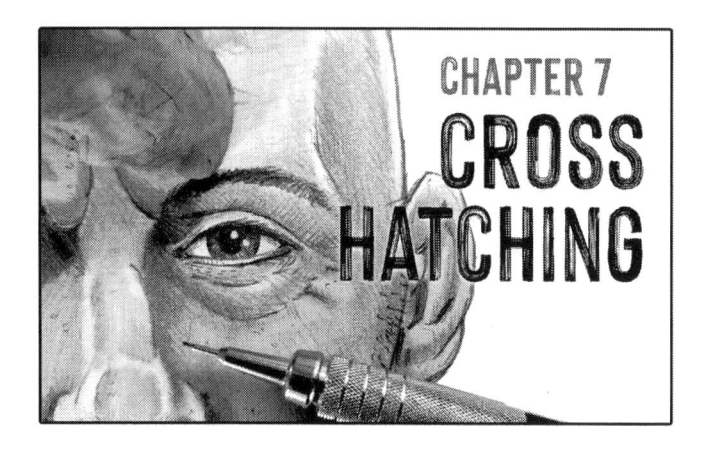

THE MALL WAS abuzz on a cloudy Saturday afternoon.

Freddy licked his dripping cone of mint chocolate chip ice cream. Charlotte had pistachio. They strolled through the lower level of the modest small town shopping center, looking at the storefronts and the people walking to and fro. He carried his new coat and gloves in a Target bag, and she had nabbed some goodies from Sephora and Bath & Body Works. She struggled with her dripping ice cream, much to Freddy's amusement.

"So you haven't talked to your parents at all since you moved back?"

Freddy shrugged and slurped his ice cream.

"Nah. It's kind of, I don't know, a weird situation."

"You guys don't get along?"

"No. I mean, we do, and I love them, but... I don't know. It was becoming a toxic situation. I had lived on my own after college, so when I had to move back home I was really depressed. Wasn't doing anything with myself, they started to feel like I was just being lazy and taking advantage, we fought..."

"Well, you should at least call them, like, tell them you're okay."

"They know I'm okay."

"But I mean, *eek!* Crap..." Charlotte's ice cream had run down her hand and was starting to drip onto her chest. She hurried to lick it all up, frowning at the mess. "Oh man, my shirt. *Nnnf.*"

Freddy was enjoying the show. Any time a woman dripped anything on her breasts, it was a turn-on. "You need a napkin?"

"Yeah, I should've gotten some, huh?" She chortled, her adorable nose crinkling up. She put her bag down and wiped at the spill on her shirt, trying to get it all and lick it off her fingers. She sighed, going back to the cone, lapping at it to avoid more dripping. "But I mean..." she continued, licking ice cream between words, "They're your parents..." lick, "and they still love you..." slurp, "and you should at least call them." She picked her bag back up and they continued walking.

"I know they love me, and I love them too. It's just... Ah, I don't know."

"My mom died when I was ten," Charlotte said. "Trust me. You should call your parents, try to make peace. We don't get second chances."

"Man, you should be a psychiatrist."

"And you should be a famous artist. I've seen some of your stuff. It's really good."

Freddy chuckled as they ambled along, dodging a couple of skater dudes as they blustered past.

"What, the little doodles I've done on scrap paper at work? That's nothing. Sometime I'll show you my actual portfolio."

"Totally, I'd like that. You shouldn't be working in a stock room. You should be doing something more with your art."

"Yeah, yeah. It's just... It's very hard to make a living as an artist."

"Yeah, yeah," she mocked him, giggling. "I'm still trying to get used to you with a clean shave."

"You don't like it?"

"I kind of miss the beard. But you're cute either way." She blushed.

"Oh, yeah?"

She giggled.

Freddy's phone rang. He stopped to put his bag down and dug the device out of his pocket. He didn't recognize the number, but the area code was local.

"Hello?"

"Hey, Freddy?" An unmistakable New York rasp.

"Yeah?"

"John Harney, how you doin'?"

"Oh, hey!" Freddy stammered. "Uh, yeah. Hi. How you doing?"

"You busy today?"

"I mean..." Freddy looked at Charlotte, who watched him with curiosity as she worked on her pistachio cone. "Um, I'm at the mall right now. What's up?"

"If you have time, I could use your help. I need an artist. Would you be able to come down to the station?"

"Oh! Um, okay..." Freddy hesitated. "I guess so. Can you give me an hour?"

"Sure thing. Thanks. I'll see you in a little bit."

"Okay." Freddy hung up and looked back at Charlotte, an apology in his eyes. "So, um... Remember how you were saying I should do something with my art?"

HE HURRIED to the police station and flew out of the car.

In his backpack was his 11x14 Strathmore medium surface sketch pad, and an assortment of Draft/Matic mechanical pencils, erasers, blur sticks, and three year-old cherry lozenges. He held his portable drawing table under his left arm, its cushioned bottom hugging his ribs. He hustled through the front door and into the lobby.

Donna was sitting at the left window.

Freddy stepped up to the glass, catching his breath.

"Hi, Donna, um, I'm here to see..."

She rolled her eyes and buzzed him in.

He moved through the stark halls and composed himself. Harney's office door was ajar and there were voices inside. He peaked his head in.

"Hello?"

"Come on in, Freddy," Harney waved him in.

Freddy walked into the room, his shoulders tense. Harney sat at his desk, and a middle-aged married couple sat across from him. They turned to greet him, and the lingering effects of fear and stress were in their eyes. Mr. and Mrs. Marco and Eva Andujar were in their mid-fifties, portly, and absolutely adorable huddled together. They all stood to greet Freddy as he came in.

"Hi, guys," he said.

"Marco, Eva, this is Freddy, our sketch artist."

"Oh, oh. Hello," Mr. Andujar said, shaking his hand, "Nice to meet you."

"Hello," Mrs. Andujar said.

"Here, take a seat and get set up, Freddy." Detective Harney pulled up a third chair. Freddy smiled politely and started getting ready. Harney crossed back to his chair, turning to face the room. "So, last night Marco and Eva are in their house, sleeping. They heard a sound so Marco took a baseball bat and went down to investigate. There in his living room is some asshole kid trying to run off with his TV. The punk bailed, but Marco says he got a good look at him. Right, buddy?"

Mr. Andujar nodded nervously. "Only for a second, but yeah. I saw him good."

"Okay," Freddy slipped out of his coat and put it on the back of his chair. He sat down and opened his bag, taking out his sketch pad and pencils. Everyone quietly watched as he shifted unevenly in his seat and meticulously set up his maise-en-plasse of art supplies. "So, uh... First of all, I'm so sorry this happened to you. But these guys are the best, and they're gonna catch 'em. Don't you worry."

Freddy smiled, putting the lap desk over his knees, turning the pad to a blank page and getting his favorite pencil set in the crook of his hand. "I'll do my best to do something light and rough, then show it to you. And I'll ask you on a scale of one hundred percent how close it is to what he looked like. And then I can revise it, show it to you again, and so on. Now tell me, what did this guy look like?"

"W-Well..." Mr. Andujar began, looking over at his wife who was gripping his arm, "He looked like college age kid, maybe high school. He was Latino, or maybe light skin Black. Um, he had like a buzz cut..."

"Tell me about the shape of his face."

"Um, well, it was kinda like, long? Real skinny. Uhhh, kinda like droopy eyes, y'know? One of those little beards that don't grow in all the way..."

Freddy cleared his throat and hovered the tip of the pencil over the paper.

Harney watched with keen interest.

"Okay," Freddy said, "Let's do this."

His pencil came to life.

CHAPTER 8
THE WATCHER

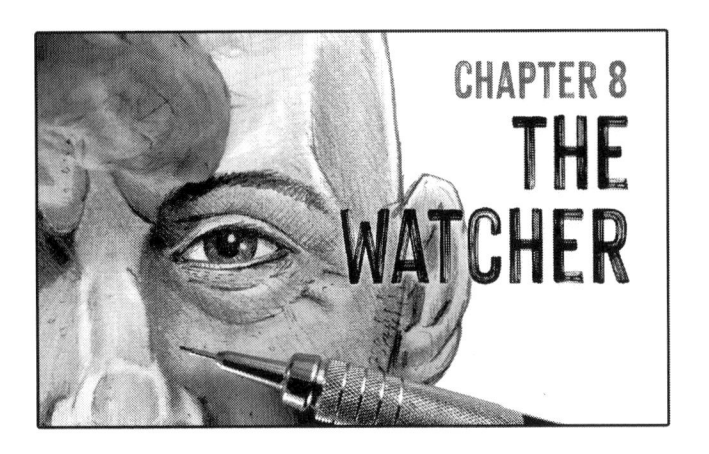

HE SAT in his car and watched.

The engine was off. The street was quiet. It was night. The lights were still on in the house and two cars were in the driveway. He tapped on the steering wheel with big sausage fingers. He heard something and his eyes ticked over to the driver's side mirror. A car came up from behind and drove past. His eyes went back to the house.

Come on, come on... It's Saturday night, fuckers. It's date night. Time to grab your shit and go out to dinner and a movie, or whatever the fuck you yuppies like to do. I don't care, just get out of my way. Come on, it's time. You guys always leave at seven sharp. What the fuck? Oh wait, okay. Here we go...

The light turned off in the house and a moment later the front door opened. A middle-aged woman dressed for a night on the town emerged onto the porch, smiled and adjusted her purse onto her shoulder. The porch light turned on and her husband came out, smiling as he locked the front door behind him. She shivered and he put his arm around her, rubbing her shoulder as they trotted down the front steps.

Hello there, Mr. and Mrs. White. About fucking time. Yes, you both look so nice, look at you. Look at you. Hope you both have a lovely evening. Don't worry, everything's gonna be just fine. Juuuuust fine.

They reached the two parked cars, a black Acura MDX and a cardinal-red Mercedes E-Class C238, and chose the Mercedes. He said something funny and she laughed. They slid into the sedan and the husband started it up. There was movement inside, the buckling of seatbelts, adjusting to get comfortable. A minute passed, then another.

Come on, come on! What the fuck are you guys doing in there? Just go.

Finally, the tail lights came on and the car began to back up. It pulled onto the street, stopped a moment to change gears, then pulled forward. The man watching from his car stayed perfectly still as the headlights swept over him, and the car disappeared down Hazelnut Lane. Within seconds its taillights had vanished and the street was still and silent.

Bye bye. Have yourselves a lovely night.

The man sat motionless in the car, a hulking shape in the shadows.

He looked straight ahead up the street, then into the rear-view mirror. Then both side mirrors. Someone was approaching from behind him on foot. It was an old lady walking her dog, a cocker spaniel. She passed the car and kept on going up the street. His eyes did another scan. Straight ahead, straight behind, side mirrors. All clear.

The man took his car keys from the ignition and slipped them into his coat pocket. When his hand came out he was holding a pair of leather gloves. He pulled the gloves on over his grubby fingers until they were nice and tight.

Heeeeere we go...

The man got out of the car and gently closed the door. He looked both ways again. Coast still clear. He strolled across the street to the White's house, bypassing the front door and heading around the side. The neighboring houses were all dark and silent. He strolled past the gas control panels and the spooled garden hose, past the small flower garden, and into the darkness of the back yard. He checked the back door and windows. All locked.

Not a problem.

The windows would break easily but he was too big and bulky to try sliding through a small frame like that. It would have to be the door. He looked left and right, and the coast was still clear. He stood back, raised his foot and kicked with his heavy boot. The door frame cracked and splintered but did not give entirely. He loaded up again, aiming for the lock, and launched another powerful front kick, this time shattering the door frame. The door flew open, inviting him into the darkness of the family home.

Why, thank you. Don't mind if I do. Later on when you're screaming and crying you can blame yourselves for not installing an alarm or security cameras.

He stepped across the threshold and into the kitchen. In the darkness he could make out the fridge, an island, a counter with a dishwasher, cabinets, four stools. He casually looked around, taking in the details. Pot holders that looked like avocados. Dish towels with cartoon kitty-cat designs. Far too many family photos, drawings and postcards clung to the fridge, decorative magnets barely holding them all in place.

He looked closer, enjoying the collage, spying in on the family via their printed memories. There was a Christmas card with a photo of a smiling young couple holding their baby. A postcard said "Hello from Miami, Florida!" Photos of grandparents long dead.

Then there were photos of the Whites themselves. Mommy and Daddy dressed up for some gala event. Mommy and Daddy years ago, posing with their beautiful two year-old girl. A high school graduation photo of that same little girl many years later. The dark figure leaned in to see better.

Ohhhh, there you are. Hello, Katie. God, look at you. Look at that smile. Those cheeks. Those eyes... Mm! Look at this one. Looks like y'all are on a family camping trip or something. Look at her in those little shorts, that little cut-off top. Oh, sweet baby girl, the things I'm gonna do...

He squeezed his crotch and felt himself getting hard.

The inside of the fridge offered him nothing he wanted. No beer. Just a bunch of health food. Eggs, vegetables, low-fat yogurts. He grunted and closed the door, turning back to the darkness of the house. Continuing inside, his eyes adjusted to the dark. He moved into the hallway, the foyer, the living room. Everything was clean, orderly and in its proper place. There was a fifty-inch flat screen and shelves of books, DVD's and Blu-Rays. Family photos lined the walls and there were far too many decorative pillows on the couch and love seat.

He scoffed and continued upstairs.

The shadow reached the second floor, looking both ways down the hallway. One door was obviously the bathroom, and another was the towel closet. A closed door looked like it could be a bedroom, so he opened it. There was a bed, a dresser, and a bedside lamp, but it was plain and without personality. A guest room. He closed the door and walked to the far end of the hall.

He crept into a large bedroom. King-size bed, another big TV, photos on the wall, a hamper half-full of dirty clothes. The master bedroom. He saw movement in the corner and heard a grumble, and the family cat scurried fearfully out the door to find a hiding place. He chuckled and backed out of the room, closing the door behind him.

He walked to the far end of the hall and reached the last door. A whiteboard with scribbled notes was tacked in place, along with several old stickers of boy-bands and former teen heartthrobs. He opened the door and slid into the darkness.

Yessss.

His heart pumped faster. He was instantly intoxicated, feeling a euphoria washing through him as he knew he was here, inside her room, her private space. He was already inside of her. It was too dark to make out much detail, but the small bed needed to be made, and the hamper was overflowing onto the floor. The walls were plastered with posters and photos and every inch of counter space was occupied with everything from beauty products, to dirty plates and silverware, to old stuffed animals from childhood.

Mmmm, hello, Katie. Man, it's so nice and warm in here. Nice and cozy.

He went to the hamper and reached in, his hands pulling out a bundle of assorted garments. He pressed them to his face and breathed in deeply. The high was better than alcohol, better than drugs, more potent than anything. He could smell her, every bit of her, like she was right there with him. Overwhelming youth, warmth, femininity. She was like a hot, steamy, juicy steak. His mouth watered and his penis was rock hard as he rubbed her panties around on his face.

Oh, sweet little girl. I can smell your little pussy, your tight little asshole. So soft, so warm and smooth... Ohhh, yeah. I can't wait to see the look in your eyes when I grab you, when I take you. Just rip off your clothes, fuck you so hard, make you cry. Bet you never had a grown man pound that perfect little asshole, whore. Dirty little fucking whore. Pound that ass balls deep and fucking cum deep inside of you... Wait, no no. They got that DNA shit now. I'll blow my load all over your face instead, that way I can clean it all off when I'm done...

He looked down at her bed and let himself fall backwards into it. The soft warmth engulfed him. His body was relaxed, perfectly comfortable. This was where she slept. This was where she felt safe. Her smell was on the bed, her hairs. She was there with him, naked, soft, smooth, pure, young, wet.

Gonna make you mine, little girl. No mistakes this time. You're gonna know that I own your little ass. And when I take out my club and start hitting you, and you feel your skull crack, you're going to know that you're about to die. And then I'm gonna whisper in your ear, and let you know that after you're dead, I'm gonna do it all again. Just smash your fucking brains into a pulp and then fuck your dead little holes one more time... Oh my God, little Katie, I need you so bad...

Time passed, and the man got off the bed. It was getting warm, and he took off his coat and gloves. He began to pace, and checked his watch. *Getting late. She should be home any time now.* He peeked out her bedroom window, looking down at the street below. He could see anyone who came to the front door. *Any time now.* He paced, swinging his arms, fantasies swirling in his mind. He rubbed his cock, looking at another picture of Katie on the wall.

Come on, come on. You're late. Get home already. Once you get here, we won't have very much time until your parents get back. Hurry the fuck up, bitch.

He paced, he looked out the window, he waited.

He paced, he looked out the window, he waited.

After what seemed an eternity, a familiar silver Honda pulled onto the street and parked across from the house. The man's body tightened as he watched. The headlights turned off, the engine cut, and Katie White stepped out of her car. She looked beautiful and young and completely carefree. With a few trotting strides she was up the steps and at the front door.

The watcher withdrew from the window as he heard her unlocking the door downstairs and coming inside. She closed and locked the door behind her, and then there were the sounds of her moving around. Taking off her shoes, opening the fridge, getting herself a drink.

Please don't notice the back door is broken!

The footsteps moved out of the kitchen and reached

the stairs. She was coming up. The man grabbed his coat from the floor and withdrew into her bedroom closet, waiting in the blackness, his heart pounding. *Thump, thump, thump,* he heard each footstep as she ascended. He waited, taking deep breaths as she reached the second floor. There was the sound of the bathroom door squeaking open, then the fan.

The stocky figure waited in the dark womb of the bedroom closet, listening through the walls as the young woman used the bathroom and brushed her teeth. His heart beat like it wanted out as his moment drew nearer. He took deep breaths, fondling himself. He reached into his coat pocket and produced a small club. It was an old truncheon, a leather laniard strung through a hole drilled at the base. He squeezed his club with one hand and his cock with the other.

Come on, baby. Come to me, little girl.

The bathroom fan cut off and the door creaked open. He heard her footsteps coming down the hallway.

This was it.

Katie came into her bedroom and turned on the light. She took a sip from a can of lime-flavored LaCroix and put it down on her bedside table. She took her sweater off and tossed it into the pile of clothes. Her chestnut hair flowed. Her skin was smooth and unblemished. She did not notice that behind the crack in her closet door, a strange man was ready to pounce.

Oh, yes baby. Yes yes yes yes, little girl.

She took off her blouse, now down to her jeans and a bra. Then she started on the jeans, unbuttoning and unzipping. She pulled the tight denim over the soft curves of her buttocks, revealing frilly panties with a printed pattern of strawberries.

One...

She kicked away the jeans.

Two...

She unclasped her bra.

Three...

The closet door burst open and he was on her in a flash.

CHAPTER 9
THE DEEP END

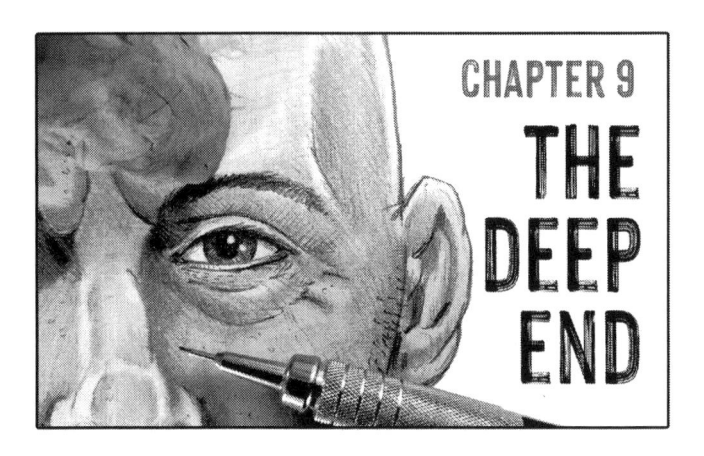

PENNY CRACKED open the oven to check on her casserole.

The smell of chicken, cheese, and vegetables floated up to greet her along with a pleasant surge of heat. She smiled and closed the oven, dancing across the kitchen to the sounds of Patti Smith, and scooped up her glass of merlot. Red lipstick rimmed the wine glass, and she gulped the rest down in two swigs. She went to her trusty box of wine, switched on the tap, and poured herself another glass.

"Freddy? You almost done settin' the table?"

"Yeah," he called from the other room. "What do you want to watch, *The Great British Baking Show* again?"

"Sure, unless you want to watch something else."

"Nah, that's fine." Freddy came back into the kitchen, collecting silverware and laying it on napkins. He smelled the meal to come and his mouth watered. "Oh my God, that smells so good, Aunt Penny."

"Be done in just a minute. You want some wine?"

"Nah, I'm good."

Stella watched them from the doorway, idling like a tiny motor.

"So how's it goin' with this new girl? You like her?"

"Charlotte? Yeah, she's cool."

"Yeah, she's cool," Penny mocked him. "What does that mean? You either like her or you don't."

Freddy chuckled as he pulled two large bowls from the cupboard and set them on the counter. "Yeah, I like her. Jeez. She's cool. She's pretty, and she's shy. Very sheltered. I don't know... She's cool."

"You gonna put a ring on her finger or what?"

"Would you give me a break? We've only been out on one date."

"I know, I'm kiddin'. Here, watch out..." Penny opened the oven and grabbed two pot holders, pulling out the ceramic platter covered in aluminum foil. "Oh boy, here we go. Penny D's famous chicken casserole!"

"Mmmmm."

"How did it go with that police thing? You didn't tell me about that."

"Oh, yeah. That was cool. I talked to these people who saw a guy in their house. I did a drawing for them, I got it to where they said it looked enough like the guy... Gave it to the cops. It was cool."

"Well, that's great. So they can use that sketch to help find him."

"Yeah, it's a good feeling. I don't know. To use my art to do something good. To actually feel helpful in some way... Feels like this is a field I could get into more. I like it."

"That's great. I'm so glad to hear that, Freddy. The salad's already on the table?"

"Yup."

"Good. Let's see what we got here. Ohhh, would you look at that..." Penny peeled the foil off the platter to reveal a bubbling, golden brown chicken and veggie casserole, steam dancing off of it. "So, are you two goin' steady now, or what?"

"Man, you don't let up. I don't know!"

"You goin' out again?"

"Yeah."

"You goin' out with anyone else?"

"No."

"Then you're goin' steady."

Penny scooped a helping of casserole into Freddy's bowl, then filled her own. Freddy chuckled and picked up his food. "So what about you? Any new men you like?" Penny shot him a sideways scowl as she grabbed her bowl and wiggled into the living room.

"Come on, Freddy. I'm too old for that," she said, taking her seat on the couch. "I been married once, and I'm not goin' down that road again. Nobody can ever replace my Bill."

"Well, I don't want you to be lonely."

"I'm not lonely, I got you! And I got Stella. Come on, girl! Where are ya? Come on, Stell." The little dog scurried into the living room and jumped onto the couch next to her mommy.

Freddy smiled and sat beside his aunt, placing his food on the coffee table. "You got the remote?"

"Yeah, here we go." Penny turned on the TV and

switched on Netflix. She took a bite of her food and her eyes rolled back. "Oh my *gawd!*"

"That good, huh?"

"Oh, yeah. Careful, it's hot."

Freddy took a bite and it nearly burned his mouth. He hooted and rolled the morsel around, letting it cool down. "Wow, that's so good."

"You want more parm?"

"Nah, I'm good."

"Here, let's start the show. I hope Francis wins."

"Oh, she's annoying."

"No way, I like her!"

Freddy had not finished chewing his first bite of food when his phone rang. He rolled his eyes. *Who the fuck can this be?* He picked up the phone and looked at the screen. *Restricted number.* He looked at Penny and shrugged, then hit the answer button and held the phone to his ear.

"Hello?"

He listened, and his face began to sink.

The color left his cheeks. His mouth dropped open.

THE VOLVO'S tires shrieked as Freddy swerved into the parking lot of the Everett Falls County Hospital at 7:42 p.m. His hands trembled on the steering wheel. He found a space near the ER entrance and parked, his mind racing. *Holy shit, what is going on here? What the hell am I getting myself into?*

He jumped out of the car and grabbed his backpack and lap-desk, then turned to face the imposing building.

There were four main wings connected at the center, and a bridge spanning over Hudson Ave which connected to another building of private doctor's offices. A large crucifix was mounted above the main entrance, lit from behind to give it an ethereal and majestic presence. Freddy's eyes locked on to the red sign for the ER and he hustled in that direction.

There were two police cruisers parked outside the entrance and two uniformed officers stationed at the automatic doors, along with four hospital security guards. When they saw Freddy jogging up to them, the two officers held up their hands to stop him, their faces dead serious.

"Who are you here to see?"

"Uh, um, I got a call to come. I-I'm supposed to..."

The automatic doors slid open and a tall man walked outside to greet Freddy. He was six foot-four, wearing a beige suit and tie, a badge clipped to the front of his belt. His hair was black and his features chiseled from Mediterranean stone, only a few years older than Freddy. He looked the young man up and down with somber brown eyes, noting the lap-desk under his arm.

"You Freddy Luccio?" His voice was a full-bodied baritone.

"Yeah."

"Detective Ron Bagnarol."

They shook hands. Freddy noted how large and strong the detective's hand was, and was grateful he didn't feel the need to impose his dominance with a bone-crushing handshake.

"Good to meet you," Freddy said.

"Come on. Harney's upstairs in the ICU."

One of the security guards stepped forward with a metal detector wand and pointed it at Freddy. "Please raise your arms."

Freddy did as instructed, and the guard waved the device under his arms, down his body, and over his legs. Satisfied, the guard stepped back and nodded.

The uniformed officers and security guards stood aside as Bagnarol led Freddy through the sliding doors and into the ER reception area. A nurse greeted him with a polite smile and gestured to a box of medical masks on the front counter.

"If you would please put on a mask," she said.

"Sure, sure," Freddy said, pulling a small cloth mask from the box, placing it over his face and pulling the loops around his ears. He glanced around at the ER waiting room, a bleak and depressing sight. Suffering people sat on hard plastic chairs under florescent lights while *The Price Is Right* played on a wall-mounted TV. One old man was suffering from kidney stones as his wife held his hand. A woman in a wheelchair groaned in pain and gripped her swollen knee. A young boy had some kind of head wound, and his parents flanked him, applying pressure with a bloody towel.

Bagnarol already had a mask in his hand, and put it back on. He cocked his head to the side, indicating for Freddy to follow, and the young artist was all too happy to get the hell out of there. The nurse buzzed them through the inner door, and Freddy found himself in a long hallway, trailing behind the much larger man. He sped up, trying to match the stride of Bagnarol's long legs.

"So, what's going on?" Freddy asked. "Harney didn't tell me much over the phone."

"A young woman was raped and badly beaten in 'er home last night. She survived, but she's hurt pretty bad. The doctors said it's okay to talk to 'er now."

"Jesus!"

Bagnarol's eyes were locked in a sullen scowl as he led Freddy forward. His deep Brooklyn accent struggled to retain a detached, professional tone. He was clearly angry. Pissed. They reached an elevator at the end of the hallway, and the detective pressed the button.

"Apparently, she'd just come home from work, and the bastard was just waitin' for 'er. Good thing 'er parents came home when they did, scared 'im off. Otherwise..." He stopped himself from finishing the thought. *Ding!* The elevator doors slid open and they stepped inside. Freddy found himself breathing heavy, his heart racing.

Holy shit, is this really happening?

The elevator lifted them to the next floor, and the doors opened with another *ding*. Bagnarol led Freddy down a long hall, past a sign directing them to the ICU. More armed officers guarded the entrance at the end of the corridor.

"Needless to say," Bagnarol continued, "we brought you 'ere 'cause the girl got a good look at 'er attacker. So whatever you can do to give us a good picture of this scumbag..."

"Right, right. Of course."

They reached the door to the ICU, and Bagnarol nodded to the two officers, who returned the gesture. The doors opened and the two men strode into the busy medical unit. Freddy's head was spinning, and he focused to control his breathing as they drew closer to their destination.

"Listen," Bagnarol said. "Just so you know, this girl looks pretty bad. I want you to be prepared. Just try to keep your cool. Just... Y'know."

"Right. Sure. I'll, uh, I'll do my best."

They reached the door.

Bagnarol turned to give Freddy one last look. Freddy nodded. Bagnarol took a deep breath, then opened the door.

CHAPTER 10
COMPOSITE

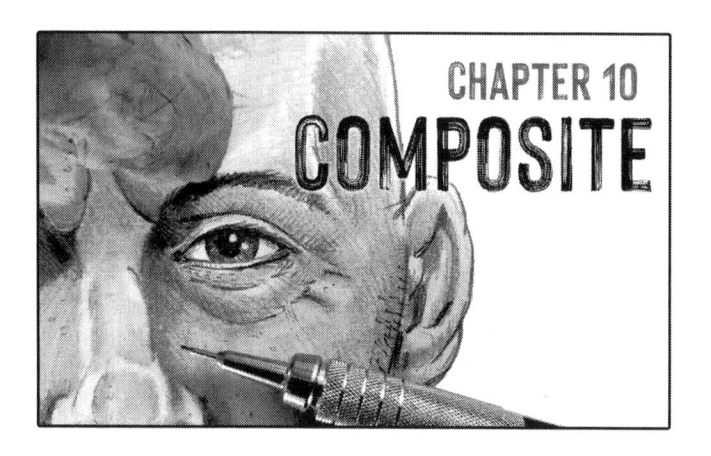

FREDDY AND DETECTIVE BAGNAROL walked into the dim room.

Lying on the hospital bed was what remained of a beautiful young girl. Katie White's left eye was bandaged over, as was the entire top of her head. Her split lips had been stitched up, her front teeth knocked out. Her one good eye was bloodshot and bruised deep purple. Her right arm was in a cast and a sling, her left arm the entry point for two IV's.

"Hey, Bags. Freddy," Harney whispered.

The tree trunk of a detective sat beside the bed reverse-style on his chair. Standing beside the bed was a Black female doctor checking Katie's vitals. Crouched next to her on the right, her parents were a mess. Mr. and Mrs. White clung to their daughter, their bloodshot eyes reflecting the day they'd had, after their world had been turned upside down and then shit on. They looked at the young newcomer with those glazed, desperate eyes.

"Everyone," Harney said, standing to shake Freddy's

hand. "This is Freddy Luccio. He's the artist. Freddy, this is Katie White and her parents."

"Hi, Katie," Freddy said, nearly whispering. "Mr. White. Mrs. White."

He tenderly shook their hands.

"Thank you for coming," Mrs. White said.

"Hi..." Katie whispered, her sweet voice now a croak.

Keep it together keep it together keep it together.

Freddy found a chair and pulled it up to the side of the bed. He took his jacket off and hung it on the back of the chair, then sat and began unloading his things. Everyone else quietly watched his process. He pulled his sketch pad from his bag, followed by his carry case of pencils, erasers, and smudge sticks.

"Could we turn up the lights a little, please?" Freddy asked. "Would that be all right?" Katie nodded and the doctor flipped on the main light switch. Freddy scooched around in the chair until he was comfortable, then laid the lap-desk over his knees. Mrs. White stroked her daughter's hair, fighting back tears. Freddy gently held Katie's hand and looked her in the eye. "Don't you worry, Katie. You're gonna be all right. These guys are going to take great care of you. I'm gonna draw a picture of this bastard, and these detectives are gonna find him and put him away. These guys are the best at what they do."

Bagnarol looked over at Harney, and the superior officer shrugged.

Freddy sat back into his chair and placed the large sketch pad on the desk, open to the first blank page. He got his pencil ready in hand. "Okay now, Katie. I want you to start telling me the absolute basics about this guy.

I'll start off drawing super light, then show it to you, make some changes, show it to you, until you think it looks like him. Then I'll detail it. Okay?"

"O-Okay."

Jesus, this is too much! This poor fucking girl!

"Okay," Freddy began, "what ethnicity was he, and about how old?"

"H-He was a white guy," she trembled, "I-In his like, fifties..."

"Now, what kind of shape was his face?"

"He was... kind of chubby looking. Like, chubby cheeks, round nose..."

Freddy had enough to start.

His pencil took off like an ice skater.

Fast, loose, and light, the graphite strokes swooped across the Strathmore medium-surface paper. The Whites, along with Detectives Harney and Bagnarol, watched with vested interest. Katie squirmed and cringed as she forced herself to remember the nightmare, to remember his face.

"He had kind of like... a big cowboy mustache, messy hair..."

"Okay," Freddy said, his pencil whizzing across the white surface. Using very light lines, the .5 pencil tip barely kissing the paper, he created the rough shape of a man's head, with round features, and a large mustache. He leaned forward and held up the pad for Katie to see. "How does this look as far as the general shape of his face?"

Katie scanned the page with her one eye.

"He wasn't quite that chubby," she said.

Freddy nodded and reclined again, going back to work. Out came the kneadable eraser and it went to work slimming down the subject's face. Harney cleared his throat and began to speak.

"Now, when you guys got home last night, did you notice anything strange or out of place?"

"Not right when we walked in, no," Mrs. White replied. "But when we were waiting for the paramedics and the police, we noticed the back door had been kicked in." She trembled and stroked her little girl's hand.

Mr. White seethed with anger. "The only thing we noticed when we walked in was the sound of our daughter upstairs, *screaming*."

Freddy stopped scribbling long enough to lean in again, showing her the progress. "How's that?"

"Yeah, that's better..."

"Okay, you're doing great, Katie. You're gonna be just fine." Freddy wondered if he was reassuring the girl or himself. "Now, what would you say is the most distinctive feature this guy has? Does he have a big hook nose, a scar on his cheek, big ears?"

Katie recalled the face, the man on top of her, pinning her down, breathing on her. Raping her. Beating her. Her eyes swelled with tears remembering him.

"His-His eyes... He just had these like, tiny, evil little eyes. A-And the way he was looking at me... W-When he said he was going to k-kill me!"

She broke into uncontrollable sobbing, and her mother was right there to cradle her. Her father rose to his feet, fists clenched, face beet red. Unable to take anymore, he screamed and stormed out of the room.

"Son of a bitch! God damn *son of a bitch!*"

Nobody stood in his way.

Freddy sketched, applying more pressure with his pencil. The lines grew darker. He showed Katie again, and she said the nose was too small. He showed her again, and she said the eyes were too big. He kept refining and shaping the image, and the composite sketch began to take shape.

Beady little eyes, round features, big mustache and shaggy hair hanging down in front of his eyes. Freddy turned the paper left and right, hitting it from different angles. His pencil flew, adding more detail, shading, and textures. The portrait of an evil man came to life. The hair had volume, weight, and dimension. Even the texture of skin and beard stubble brought an air of realism.

Freddy stopped drawing and leaned in once again.

"Okay, take a look at this now. And tell me how close, percentage-wise, this is to the man?" A shiver shot through Katie's nervous system. She couldn't help but break down again. Everyone leaned in closer.

"Is it close?" Freddy asked.

"Yes! That's him! That's *him!*"

Mr. White hurried back into the room, joining the family huddle.

"How close?" Bagnarol asked, stepping forward. "Seventy-eighty percent?"

"No, ninety percent. That's him!"

Harney and Bagnarol shared a steely look and peered down at the finished drawing. "Guess you're done here, Freddy," Bagnarol said.

Freddy nodded and tore the page out of the pad, signing his name at the bottom and handing it over to them. "Here you go, detective."

Harney gave the portrait a good, hard look, then slapped Freddy on the shoulder as they walked to the door. "Good job, Freddy."

The Detective Sergeant signaled to one of the uniformed officers standing guard. He handed the illustration to the officer, urgency in his eyes. "Get this to the station. Tell them to make a million copies, you hear?"

"Yes, sir."

"I think that's enough for tonight," the doctor said.

Freddy nodded and quietly packed up his things.

THE ER DOORS slid open and Bagnarol led Freddy back outside, the detective hand-rolling a cigarette and lighting it up as they passed the police and security detail. He exhaled in relief. Freddy was in a haze.

"That was crazy. You worked a lot of cases like this?"

"Back in the city, yeah," Bagnarol said. "Never 'ere. And I been workin' in this town for seven years. Came 'ere to get *away* from bullshit like this."

Freddy fumbled with his art gear as he walked and searched to find the car keys. "That poor girl," he said. "I could barely keep it together in there, man."

"Oh, you done real good work. I worked with a lot of sketch artists, and you're better than most. I can't fuckin' believe this was your first time."

"Well, second. But that first one was... nothing like this."

"Ah, all right," Bagnarol said. "Well, you did good."

"Yeah? Thanks. Talk about jumping into the deep end, huh? I don't know, both my grandparents were cops, so maybe it's in my blood."

"Oh, is that right? Blue-blood, huh?"

"Yeah." They walked through the chilly parking lot, approaching the Volvo. Freddy opened the doors and tossed his stuff in the back seat. "That and I watch a lot of cop shows."

Bagnarol laughed and took a drag.

Freddy opened his driver's door and stopped, turning to face the detective with worry in his eyes. "Y-You don't think this guy will...?"

Bagnarol gave him a solemn, somber look, exhaling smoke through his nose.

"You been a very big help, Freddy. And I want to thank you for that."

The big man offered his hand and Freddy shook it. A silent moment of understanding passed between them.

This was far from over.

"Take care, Detective."

"You too, Freddy."

The young artist got in his car and started it up, and Bagnarol watched as he drove off down Hilliard.

CHAPTER 11
BREAKING NEWS

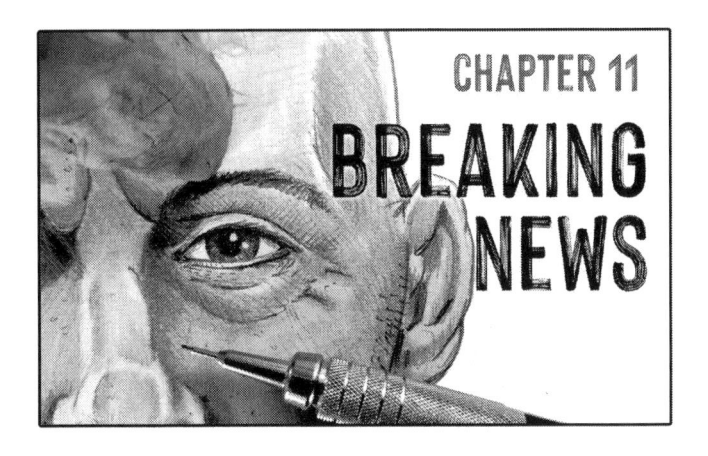

EVERETT FALLS WAS CONSIDERED A HAMLET, not even large enough to warrant a newspaper more extensive than a monthly newsletter. For their daily news, residents relied on the Putnam County Courier, as well as the Local 2 News on TV, and of course the internet. On this particularly brisk, gray morning there was only one story that anyone was talking about.

Freddy helped Dave and Charlotte open the store.

He unlocked the front door security gate, letting the fall morning air sweep in. On the front step as always was a stack of Putnam County Couriers. He hefted up the bundle and carried it inside, placing it beside the Pennysaver and daily coupons. Out came his pocket knife and Freddy eagerly cut the strings binding the stack and picked up the first copy.

"Local Girl Raped and Battered in Own Home."

Beneath the bold headline were two images; the first was a photo of Detective Harney being interviewed outside the hospital, and the second was Freddy's composite sketch. Those gray graphite eyes looked back at him with a cold malice. Freddy nodded with pride and began to read the article.

"SO THIS IS your favorite place, huh?"

"It's one of them," Charlotte answered. "Really good orange chicken."

She and Freddy paced and strolled around the entrance to Mandarin Garden, along with another couple and a young family, all waiting to be seated. Through the windows, the dining room was bustling. She shivered, her shoulders tensed, hands buried deep in the pockets of her green wool coat.

"You okay?" Freddy asked.

"I'm cooooold."

"It's not that bad," he chuckled, checking the light-up pager given to him by the hostess. "I'm sure they'll call us in soon." *Okay, enough small-talk, Freddy. Jesus.* "So, is this where you take all your dates, y'know, before sacrificing them to the dark lord?"

She frowned, confused. "What?"

"Sorry, I'm kidding. Just... Bad joke. Stupid." *Smooth, Luccio, smooth.*

"You're weird." She shivered again, hopping up and down. "I'm *cold*."

"Oh, you poor thing..." *Do it, pussy! Do it!* "Come here."

Freddy wrapped his arm around Charlotte and held her tight, rubbing her shoulder. She did not object. They made eye contact and she looked away, cheeks flushed with red. "Thanks," she squeaked.

"We gotta fatten you up," Freddy said. "Extra orange chicken for you tonight."

"Oh, so you think I'm too skinny."

"No no, not at all... I think you're adorable."

She looked back at him, this time holding his gaze.

"Yeah?"

Okay, here we go. Do it, do it...

"Yeah."

Freddy pulled her in even closer, holding her against him. He moved in, lips inches away from hers. They each closed their eyes and parted their lips, and kissed for the first time. They pulled away a little, giggled, then went in again for more. Deeper. His hands caressed her back. Her knees went weak.

The restaurant's buzzer went off in his hand.

"C'MON, TRY IT. C'MON!"

A steaming shrimp hovered in front of Charlotte's face, held between a pair of chopsticks. She rolled her lips inward as Freddy held the savory morsel up for her to taste. She giggled and shook her head.

"No!"

"C'mon, it's just shrimp. Try it, you'll love it."

"I told you, I don't like seafood. Let me just eat my chicken and rice."

Freddy laughed and waved it in front of her face.

"It's reeeeaaally good. C'mon, just one bite. Expand your horizons." This tactic was still not working. He switched to one of his favorite silly voices. *"Eat me, Char-*

lotte! I taste soooo good! Oh my, look at how good I look! Oooooh!"

She cracked up laughing and gave up.

"Fine, fine. You're such a jerk."

With a tentative grimace she parted her lips and opened her mouth. Freddy placed the shrimp on her tongue and sat back, awaiting her reaction. She chewed slowly, her eyes looking around as if searching for an answer, analyzing this strange, foreign substance in her mouth. Her eyebrows remained furrowed as she swallowed it and flushed it down with a gulp of water.

"Well?" Freddy leaned in.

"I don't like it."

Freddy exploded with laughter. *God, she's like a little kid, but it's so cute!* The young family sitting beside them looked over, distracted by the booming laughter, before returning to their own conversation.

The dining room was nearly at capacity. The decor centered around a deep red and gold color palette. The lights were dim, and Chinese knock-off sculptures and paintings adorned the walls. Traditional music played softly as servers in white shirts and black ties buzzed around taking care of the patrons. At the end of the dining room was a large fish tank, and beyond that, the bar, with the local news playing on the wall-mounted flat screen TV.

Freddy took a sip of beer and chuckled again.

"Ahhh, I tried. You're funny. How does a person *not* like shrimp? Whatever, you're entitled to your wrong opinion."

"Oh, look at me! I'm Freddy! I'm like sooo funny!"

He laughed and continued eating his shrimp fried rice. "So what *do* you like?"

"Well..." she took a bite of chicken and thought about it. "I like chicken, spare ribs, Hot Pockets, Dunkin' Donuts..."

"Okay, all right. Health food."

"I don't know. I have simple tastes, okay? I grew up in a small town, I go to church every Sunday with my dad... I'm boring."

"Oh, I don't think you're boring."

He smiled and locked eyes with her. His brown eyes met her blues, and she blushed, looking down. "Sorry if I seem nervous," she said. "It's just that nobody's asked me out in a long time."

"Yeah, well me neither."

"Oh, no? You didn't have all kinds of hot girlfriends in Hollywood?"

Freddy chortled and rolled his eyes. "Oh, yeah, all those hot babes in Hollywood. God... No, they're all so shallow, materialistic. I mean, I know not all women in LA are that way, I know I'm generalizing, but... Let's just say I couldn't find a woman of substance, someone who liked me for me."

"I don't know why," she forced herself to look him in the eye, "you're adorable."

"Maybe I just needed to meet a good girl for once."

"Well, I'm definitely that." She seemed to deflate a bit, eyes looking down at her plate. "Maybe a little too good."

"What do you mean?"

"Never mind. I just... I don't... No, never mind."

"No, what is it?"

"I mean, it's not really something I should, I don't know, talk about on a first date. Or maybe it is. I don't know."

"Spit it out, woman."

"Well," she hesitated. "I told you I go to church every Sunday."

"Yeah?"

"I mean, I haven't... I've never..."

"Aha. Okay." *Daaaaamn, dude!*

"I guess it's only fair to let you know. I don't want to waste your time if you're not cool with that." Her eyes searched his, seeking approval.

"Of course that's cool," he smiled. "I'm not exactly a Casanova here. I don't usually go around asking girls out. I'm too shy."

"You don't seem shy to me."

"Well that's because you're even more shy than I am! So, you're waiting for marriage, then?"

She shrugged. "I mean, I don't know. Kind of... Not really? I guess I'm just waiting for the right person. Waiting for it to be special... You know?"

Freddy nodded and smiled.

At the bar, employees and patrons alike began to stir, gathering around the TV. Freddy could see it happening behind Charlotte, but paid it no mind. He was focusing on her blue eyes behind those wire-rimmed glasses. Those rosy cheeks. That smile.

"Well, maybe I'm shy, but you're a goober."

"Oh, I'm a goober, huh? What does that mean?"

"It means you're weird." She giggled.

"Oh darling, you ain't seen nothing yet. I have yet to unveil the full arsenal of my weirdness. I don't know if you can handle it."

"Mm hm. This is what I mean."

Freddy laughed and took another swig of beer.

"Turn it up! I can't hear!" called a voice behind Charlotte at the bar.

Freddy looked over her shoulder at the bar area, noticing people huddling around the TV. The local news was on, but he couldn't make out more than that. He could tell, however, that something was wrong. Restaurant workers and customers alike watched the screen with astonished looks in their eyes. Freddy scooted back in his chair, curious.

"Um, excuse me just a minute," he said as he stood up.

He touched her shoulder as he walked past, and she continued to eat. He made his way across the dining room, closing in on the bar. A graphic on the TV screen read "breaking news"and the live video was that of a crime scene. Several police and CSI units were converged around a local home, the area sealed off with yellow tape. A crime scene reporter's voice became clear as the bartender turned up the volume.

"—And although extra security and precautions were taken by the White family since last week's assault, the perpetrator was able to break into the house again to brazenly finish what he started."

Freddy's face dropped. Two EMT's rolled a gurney out of the house, gently transporting a sealed body bag. They rolled it to the tailgate of an ambulance and loaded it in as an astonished crowd of neighbors looked on in horror.

"This time, the attacker succeeded, beating Roy White unconscious, then raping and murdering the helpless Katie White with a blunt instrument—"

"Jesus Christ..." Freddy's hand clamped over his mouth and his heart sank. On the screen, paramedics rushed a critically injured Roy White into another ambulance and raced off to the hospital. Harney, Bagnarol and other law enforcement officers he recognized were on the scene as well.

"A graduate of Manhattanville College, Katherine Anne White was twenty-two years old. No evidence has been made public at this time, but police urge citizens to be vigilant. And that anyone with any information that could lead to the arrest of this individual, please come forward. Tonight, a shocked community grieves the loss of one of its own."

Freddy could not feel his own legs.

He watched in shock as a reporter tried to question Detective Harney, who was too busy to be bothered. The bar buzzed with worried and terrified people, aghast at the horrible news. Freddy felt a hand on his shoulder. Charlotte leaned in to see what all the fuss was about.

"What's going on?"

Freddy could not answer.

CHAPTER 12
GRAVITY

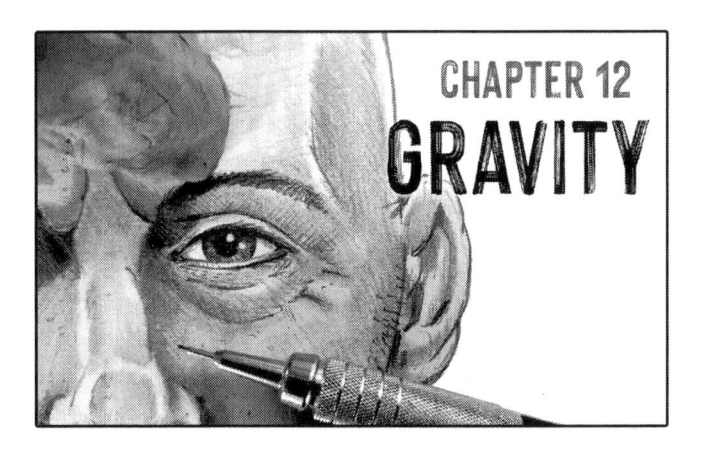

LITTLE FREDDY RAN.

He wore his favorite Winnie The Pooh pajamas. To his left and his right and all around him were dog cages, and in each cage was another little boy like him. They cried and begged him to let them out. There was filth and steam, a low ceiling, a concrete floor. Some kind of basement or abandoned factory.

The Shadow was in there as well.

He was somewhere around. Little Freddy could feel his presence. Infinitely dark and impossibly strong. He was coming, hatchet in hand. The child darted left, right, left again, zipping through the maze of cages and terrified boys. Little Freddy could hear the heavy footsteps behind him, and though he couldn't see his face, he knew the bastard was smiling. The imprisoned boys screamed *Help us, Freddy* as he plunged through the madhouse.

He skidded to a stop at the edge of a cliff. He was suddenly outside and everything was covered in snow. He looked down and saw nothing but an endless abyss.

He looked back and saw The Shadow coming. He gripped the hatchet, raised it high over his head.

Little Freddy screamed and fell backward into darkness.

FREDDY WOKE UP.

He had barely slept that night, and when he did... Terror. Horror. The rest of the night had been a blur after seeing that news report. He had driven Charlotte home, gone back to his Aunt Penny's, somehow drifted up the stairs to his bedroom, and found himself in bed, staring up at the ceiling. Images and thoughts swirled in his skull like a dust devil. There was no rest.

Morning light crept through the blinds. He lay still, staring at nothing. Birds were starting to chirp and the sounds of traffic increased. Between the shock and the sleep deprivation, he was unsure if he was asleep or awake, floating in an exhausted haze. He wanted to just stay there forever, to float away into a coma and sleep, but he needed to use the bathroom. He also needed answers. *Must have coffee.*

He lurched out of bed, his hair like a bird's nest, his chin in need of a razor if he was to stick with the clean-shaven look. But none of that mattered now. *Answers.* He quickly brushed his teeth, brewed some coffee and got dressed. Stella yapped at him as he flew out the door.

THE VOLVO SPED through Everett Falls. Every tree was bare, every leaf on the ground. The sky was cold and gray. The storefronts and houses displayed their finest seasonal decorations; pumpkins and ghosts, witches and ghouls. Monsters. Freddy shivered and blinked away the delirium of sleep deprivation as he turned onto I-22.

He parked at the police station and sprang from the car, taking long strides up to the front door. Stalking into the lobby, he saw Donna at her workstation and went up to the window. She was busy fielding calls, too preoccupied to even roll her eyes at the sight of him. Freddy waited, impatient. Donna glanced up and saw the urgency in his eyes, sighed, and waved for him to come.

The buzzer rang and Freddy ran in.

He slipped through the door and headed down the long hallway. The offices were empty, as was the break room, but he heard voices further down. He turned a corner and went down another hall, finally arriving at a conference room. The door was open, and sitting at the large table were Harney, Bagnarol, and Miller, each busy on a phone call.

Bagnarol took notes on a pad of paper while Harney scanned mug shots on his laptop. Miller tapped his foot, apparently on hold. The countertop hosted a collage of photos, notes, and evidence, and amongst it all, the composite sketch. Freddy stood in the doorway, awkwardly shifting his weight from foot to foot, not wanting to disturb the detectives at work. Bagnarol noticed him standing there and held up a finger, indicating for him to wait a minute.

Freddy nodded and stayed put, his eyes unable to resist scanning the evidence on the table. Crime scene photos. Katie White. Her home, her body. Her blood. He didn't want to look, but he couldn't help himself. His eyes were drawn to the red. One shot in particular nearly stopped his heart. Katie was on the floor, naked. Her head was utterly destroyed, smashed into a grisly tapenade. Freddy forced himself to look away, his hand reflexively covering his mouth.

Oh my fucking God. This is real. This is really real.

The detectives hadn't slept, as evidenced by the dark under their eyes. They were tasked with the unimaginable, to confront the dark side of humanity. The ugly, the evil, the worst of us. They were tasked to bring closure, to get justice, to catch the devil himself. Freddy suddenly felt very silly standing there.

What the hell am I doing? These guys have real work to do. I shouldn't be bothering them. Oh my God, that poor girl... What the fuck, I'm such a moron!

Bagnarol finished his call and hung up, taking a deep breath and briefly closing his bleary eyes. He looked up at the young man fidgeting in the doorway. "What's up, Hollywood?"

Freddy tried to find the words. "I just, I... I held her hand. I told her everything was going to be all right..." He felt his throat tighten and his eyes burning. The tears wanted to come but he fought them back. He swallowed hard, trying to compose himself. "I mean... *How* could this have happened? She was under protection, wasn't she? What the hell...?"

Bagnarol sighed, doing his best to remain stoic and professional, though it was clearly eating away his insides. "This guy is very slick, very smart. We think he was already in the house when she came back from the hospital, just waitin' for the right time. Then when it was just her and her father alone..." He shook his head and rubbed the bridge of his nose.

"And Mr. White?" Freddy asked. "How is he?"

"He's in a coma at the hospital, plugged into life support."

"*Fuck*... So you got no fingerprints, no DNA, nothing?"

Bagnarol debated sharing information with the civilian. Harney glanced up briefly from his computer screen and noticed Freddy, then returned to his phone call. Bagnarol let out a sigh and leaned forward, inviting Freddy to take another step closer.

"No fingerprints or semen, no. But we believe that Katie scratched the fucker during the assault. We found blood and skin cells underneath her fingernails, even traces of make-up. We should be able to work up a genetic profile from it... But that don't leave this room, got it?"

Freddy held up his right hand as if taking an oath. "No, of course not. I won't tell anyone, I swear... But do you... Do you think... like, is this over? Is this guy gonna keep...?"

The detective sighed and looked at Freddy with tired eyes. That look said it all.

"I got a lot of work to do here, little brother." Freddy nodded and backed out of the room. Bagnarol dialed another number and held the phone to his ear, focused and determined. "Yeah, hello. This is Detective Ron

Bagnarol, Everett Falls Police. Can I speak with Doctor Pierce, please?"

Freddy quietly drifted back into the hallway, deflated.

"Good luck, you guys..." he said to himself.

CHAPTER 13
THE BASHER

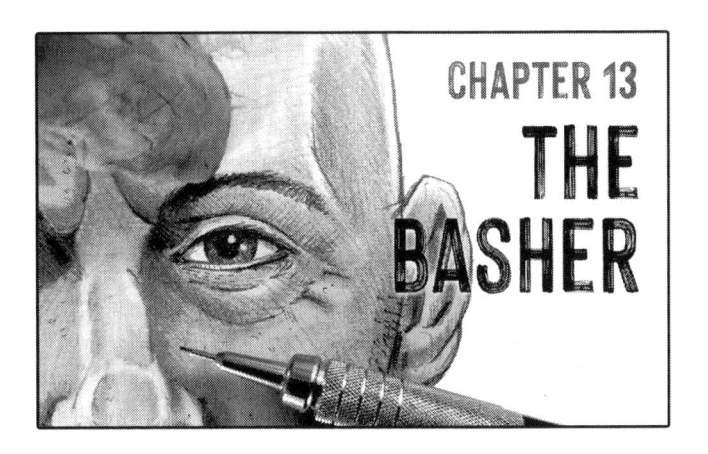

HALLOWEEN WAS THE NEXT DAY.

Porches and front yards were decorated with the expected pumpkins, skeletons, and cardboard-cutout ghosts, but the streets were uncharacteristically quiet. The kids in this town loved Halloween, but this year a specter of dread seized Everett Falls. There was a shadow, a shape, a figure moving amongst them. Few kids dared to trick-or-treat, and those who did went with the protection of both parents.

The mall was buzzing. People felt safer indoors with a team of security guards than they did outside. They had no idea the wolf was in their midst. He carried two shopping bags in his massive hands. The wolf wore a cute bunny mask, gliding through the river of consumers.

I love hunting at malls. So many people, so many sounds, so many ways to be sneaky. Especially today, having an excuse to wear this mask. I feel them rush past me. Sweet, sweet little girls... There's one I like who works at the little beauty kiosk upstairs. Little Latina. She parked where she always does in Lot C, and tonight I made sure to get the parking space right next to her.

The man strolled along.

He took his time. He watched humanity swirl around him. He liked to watch. The cute bunny mask betrayed no emotion. A five year-old boy nearly ran into him before the father yanked him back.

The man stepped onto the escalator, observing these humans from above as he moved to the second level. Watching them scuttle about like ants. He made his way down the corridor, casually observing the shops, products, people, smells, and sounds all around him. He reached the beauty kiosk.

There she is. Nicole. Mmmm... Long black hair, dark eyes... My God, look at that fucking ass! You and me tonight, baby. You and me. Maybe you've heard of me. I got a bad reputation. And it's about to get even worse. I'm just getting started, little girl. You're next, and there will be many more after you. Mmmm, those lips. Those tight little pants... Oh, brother! Just wait and see what I do to this one! Mm! You and me tonight, baby. You and me.

She sold a travel pack of makeup to a woman and handed her the receipt. She smiled and waved to the customer, then returned to texting her friend. The man checked his watch. 9:35 p.m.

She gets off at ten. She comes to her car, whack! Throw her in the trunk, drive out to one of those empty condo's off Shallow Circle... Have us a little party. Mmm... Think I'll pick up a slice of pizza and go wait by the car.

. . .

NICOLE WALKED into parking lot C.

There were shadows and echoes of other people in the massive structure, but none close by. She buttoned her coat as she trotted through the dark, concrete tomb. She reached her car and dug into her pocket for the keys. A man casually strolled the opposite direction and she thought nothing of it.

He whipped out his arm and clotheslined her.

She slapped back into the pavement, her brain buzzing and her world upside down. Her nose and front teeth were smashed, her face a splatter of blood. She coughed and choked and tried to move, but her body was seized in shock.

The Shadow stepped over her.

Oh yeah, baby. Hi, Nicole. Little sweetie. Look at your pretty face bleeding. Look at that pretty little face all smashed the fuck up. Oh sweetheart, you look so beautiful...

She sputtered and tried to pull herself backward, tried to crawl. The Shadow took his time. Nobody was anywhere near them, and they were obscured between their two cars. She was trapped. He bent down to see her better through his twisted bunny mask. She trembled in terror, unable to scream.

Oh, I'm gonna have fun with you, little darlin'. Gonna have my way. Those pretty brown eyes. Can't wait to see those eyes squirt out of your skull as I smash your fucking head until it looks like a pile of ground beef. Sweet, sweet little girl...

Nicole swatted absently at the air in front of her, like that might stop him. He reached down and grabbed her by the collar. She cried and searched his eyes for mercy. He smashed his fist into her face three times. She fell back unconscious, her jaw, nose, and orbital socket broken, blood flowing onto the cold concrete.

He dragged her to his open trunk, looked both ways, then hefted her up and tossed her in. He calmly closed the trunk and went to the driver's door, plopping down inside. He took off his mask and tossed it onto the passenger seat. He started the engine and pulled away, leaving her purse lying beside her car.

I got you now, baby. No mistakes this time, no fuck-ups. I'm getting better at this.

"THE EVERETT FALLS BASHER STRIKES AGAIN!"

The headlines were not subtle. Crime scene photos and Freddy's sketch were on every front page and news broadcast. They were doing what the media does, sensationalizing tragedy. They had even given him a name. The Basher. Now everyone was talking. Two of their own girls brutally murdered. A devil among them.

Who can it be? What can we do?

November swept in like a cold breath. Parents locked their doors at night. The few gun owners in the area kept shotguns and .38 snub-noses by their bedsides. Young women traveled in pairs everywhere they went. The community held together, remaining strong and vigilant. But it wasn't enough.

"Basher Claims Third Victim!"

Freddy went to work, cutting loose the stacks of

newspapers in the morning. *"Still No Leads"* and *"A Community in Fear"* were typical examples of headlines. He organized the newspapers, swept the floors, cleaned the back room, and helped customers. He watched the news, read the papers, and waited helplessly. He went through his days, looking for a man with the right face. A man who matched his sketch.

A thick, round face. A large nose, a bushy mustache. Cold, beady eyes. A shaggy head of hair. Freddy's eyes scanned every face, his artist brain calculating the angles and planes of every feature. Nothing. The days went on. He went to work, hung out with Charlotte, and sat in suspense waiting for the next headline.

"Fourth Victim Found!"

That November was truly gray and miserable. Cold and wet. If it wasn't raining, there were puddles and mud from the previous shower. A bleak, penetrating, lonely cold. Harney and Bagnarol made their appearances around town, tracking down leads and interviewing witnesses. Freddy caught glimpses of them on the news, but he didn't reach out to them. What could he say?

Freddy and Charlotte continued to see each other. After every date, he would drop her off and make sure her father was home and that everything was okay.

One night, Charlotte asked if she could stay over with Freddy. She told him she was still scared, but she'd finally found the right person, someone special. She was ready. They made love for the first time that night.

Aunt Penny didn't seem to mind. Between Freddy and her father, Charlotte was well worried over.

"Elusive Basher Claims Fifth Victim!"

Freddy's heart sank reading the headline. There was nothing he could do. So he straightened the papers and continued stocking aisle one.

LITTLE FREDDY RAN through a maze of rocks.

A city of bridges and boulders and cobblestone paths. His eyes were glazed with terror. He ran through the dark. The man was behind him. The Shadow. The shape. He was so big, so imposing, a mountain. His heavy footsteps echoed as the young child dashed through the maze of caverns. He screamed as he ran into a wall.

He turned to see The Shadow closing in on him. Nowhere to run. Trapped in a corner. Death closing in. He raised his hand—a club instead of a hatchet this time—and lunged at the boy. Little Freddy shrieked as the hulking fiend swung the weapon.

"Nooooooo!!"

FREDDY BOLTED UP in bed screaming.

Charlotte startled awake to find him covered in cold sweat, his eyes wild, shivering. She sat up and cuddled next to him, stroking his back.

"Babes, are you okay?"

He struggled to compose himself, catching his breath.

"Yeah... No. I don't know..."

She ran her fingers through his hair and kissed him on the cheek. "Poor baby." She pushed away the comforter and slid to the edge of the bed. "Stay here. I'll get you a glass of water, okay?"

Freddy nodded.

Charlotte scooped an oversized night shirt off the chair beside the bed and slipped it over her nude body. She tip-toed through the darkness of Freddy's guest room, creaking open the door and heading for the kitchen. Freddy allowed himself to fall back into bed, feeling the cold dampness of his own sweat. He looked at the ceiling, finally calming down.

The sound of a terrified scream jolted through his spine. Freddy bolted up in bed, every muscle tensed.

Another scream. Glass breaking. The kitchen.

Freddy leapt out of bed in his boxers, crashing through the bedroom door, hurtling down the dark hallway, spilling down the stairs.

"Char? *Charlotte?!*"

The sounds of heavy thudding, of smashing something dense and wet. Freddy flew around the corner and crashed into the entryway to the kitchen. There before him, crouched on the floor was a massive figure, cloaked in a hooded black raincoat. Beneath him was Charlotte's lifeless body. He had smashed her head into a mound of bone and blood and viscera and brains. He continued bashing and bashing what was once her beautiful face.

"CHARLOTTE!!!"

FREDDY'S EYES snapped open as he suddenly woke up in bed. Again.

He wanted to instantly bolt up screaming, but found himself completely paralyzed. Charlotte lay beside him in bed, fast asleep. He tried to call for help but had no voice. Tried to roll, to sit up, but his entire body was locked in spasm.

His muscles were tight as bunches of cables. His eyes bulged, teeth grinded.

Please God, let me move! Snap out of it, Freddy!

He fought back, forcing himself to break the spell. Finally, it was like a switch flipped and Freddy could move. He sprang out of bed like a slingshot, tumbling onto the floor in a mess of sweat-soaked sheets.

"*Ghck-Haaaaa!! Ah!* Oh, God! Oh, fuck..."

Freddy gasped air into his lungs, sitting in the dark against his bed. He rubbed his face and head, trying to calm down. The digital clock on the counter read 3:30 a.m. He glanced at Charlotte and was glad to see he hadn't woken her. He let his head lean back against the bed, looking up at the ceiling.

"Fuck me..."

CHAPTER 14
THE BALD MAN

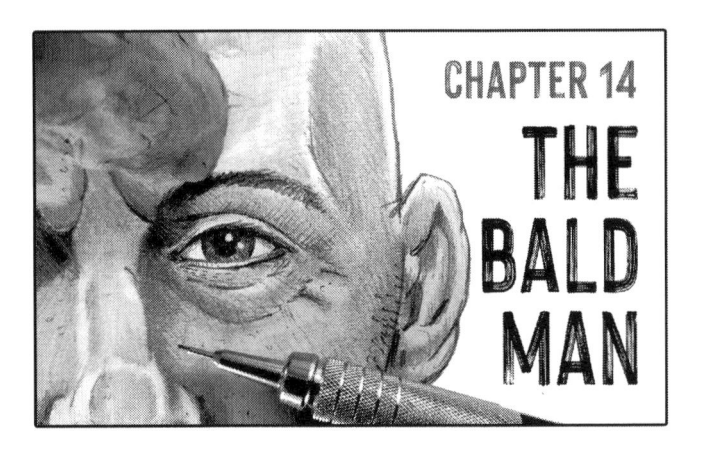

IT WAS mid-shift at Clarkson's and he sluggishly tied up the final Hefty garbage bag to be thrown into the dumpster. It was near freezing outside, but Freddy didn't bother with his jacket as he lugged the bulging sack through the loading dock, into the back parking lot, and tossed it in the battered steel receptacle. Seeing his breath, he briskly hurried back inside.

He shook off the cold, blowing warm air into his hands. He went to the bathroom and relieved himself. His phone beeped, *Close Encounters*. A text. He finished his business, then checked the message. It was from Rick.

Tell me more about this girl ur seeing

Freddy shook his head and typed. *Not now Rick, I'm working*

He pocketed his phone and went to the sink to wash his hands. *Do-de-do-do-doo*. Freddy chuckled and shook his head, tearing a length of paper towels from the dispenser and wiping his hands clean as he walked back out into the store room. He checked his phone again and sighed.

Don't be a cunt! What's her name again? Chartreuse?
It's Charlotte, okay?
Does she have a nice smoke wagon??
Dude, give me a break lol, I'm at work

Freddy ducked into the maze of boxes to conceal himself, pacing absently as he awaited the next text. It came right away, and Freddy found himself smiling despite the annoyance. He checked the message and laughed.

Don't give me that work shit! Does she have a nice pressure cooker, yes or no?

Rick, I'm not about to describe my girlfriend's ass to you, mkay?

Well, can you at least send me a picture then??
No, Rick lol
What about her feet? Does she have nice feet?

Look, she's a nice girl and things are going well, okay? It's a real difficult time right now, everybody's stressed. We're both helping each other, propping each other up. She's good for me. I like this girl.

FEET!! What about her FEET???

David plodded through the swinging doors and into the store room.

"Freddy?"

The tired pharmacy manager shambled through the back room, peering down the aisles of pallets and products, looking for his employee. Freddy held his phone down at his side and came out from his hiding place.

"Yeah, Dave?"

"You done with the garbage?"

"Yeah."

"Okay, I need you to stock the cereal aisle when you get a chance. It's uh, you know. Needs to be stocked."

"Gotcha. I'll get right on it."

David nodded with a polite smile and awkwardly stalked away, back to the storefront. Freddy sighed and looked at his phone screen again. He chuckled and shook his head, typing his reply.

Yes, Rick. She has nice feet, okay? Now I have to get back to work. Leave me alone you infernal pain in my asshole lol

FREDDY STOCKED THE CEREAL AISLE.

He cut open a large shipping box filled with Fruit Loops and began unloading the small rectangular boxes. Two at a time, he stacked them on the shelves, replenishing the empty spaces. He tossed aside the empty box and went to work on the Rice Krispies. His eyes drifted past the packaged breakfast treats. His mind wandered, hands moving on their own. Eyelids were getting heavy. Freddy yawned, grabbing more boxes of cereal and stacking them neatly.

Through the cereal boxes, he could see shoppers passing by in the next aisle. There was an elderly woman with bright red hair, deciding on which flavor of chewy granola bars to purchase. A young father and his three year-old son. They had matching close-cropped blonde hair. The father had a sharp nose, sporty eyeglasses, and a fashionably well-trimmed beard. A fat bald man stopped pushing his cart and looked down at a handwritten shopping list.

Freddy knelt down, scooped up a few more boxes of cereal, and continued stacking them in orderly rows. His eyes shifted focus into the next aisle again and the fat bald man was still there. He had powerful shoulders beneath his red and gray North Face coat. His stomach was a massive keg, his legs tree trunks. What little hair remained on his head was buzzed nearly to the skin.

Freddy found his eyes staying on the man.

Through the stacks of cereal, his view was obscured. There were big fleshy cheeks and jowls, a clean-shaved face. Freddy watched the man as he slowly pushed his cart. Small glimpses of his face were revealed. A bulbous nose. Beady eyes behind wire-rim glasses. He pushed the cart to the end of the aisle, then turned towards the pharmacy area. Freddy followed, noticing a rumbling in his stomach.

Do I know this guy? Something so familiar...

He pretended to straighten up as he kept his distance. When the subject turned to check prices on toothpastes, he revealed his whole face for the first time.

Freddy Luccio had a secret.

He had a super power. He had x-ray eyes. He had the ability to see through anything, to calculate angles, to perceive complex lighting patterns, and put it all down on paper. In order to draw at a professional level, he had to learn to see through everything. It was all in the eye. Freddy's eyes could scan the planes of a face, seeing through it as if it were made of glass.

He never forgot a face.

All sounds and sensations faded away as he watched the bald man take his items to the front register. Freddy followed him, his eyes glued to the husky customer. *His face, those eyes! But he's bald and clean shaven... Oh, fuck that, look at the bone structure, gavonne! Oh, man, I don't feel so good. I got a bad feeling. Oh, shit... It couldn't really be him, could it? I mean, there's no way, right...?*

A bulbous nose and a red Irish complexion. Small eyes, that pronounced downward slope of the upper eyelids. That furrowed brow. Late fifties, early sixties. Freddy's stomach tightened, a feeling of dread brewing inside of him. He knew.

He just knew.

Motherfucker... Mother. Fucker.

He watched, pretending to tidy the Red Bull front display shelves.

What the fuck are you doing, Freddy? I don't know, Goddamn it! I'm gonna follow him! And then what?... I don't know!

Freddy crept forward, positioning himself to follow the man into the parking lot. A little elderly lady in post-yoga gear had other plans for him though, cutting in front with a histrionic wave and a smile.

"Excuse me, young man. My eyes aren't what they used to be. Can you show me where the suppositories are, please?"

"Uh, yes. Of course, ma'am, it's right this way."

Freddy gestured for her to follow, catching a glimpse of the bald man walking towards the exit. *Shit shit shit!*

He tried to up the pace, but she dragged along at her own tempo. He drummed on his legs, his heart racing, ready to spring into action.

Have to catch him! Have to catch him!

"It's right down here on aisle six, ma'am." Freddy jogged ahead and pointed the rest of the way rather than taking her the whole distance. "Right down there on the left, okay?" She struggled to hustle but waved to him that it was okay and that she'd take it from there.

"Thank you, thank you."

Freddy nodded with a forced smile, then shot for the front door.

He dodged two more patrons and ran outside into the parking lot.

The cold air slapped him across his face. Late November New York wind. He looked left and right, scanning every car in the lot. Nothing. The bald man was nowhere to be seen. Freddy's fists clenched.

Motherfucker.

CHAPTER 15
GUT FEELING

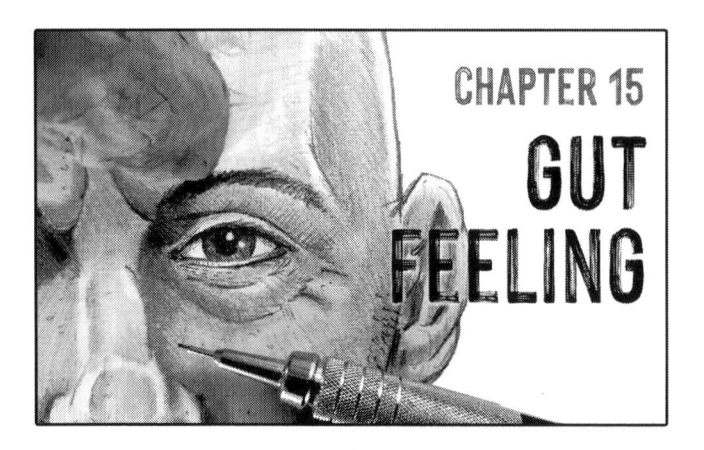

"LISTEN, I know he doesn't exactly match the description or the drawing, I know that. But you have to be able to read between the lines!"

Freddy followed Bagnarol through the hallways of the police station as the detective smoked a cigarette and absently flipped through a stack of paperwork.

"Mm hm," Bagnarol managed.

"I mean, his eyes, his bone structure, *that's* what matters!"

"Listen, Freddy. I know you want to help, but this is a real stretch. Sayin' this guy *would* look like The Basher *if* The Basher looked completely different... I mean, come on. That's pretty thin."

"I know, I know," Freddy's heart pounded, his mind racing like a wind turbine in a storm. "I just think it deserves some looking into. I mean, if you were The Basher, and there were posters of you everywhere with shaggy hair and a 'stache, wouldn't you shave it all off?"

"Good point. But—"

"Shit, maybe he wears a wig and a fake mustache as a

disguise when he goes out hunting. I mean like, you did find traces of makeup under Katie White's fingernails, right? I'm telling you, I just have a feeling about this guy."

"Oh, you have a feelin', huh?" Bagnarol held up the stack of paperwork. "Ya' see this? There's hundreds of tips from the public in here. People sayin' they saw a guy who looks like your composite. Sayin' they suspect this or suspect that. So we gotta run down every single one of these fuckin' leads, and so far none of it has turned up jack shit. But I'm so glad you have a feeling."

Freddy followed the detective into the conference room, where Harney and Miller were feasting on pizza and poring over a mosaic of evidence. Harney took a bite from his slice of pepperoni and glanced up at their guest.

"Hey, Freddy," he said with a mouth full of food.

"Hey, hey," Miller added.

"Hey, guys," Freddy said, his nerves on edge. "Listen, I'm just saying this guy should be looked at. That's all."

Harney shot a look at Bagnarol.

"What's goin' on, Bags?"

Bagnarol put down his stack of papers and extinguished his cigarette in a cheap plastic ashtray. "Freddy's playin' Columbo," he said, lifting a slice of pizza from the box and chomping into it.

"Come on, Ron. I—"

"Hold on," Harney said, sipping his drink. "What's the story, Freddy?"

The young man collected himself and focused his words. "Okay, I was at work earlier today. This guy comes in I've never seen before, and something just feels off about him, right? So I follow him around a little, get a better look at him, and I swear... It's the guy you're looking for. I-I mean, he had a bald head, glasses, clean-shaved, but I saw through all of that. The shape of his cheeks, his chin, his nose, his *eyes*. I could just feel it, I can't explain. I think... I *know* this is the guy. Maybe he wears a wig and fake mustache when he hunts? I don't know..."

"Shit, that's all I need to hear," Miller shrugged. "Let's go get him!"

"Shut up, Miller," Harney said. "You got a name on this guy?"

Freddy deflated a little. "...No."

"Address? License plate?"

"No. It was real quick. I didn't have time to—"

"Listen, Freddy," Harney said, swallowing a bite of pizza. "At the moment we got about forty-five active suspects in this case. All of whom at least somewhat match the description and your drawing. Here, let me see those files."

Bagnarol passed the papers over and Harney began to flip through as he took another bite. "Mm. You were right, Bags. Mario's really is better than Dante's."

"Oh, yeah. Told you."

"Bullshit," Miller scoffed. "Dante's kicks ass."

"You don't know good pizza," Bagnarol scoffed. "You ain't even Italian."

"Neither is Harney."

"Yeah, but he agrees with me."

Harney stopped flipping when he came upon the mug shot and rap sheet he was looking for, holding it up for Freddy to see.

"Here we go. Check this out. Farley Thomas. Forty-two years old. Two prior convictions for assault, three for grand theft auto."

Freddy leaned in to study the photos. The man did look similar to his composite sketch. A roundish face, mustache, scraggly hair. Harney continued flipping through the files, stopping again at another mug shot and holding it up to see.

"William Henry Rayburn. Fifty years old. Multiple past convictions, including sexual assault. Just moved here with his family two months before the murders started." The man's mug shot also resembled Freddy's drawing, but with a slimmer face and pock-marked skin from a lifetime of acne. Freddy swallowed his Adam's apple.

Harney flipped to the next mug shot. "Now this piece of shit. Lawrence Brian Stewart. Forty-five. Charged twenty years ago but never convicted on child molestation charges. Looks *a lot* like your picture. And the list goes on. Most of these scumbags have alibis that we're chipping away at. Some haven't even been catalogued into the national DNA database yet... You startin' to get what we're sayin', Freddy?"

"Yeah... I understand."

"Look, we know you want to help," Bagnarol said. "But trust me, we're doin' everything we can to catch this scum-fucker. Now if you really want us to check out the guy you saw, we need to know who he is. His name, address, license plate number, anything. Then we can check 'im out, okay?"

Freddy sighed, humbled and deflated.

"Yeah."

"You okay?"

"Yeah, just... It's a strong feeling. Y'know?"

"Oh, believe me, kid. I know."

Harney allowed the corners of his mouth to curl up into a polite, empathetic smile. His rich blue eyes watched as Freddy nodded and turned for the door.

"Hey, wait a minute," Bagnarol said. "You wanna weigh in on this debate or what?"

Freddy stopped and turned to face them.

"What debate?"

"Who's better? Mario's or Dante's?"

Freddy smiled.

"Pfft. I make better pizza than both of them."

CHAPTER 16
GIVING THANKS

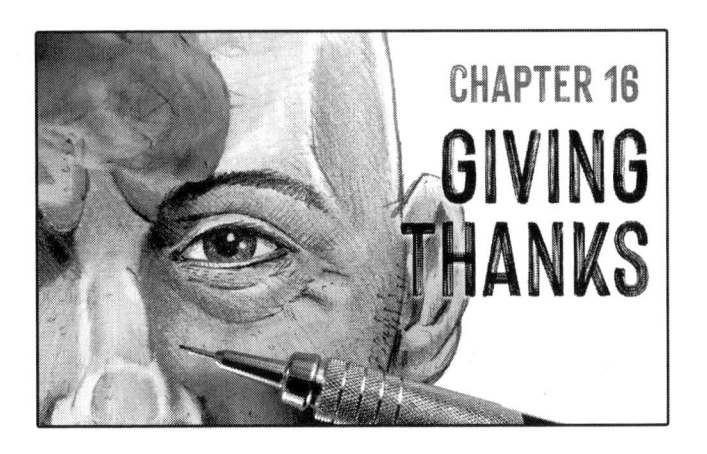

THE SMALL TURKEY had been nearly decimated, and the rest would make for some good leftovers in the following days. There was an almond stuffing, a dish of green beans, sweet potatoes, pecan pie, and ice cream. Freddy, Charlotte and Aunt Penny sat in Penny's dining room, candles lit, Vic Damone crooning through the stereo. Freddy took the last bite of his pie and sat back, closing his eyes.

"I'm dead."

He wore his polite, happy mask, but his mind swirled with one thought. It had found a space inside of his skull, and it lived there now, a deadbeat tenant, an insistent, unshakable nuisance. It was a thought laced with fear, with mystery, deriving pleasure from taunting Freddy and holding his mind hostage—

Him.

That face. Those eyes. The murders. Freddy fought to push it away, to focus on the good things in life. A beautiful girlfriend, a roof over his head, people who loved him, good health, good food to eat... But the darkness had crept in and made a home for itself, and the thought continued to claw at his brain.

Him.

"This pie is so good," Penny said. "Thank you, Char."

"My pleasure. Thank you, this was a great meal."

Yip! Yipyip! Rrrrrrr...

"I think Stella needs to go out," Penny chuckled, scratching the petite animal's head. Charlotte smiled and took a sip of wine.

"Here," Freddy pushed his chair back and stood, starting to gather dishes. "I'll help you clear this stuff."

Penny waved her hand, dismissing his effort. "Oh, stop. I got it. I know you guys gotta run. You can help me clean up later. Charlotte, I hope you have a wonderful Thanksgiving with your family in Vermont."

"Thank you."

"Come on," Penny said, holding up her glass of wine. "One last toast for the road." Freddy and Charlotte smiled, raising their glasses. "As Nonna Rosalinda used to say: Cheers to us, to hell with them! Salud!"

Freddy and Charlotte laughed and clinked glasses.

"Salud."

"Cheers."

FREDDY PARKED in Charlotte's driveway.

She looked at the house and could see her father inside. She sighed and turned to face him, stroking his hand.

"I wish you could spend the night."

"Yyyyeah, I don't think your dad would appreciate that."

"I know..." she giggled. "Wish you could come with us."

"Me too. But I'll see you in a couple days. You'll have a great time."

"Ugh, I don't know, babes. Trapped in a cabin with my Uncle Joe and my cousins for two days?" She laughed and sighed.

Him.

"Ah, you'll be fine. C'mon, I'll walk you to the door."

Freddy left the engine running as he hopped out and met her by the passenger door. She climbed out, holding her coat closed and shivering. Freddy chuckled and put his arm around her shoulders, leading her up to the house.

"You okay?"

"I'm cold!"

"I know, poor baby. You're always cold."

"I can't help it!" She shivered and turned to face him as they reached the front door. "I'll miss you."

"Aww, I'll miss you too."

Freddy kissed her and held her tight.

Him.

Freddy pulled back, forcing a smile as he stroked her hair.

"My little sweet-cheeks," he cooed.

"My little hottie," she answered, and leaned in for another kiss.

"Goodnight, sweetie. Text me when you get there, let me know you're okay."

"Okay." She gave him one last peck on the lips before turning to the door and taking out her keys. Freddy stepped back and watched her unlock the door and go inside. She turned with a smile and said, "Goodnight," before closing the door.

Him...

Bastard. Leave me alone!

FREDDY PACED AROUND the living room later that night in his t-shirt and sweats. Penny was asleep. All was quiet. He could watch TV. He could read a book. He could jerk off. But he wasn't alone. There was always *him*. A hulking figure lurking in the shadows of his mind.

Son of a bitch!

He went upstairs to his room and opened his backpack, pulling out his sketch book. He flipped through until he found the page he was looking for. *Him*. His sketch of The Basher stared back at him. The face of The Bald Man lingered in his head. So close but so different. A thought came to him, an experiment he felt compelled to try.

He opened his suitcase and found his 10x12" Artograph Light-Tracer. Tucking the rectangular light box under his arm, he grabbed up his backpack full of art supplies and headed back downstairs.

"Here we go, motherfucker. Here we go..."

Freddy padded down the steps and set up a workstation for himself at the living room coffee table. He put the light box down and plugged it in. He took out his sketch pad, pencils and erasers. He put the composite sketch of The Basher on top of the light box, then tore a fresh sheet of paper from the pad and laid it on top.

With a flip of the light switch, the living room was dipped into darkness. Freddy crossed back to the coffee table and sat down cross-legged on the floor. He scooted up to the edge of the coffee table, made himself comfortable, then hit the power button on the light box. The small flat screen lit up with an LED glow, creating a perfect surface for tracing.

"Okay... Okay..."

Freddy adjusted the blank sheet of paper over the composite sketch, seeing his original pencil marks clearly. He selected a Pentel 0.7 mechanical pencil, took a deep breath, and began to draw.

What is this fucker going to look like without his hair and mustache?

He traced the contours of the face, the cheeks, jowls, neck, nose. Imagining the curvature of his head underneath the hair, he penciled it in. Freddy imagined what his lips would look like beneath that big mustache, creating the proper curvature.

The face began to come to life.

No more beard stubble, he was now clean shaven. A pair of wire-frame glasses appeared over his eyes, stroke by stroke. Freddy's pencil whipped and danced across the glowing surface as the white light shone up at him in the darkness. He pulled back on the pressure, creating subtle shadows and highlights. He gave the eyes the appropriate black pupils and pin-point highlights to make them pop.

The details were finished and Freddy turned off the light box.

He stood up in the dark room and stretched his legs, hobbling back to the light switch on the wall. The room flooded with light and he could finally see the finished drawing in absolute clarity.

It looked exactly like The Bald Man.

Freddy smiled.

Damn, I'm good.

CHAPTER 17
DATABASE

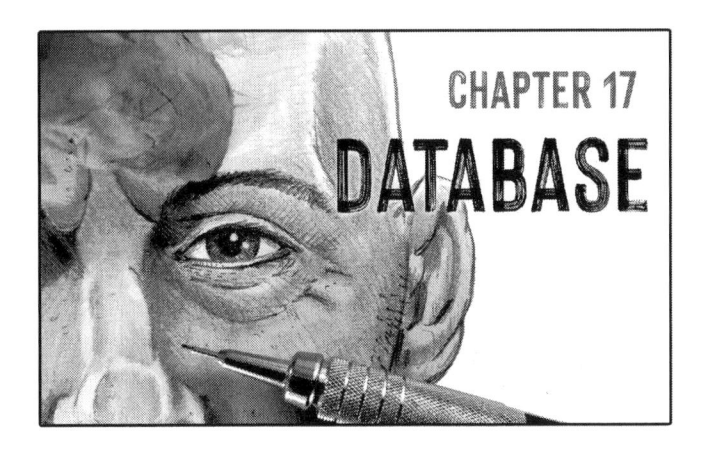

CHARLOTTE SWIPED the pricing gun across cartons of cigarettes behind the front register at the store. Their corporate-mandated playlist ran the same elevator music in a loop and it was starting to slice into her brain. She sighed, pushing her glasses up on the bridge of her nose and placed several priced cartons on the shelf.

A customer approached the register. He waited patiently for the young blonde in the blue vest to finish her task. She picked up another stack and piled them up, adjusting them into neat, straight rows. The man stood silently, basket in hand, watching her. Charlotte finished the chore and turned back around. Her whole body suddenly tensed.

It was The Bald Man.

"Hello," he said cheerfully.

Charlotte forgot to breathe. The large, husky man stood in a red winter coat and gray slacks, a pleasant smile on his face. She recognized him from Freddy's sketch right away. "Um, hello. M-May I help you?"

"Yes, you may. Oh, my my!" He beamed a friendly

smile. "What nice lip gloss you're wearing. Don't you look pretty?" His voice betrayed his appearance. It was sweet, sing-songy, almost feminine. Charlotte fidgeted.

"Um, uh... Thank you."

"Bet that helps in this cold weather. I tell you, my lips get pretty dang chapped this time of year. That and my joints keep acting up! Haha, getting old sucks!"

She forced a polite smile and nodded, gripping the counter to stop her hands from fidgeting. She couldn't place his accent, but it definitely wasn't New York.

"Well, listen sweetie, I don't want to take up your time," he continued. "I'm looking for those special shoe soles. You know, the one with the extra support? What do you call those?"

"Yeah, there's a few different brands," Charlotte pointed to the back. "They're all in aisle six by the pharmacy. Left side of the aisle."

"Aisle six, by the pharmacy. Okay, thank you very much, miss...?"

Her stomach churned and her heart fluttered. Pressure swelled inside of her, and she began to feel very warm. She fought to maintain a straight face, to not let him suspect. She forced a polite smile.

"Charlotte."

"Miss Charlotte. What a lovely name. Okay, thank you, miss Charlotte."

He tapped the counter between them and grinned at her before turning to walk away. His hand came within inches of hers and she pulled back, heart hammering, sweat beading on her forehead. She watched as the man walked up aisle six to continue shopping. Her hand went straight to the phone in her back pocket, and within seconds she was furiously texting.

You need to come in to work quick!

She waited impatiently for a moment before Freddy replied.

What are you talking about babe? It's my day off.
He's here! The bald guy from ur drawing!
On my way try to keep an eye on him
Omg yea right!

Charlotte pocketed her phone and peeked down the aisle. The Bald Man had found what he was looking for and had moved on to the pharmacy. She could barely see the edge of his head and shoulders as he dealt with Kevin at the counter. Surely picking up a prescription.

Another two customers came up to her register and Charlotte had to snap to attention to help them. She rang up their items and took their money, glancing over at the man at the pharmacy every few seconds. Kevin passed the man a baggie of medication and rang up what he had in his basket. The items were bagged and he turned to head for the exit.

Charlotte watched helplessly as the man marched toward the front doors. They slid open for him, letting a gust of early December air into the store along with a swirl of dead leaves. He was gone. She clenched her jaw and bagged items for the next customer in line. Afterwards, she found herself alone at the front of the store.

Freddy would be disappointed.

She tapped her fingers on the counter, thinking. An idea came to her, but she pushed it away. She couldn't, it was against the rules. She was a good girl. She followed the rules. Usually.

She slapped her hand on the counter as if to say *that does it*, and made her decision. She swung around the counter and headed for the back of the store to the pharmacy. David was nowhere in sight, nor were there any customers. It was now or never. She saw Kevin organizing bottles of prescriptions and came around the back to see him.

"Hi, Kevin."

"Hey, Charlotte. What's up?"

"Well, I uh... I need a little favor." She glanced over to see Meg, the pharmacist, on the phone with a customer. "You remember a few minutes ago, a customer came in to fill a prescription? Big guy, bald, glasses...?"

"Yeah, sure."

Charlotte bit her lip and rubbed her hands together, trying to figure out the best way to say this. "Well, um... I need you to look him up in the computer and give me his name and address. Uh, please."

The hipster millennial shot her a befuddled glare.

"You're kidding, right?"

"Uh... Nope. I'm serious."

"Why?"

"I... I can't tell you that, Kevin. I just need his information, okay?"

Kevin scoffed, shaking his scruffy head.

"Come on, Char. You know I can't do that. That's like, confidential information. I can't just go giving it out, I'll lose my job..."

Charlotte summoned her strength and leaned in

closer. She'd hoped it wouldn't have to come to this. "Listen, Kevin. I need you to do this for me, or I'm gonna have to tell David about you smoking pot on your lunch breaks, okay?"

The young pharmacy tech was aghast.

He swallowed his Adam's apple and turned to the computer, fingers flying into action.

FREDDY HURRIED through the front door at Clarkson's.

David was at the register helping a customer. He looked up and waved.

"Hey, Freddy. What are you doing here?"

"Hey... Just looking for Charlotte."

"Think she's in the back."

Freddy nodded and drifted deeper into the store, his eyes scanning down every aisle. There was a heavy-set old lady in the snack aisle, a young father and his two kids looking at Christmas decorations, two high school boys shopping for candy bars. But no Bald Man. Freddy had missed him. He cursed under his breath and pushed through the back doors into the stock room.

"Char? You in here?"

The space was cold, empty, and quiet. He was about to turn back to the store when the back doors flapped open and Charlotte came in. She opened her arms and they embraced.

"Hey, babes." She gave him a quick kiss.

"Hey. Did you... Is he...?"

"He left. I'm sorry."

Freddy deflated, pacing over to a palette of Dr. Pepper and taking a seat on it. He sighed, shaking his head. "Damn it."

Charlotte stepped up to him and smiled, pulling a folded piece of paper from her pocket. She waved it in front of his face to catch his attention.

"His name is James Roy Hiegren," she said. "He lives at 22 Union Valley Road."

Freddy took the paper, stunned. There scribbled in purple ink was the name, address, birth date, and phone number of the man he suspected—knew—was a monster. Freddy shot to his feet in disbelief.

"How did you get this?"

"Oh, I have my ways." She flashed a cocky smirk.

"Oh, baby. You rock, you fucking *rock!* Thank you!"

Freddy scooped her into a bear hug and began peppering her cheeks with kisses. She giggled and hugged him back.

"I know, I know. I'm the best."

CHAPTER 18
NOT MY SCUMBAG

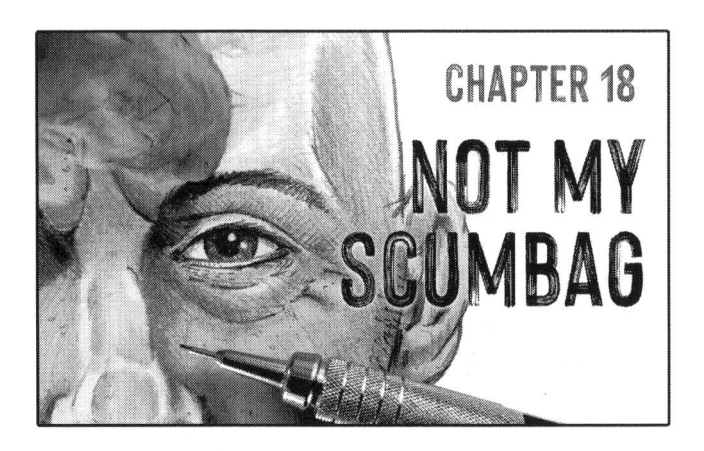

DONNA WAS busy fielding calls when she saw Freddy rush up to her window, an attractive young blonde in tow. She sighed and pretended not to notice him.

"I need to see Harney, Donna. Is he here?"

"He's busy right now, Freddy. Try leaving him a voicemail."

"No, listen. It's important that I talk to him. Please."

Donna rolled her eyes. "He's *busy*, Freddy."

"I have new information, Donna. Please, I have to talk to him."

She sighed. "Hang on. I'll see if someone can come out and talk to you. Okay?"

Freddy nodded and turned to Charlotte, who stood as rigid as a board. He rubbed her shoulders and kissed her forehead, certain this must be the first time she had ever been in a police station.

"This won't take long, I promise."

A minute passed before the door opened and a head of orange hair popped out.

"Hey, hey. It's Lucky Luciano," Miller quipped. "What's up, Freddy?"

"Hey, Detective Miller. Is Harney here?"

"What, you didn't come to talk to me? I'm hurt."

"Listen, it's important that I see him."

"Well, him and Bags are interviewing a suspect right now. I can give him a message for you if you want..."

"No, I'm sorry, but it's really important that I see him now." Freddy's eyes were determined. "I got some new information about the case. He's gonna want to see this."

HARNEY LEANED against the wall of the interrogation room. Bagnarol sat at the table in the center of the space, tapping his ballpoint pen into a yellow notepad covered with scribbled notes. Sitting across from him was a large middle-aged man with sandy brown hair, a mustache and a pock-marked face. William Henry Rayburn had cut his hair and trimmed his mustache since his last mug shot was taken, and he reclined in his chair without a care in the world.

"I just think it's weird you can't remember any of the specifics of what you did that night," Bagnarol continued to press one of his top suspects. Harney kept a close eye on the man's body language and micro-expressions, his clothes, the tone of his voice, everything.

Rayburn shrugged.

"Well, like I said, it was no different than any other night. Came home to my wife and kids, had a couple of beers... They already confirmed my alibi."

"Mm hm."

There was a knock at the door, followed by Miller poking his head in.

"Hey, boss."

"Yeah?"

"Freddy Luccio is here to see you."

"So?"

"He says it's important."

Harney grunted and shook his head, pushing himself off the wall to follow Miller. Bagnarol resumed the interview, playing with the pen in his hands.

"Look, Bill. You s—"

"William," Rayburn corrected.

Bagnarol controlled his breathing.

"You see, William, it just sounds a little bit peculiar to me that only two months after you move to town, these murders begin. A man with your record? Five counts of rape, all your victims attractive young girls? Sounds like a hell of a coincidence."

Rayburn leaned forward in his chair. "Listen to me, detective. I spent ten years in the can for some shit that I did. I *ain't* going back in for some shit that I *didn't* do. So if you're gonna accuse me of something, I believe I need a lawyer present."

FREDDY AND CHARLOTTE waited in the hallway.

"Here you go, Sarge." Miller gestured to the two civilians with a smile.

"Thank you, Miller," Harney growled. "This better be good, Freddy. We're interviewing a suspect."

"Well," Freddy beamed a proud grin, "remember that

man I was telling you about? The bald man I saw at work? Remember how you said that in order for you to do a background check, you needed some information on him first?"

"Yeah?"

Freddy reached into his coat pocket and produced the slip of paper. Charlotte slouched, doing her best to be invisible.

"Well, I got his name, address, phone number, and birth date! Boom!"

Freddy handed the paper to Harney who took a second to read it.

"James Roy Hiegren... How the hell did you get this?"

"Well, let's just say I had a little help from my ubiquitous, clandestine informant..." Freddy proudly gestured to Charlotte, stopping just short of saying *ta-daaa!*

Harney shot him a confused look.

"It's a line from *Lean On Me*. Y-Y'know, with Morgan Freeman? Anyway, John, meet Charlotte. Char, this is Detective Sergeant John Harney."

"Hi..." she mewled.

Harney did not look happy.

"C'mon, whadda you say? I did good, right? C'mon c'mon, you can say it!"

"Freddy, what're you doing? You're compromising our investigation, interrupting an interview with a suspect... To show me *this*?"

"But..." Freddy stammered. "Y-You said that's what you needed."

The door of the interview room swung open and

Bagnarol led his suspect out. Rayburn nodded politely as he strolled down the hall.

"Have a nice day, detectives."

"You too, *Bill*," Bagnarol said. "We just may be in touch."

Rayburn walked past the group standing in the hall. He smiled at Harney and Miller, then noticed Freddy and Charlotte. His eyes settled on the slim blonde, and she felt an electric jolt run through her. She hid behind Freddy as the burly man sauntered past. Freddy recognized him from his mugshot.

Yeah, this guy's a scumbag, that's for sure. But not my scumbag. I know it.

Bagnarol joined the rest of the group, hands in his pockets.

"Well, this guy's stickin' to his story, John," Bagnarol sighed. "Unless his wife and kids change their tune, his alibi is tight... Freddy, what the hell are you doin' here?"

"Freddy was just leaving," Harney snapped. "And Miller. Don't you *ever* pull me out of an interview like that. You do this shit again, I'll fuckin' have you writing parking tickets."

"Me? But..." Miller began to protest but then thought better of it.

Harney took Freddy and Charlotte by the shoulders, spun them around, and began ushering back the way they came. Freddy held up his hands, shocked.

"I'm sorry, guys! I'm just trying to help! Will you at least do a background check on Hiegren?"

"Yeah, sure," Harney scowled. "*After* we finish investigating all our other suspects who don't live in 'Freddy Luccio-Land.' Now get out of here."

In a heartbeat, Freddy and Charlotte found themselves standing out in the cold. She looked at him and his head dropped. *That was pretty fucking stupid, Luccio. God damn it.* She touched his hand, gently caressing his knuckles.

"Come on, babes. Let's get out of here."

Freddy nodded and put his arm around her shoulder, leading her back to the car. He pulled out his keys, unlocking the doors and got in without saying a word. Charlotte opened the passenger door, but noticed a man standing across the parking lot.

It was William Rayburn.

He leaned against his beat-up old pickup, smoking a cigarette. Watching her. She quickly looked away and jumped into the car as Freddy started the engine. Rayburn watched the pretty young girl through the passenger window as the young lovers drove off into the frosty evening.

CHAPTER 19
THAT'S WHAT PEOPLE DO

IT WAS JUST past ten when Freddy came home.

Yip! Yipyipyip! Rrrrrrr! Yipyipyip!

He sighed and shook his head, unlocking the door and coming in from the cold night. The lights had been dimmed and replaced with candles, setting an almost romantic mood. Van Morrison was singing about a brown eyed girl in the kitchen.

Freddy took off his coat and hung it on the wall before approaching the source of the music. Penny was doing her best to sing along with Van, and Stella provided her own unique brand of backing vocals. Freddy chuckled and cringed at her off-key performance as he walked into the kitchen. Boxes of Christmas decorations were spread everywhere, and she had begun the yearly task of decorating the house.

Penny wore a well-loved pair of pajamas and danced clumsily to the music, a half-empty glass of merlot in her hand. Her hair was down and she was barefoot, swinging and weaving to the beat.

"*Whooooa yeah yeah yeah! Ze-bop dop-dop-ditty Bop!*

Bee-babba-loo-bee- Oh hey, Freddy! Come on in! Heeeeeey!"

She swooshed over to him, her head floating in a warm river of red wine. She had been crying. Freddy's jaw clenched, but he didn't stop her when she went to hug him. He felt her frail weight draping on his shoulders, and he was nearly getting drunk just smelling her breath.

Shit, this is bad. Never seen her this lit before. What should I say?

"You okay, Aunt Penny?"

"Yeah! I'm doin' great! I'm Christmas decorating! It's my favorite time of year! My favorite time... I love Christmas. Merry Christmas, Freddy! Come on, want to help me put up the decorations?"

"Um, sure. But maybe tomorrow, huh?"

"How about a drink? Do you want some wine?" She slurped down the rest of her own glass, then nearly knocked it over as she put it down.

"Maybe we should get you up into bed."

She pulled away from him, swerving toward a box of decorations, and pulled out handfuls of tinsel. Freddy watched helplessly as she stumbled into the living room, strategically placing the shimmering eye candy.

"Eeeeevery Christmas I used to spend so much time making this place look pretty, and eeeeevery Christmas, Bill would roll his eyes at me and say I've gone overboard! *You're insane, woman!* Hahaaaa... But... We had eggnog, and gave the kids presents... You were all so cute when you were little! So precious... Sitting right over there opening your presents..." Penny's gaze went to the front of the Christmas tree, which she had not finished decorating yet. Her eyes were glassy as she remembered her ancient youth. "That year when Bonnie got her makeup set. She never looked so happy... And when Richie ate that whole cherry pie by himself... And there was wrapping paper everywhere... And... And everything smelled like coffee and roasted chestnuts..."

Penny wavered on her feet, dropping the streamers and balancing herself against a wall. Freddy went to her sides, his hands ready to catch her if she fell. Penny did not notice or care, her eyes focused on the framed family photos. One was in black and white, a candid shot of her and Bill, a million years ago. In another life. They were dancing in a park, the sun was shining. They looked happy. He was young and strong and handsome. His hair was dark and neat, his sideburns acceptable by 1980's standards. She was as fresh as a rose and on fire.

Penny swallowed a lump in her throat and touched the photo.

"This one wasn't a Christmas picture, this one was summer. It was very hot that day... I think this was the county fair? They had live music... Your Uncle Bill, he loved to dance. He could take me by the hand and twirl me around and around... Hoo!" Penny's head lulled back, her eyes flickering like an old film projector. "Oh, yes... Yes, my love... So handsome... So gentle..."

"Aunt Penny, let me help you up to bed, okay? Come on..."

Penny pushed away again, circling the room, her eyes consuming the little family museum. Stella followed at her heels, grumbling. Penny stroked the picture frames as she walked, picked up an old doll from when she was little, stroked its hair and put it back on its shelf. There were more photos of Bill, photos of Penny as a young woman and even a baby. Photos of her kids, her parents, of Freddy and his mother.

And of course, a picture of Sinatra.

Penny zeroed in on a large photo of her late husband, this one more recent. His hair was gray and his face sagged. Life had had its way with him. Still, his smile was infectious, and his eyes sparkled. Penny rested her hands against the wall and leaned in close, eye to eye with her husband's portrait. Her eyes burned, but she held it back.

"He could be a major pain in the ass too, don't get me wrong," she continued with a booming laugh. "God, you used to drive me *crazy*... Grumpy old son of a bitch... But I wouldn't have it any other way... E-Even in those last years, when things got bad... I stayed with you... I-I mean, what else was I supposed to do, ya know? That's what people do... When you love someone, and you're married, you stay by their side right... Right until the end!"

She erupted into tears.

Freddy came in and held her shoulders as she wept. Her fingers clung to the picture frame. She wailed, unable to stand on her own.

"Come on, Aunt Penny. Come on..."

Freddy gently lifted her arm and placed it around his head, unable to help getting choked up himself. Penny hung onto the photo, her eyes on fire.

"He was the love of my life... He was the love of my life..."

"Come on, Aunt Penny." Freddy reached his other

hand behind her knees and swept her up into his arms. "Come on, now. It's gonna be okay."

He turned and carried her away, her hand reaching for the framed photo, still trying to hold on. Her head lolled as Freddy slowly made his way up the steps, Stella following closely behind, worry in her little black eyes.

"He was the love of my life..."

Penny didn't seem to notice as she floated weightlessly into her dark bedroom. Her body eased onto the soft mattress, her head sinking into the luxurious fluff of her pillows. She sank into a warm, fuzzy feeling, and within seconds she was out. Stella hopped up onto the bed to cuddle with her mommy. Freddy pulled the blanket over her and stepped back, looking at the broken woman with concern in his eyes.

"Good night, Aunt Penny."

FREDDY SAT on the edge of his bed.

It was 11 p.m. He was fully dressed. His shoes were on. *What the hell am I doing? This is so stupid. Go to bed, Freddy.*

He rocked back and forth, nervous energy pumping through his body. He stood up, paced around, swung his arms a few times, sat back down. He cursed himself, unable to turn off his brain and relax. Fidgeting, he picked up his phone and turned it on. He opened up Facebook and scrolled around for a minute. No notifications, nothing interesting. He opened Instagram and scrolled around for a minute. No notifications, nothing interesting.

He switched the screen over to his personal contacts.

Starting at A, he scrolled through the alphabet, looking at all the names. So many people, yet no one to call. Ex-friends he'd forgotten were still in his phone. Family members he hadn't seen in a decade. He saw his father's name and scrolled past. Saw his mother's name and stopped. *Should I...? Nah.* He scrolled past. He saw Rick's name, chuckled, and put the phone down.

Him.

Stop, damn it. Just stop thinking about it. Just stop.

This is so stupid! This is none of my fucking business. Why am I so fixated on this one fucking guy? James Roy Hiegren... He has a name now.

Freddy drummed on his knees as he rocked back and forth.

Don't do it. Don't fucking do it. Be smart... But there's just something about this guy. It's not just the way he looks, it's... It's a feeling I can't explain. He makes my skin crawl... Just let the cops do their jobs, Freddy... Yeah, but what if I can help? What if I can actually show them some real evidence? ...Don't do it, Freddy.

He looked down at his phone again. Picked it up.

His finger swiped the screen and he opened the photos folder. He clicked on the first photo there, a shot of the slip of paper Charlotte had given him with Hiegren's information. Freddy sighed and his jaw clenched. *Fuck it.*

"22 Union Valley Road..."

CHAPTER 20
STAKEOUT

HE FOUND THE HOUSE EASILY. It was a nondescript two-story home at the end of a cul-de-sac. Cars were parked in driveways and on the streets, and Freddy found a good spot where he could sit in the Volvo 960 and see the house. Snow covered the scene like powdered sugar, and paths had been shoveled through it on the sidewalks and driveways. It was a clear night, crisp and chill, the moon and stars as bright as the Christmas lights that decorated most the front yards.

Freddy cut the engine.

He sat in the dark and watched Hiegren's house. It was flanked on all sides by Scarlet Oaks and Elm trees, and an expanse of woods in the rear. Nearly a hundred yards further back was the busy I-22 and its nearly constant flow of vehicles even this late at night. The neighbors all appeared to all be asleep. Christmas was good in places like this. Kids got presents, loved ones hugged each other, feasts were gorged.

There was no car parked in Hiegren's driveway, and the only sign of anyone being home was a light on inside.

Freddy fidgeted, waiting as the temperature in the car began to fall. He slipped his warm beanie and gloves on and continued to wait. He checked the clock on his phone. Midnight.

Come on, you fucker. Make a move. Slip up... And what do I do if he doesn't? How far am I willing to go with this? God, this is not smart...

Freddy waited. He could see his breath. He crossed his arms and shivered, rocking in his seat. A Ziplock baggie with a few Tostitos left in it was in his backpack, so he opened it and snacked away. He looked at his phone to check the time—12:34 a.m.—and noticed there was one new text message from Rick.

When are you coming back to LA? Enough of this bullshit.

Freddy put the phone down and shook his head.

"Not now, dude. Jesus."

He looked at the house. No movement, nothing.

"Oh, fuck this. What the hell am I doing? I should have my fucking head examined. Yeah sure, just sit in this freezing car all night and—"

Hiegren's front door opened.

"Oh, shit..."

The burly man trudged outside in his winter coat and hat, smoking a cigarette and carrying a bag of trash. He closed and locked the door behind him, then took one final drag of his smoke. He smashed the butt into an ashtray carved into a short stone pillar by his front bench. With heavy footsteps he carried the garbage out to the curb, and Freddy reflexively sank down into his seat.

Hiegren threw the bag into the trash can, then

headed back up the driveway. He pulled a clicker from his pocket and pressed the button, starting the mechanism to open the garage door. Freddy watched as he walked into the darkness and climbed into his car. The baby-blue Cadillac CT4-V roared to life, its exhaust steaming out into the cold air. Freddy snatched up his phone and turned it on, switching into the video setting.

"Where are you going, Jimbo? Where are you going?"

He held up his phone and began to record video.

"Um, okay, it's December 7th, approximately 12:35 a.m. Subject James Roy Hiegren appears to be leaving his house, uh..." He slid down in his seat, watching as the Cadillac backed out of the driveway, the garage door closing behind it. "License plate XJ6-2113. Where's he going at this time on a Wednesday night?"

Hiegren backed out onto the street, shifted gears, and drove off down the road. Freddy stopped recording and sat up, lingering in silence.

Should I follow him? No, don't be an idiot. Stay here. Just be patient, document his movements, see if there's any... Hey! The cigarette! That'll have his DNA, right?

Freddy looked down at the nearly empty Ziplock bag of chips in his hand and smiled. He stepped out into the cold, delicately closing the door behind him. He held the baggie upside down to dump out the rest of the Tostitos, then blew into it to get the crumbs out. He looked around to make sure the coast was clear, then crunched through the snow and up Hiegren's driveway.

This is crazy this is crazy this is crazy...

The house loomed over him, innocuous and plain. He tried to peek in the front window but the curtains were drawn. There were no bloodstains on the windowsills, no skeletons popping out of the ground, no terrified young girl screaming for help within. Just a house. His real interest was by the front door.

The ashtray was set into the top of a faux marble pillar crafted to look like an ancient Greek ruin. Inside were several crushed cigarette butts. Freddy smiled and reached in with his gloved hand, plucking out three and dropping them into the Ziplock baggie. He sealed the bag and held it up to see.

Three should be enough, right?

An engine started behind him.

Freddy spun around to see a pair of headlights turn on. It was too far away to see the make of the vehicle, but it looked like a van, and it was facing him. Freddy froze in place as the lights washed over him. The vehicle backed up a little, then pulled forward out of its parking space, slowly turning around and heading the out of the cul-de-sac. Freddy allowed himself to exhale. His heart started again.

Jesus. I better get back in the car before someone thinks I'm a burglar.

He shuffled back to the Volvo, throwing open the door and sliding back in to the relative warmth. Or at least protection from the wind. He caught his breath, looking again at his evidence before tucking it away in his bag. The seat was soft and he dug his hands into his pockets, allowing himself to sink in.

Okay, Jimbo. Let's see what time you get back. I can wait all night.

Freddy lasted another half hour before the weight of

his eyelids was too much to bear. He fell into darkness, and despite the cold, his body relaxed and went to a warm place. He was fast asleep.

TAP, tap, tap.

Someone was knocking on the window.

There it was again. Freddy's eyes strained to open, blinking away the haze of sleep. It took him a second to remember where he was. Sitting in the car outside Hiegren's house. Middle of the night. Someone was knocking on the window.

"Huh...?"

He lifted his groggy head and looked. A large, dark figure stood beside the driver's window, looking in at him. A club was in the man's hand. Before Freddy could even think to do anything, the man smashed through the window with his club sending an explosion of glass splinters into his face.

"Shit!!"

HE WOKE AGAIN, this time for real.

The window was in tact, no dark figure outside.

Freddy grabbed his chest and gasped for air.

"Jesus!"

But he wasn't alone. It was the sound of a screeching garage door that woke him up. He looked ahead to see Hiegren's Cadillac back in the driveway, brake lights glowing red. The garage door opened to welcome him home.

Freddy shot up in his seat and looked at his dashboard clock.

4:13 a.m.

He snatched up his cell, switched it into video mode, and once again began to record as the Caddy pulled into the garage.

"Okay, uh, it's 4:13 a.m. Subject is just now returning home... What have you been up to, Hiegren? Where do you go in the middle of the night?"

Hiegren parked and cut the engine. The garage door closed behind him.

Freddy stopped recording and put his phone down.

"Where do you go?"

CHAPTER 21
CLOSING TIME

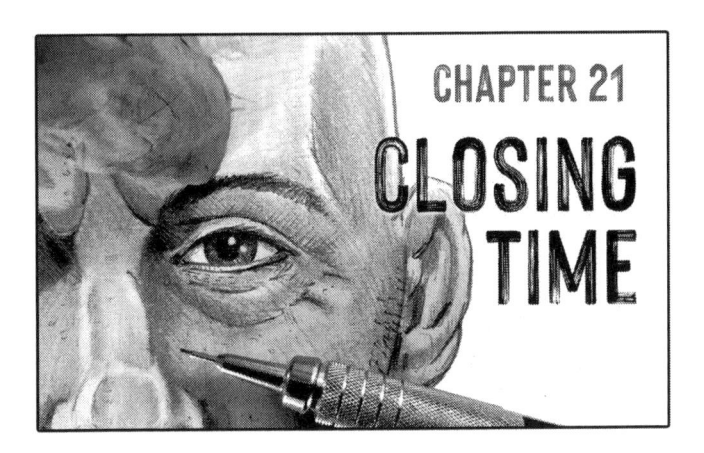

THE LAST CUSTOMER had left and Charlotte clicked off the open sign.

David locked the back door and began turning off the lights. They were the last two people in Clarkson's, and they dutifully went through their nightly ritual. Charlotte went to the Sirius control hub and turned off the monotonous loop of easy listening music, sighing with relief. Her back ached and she was dying to take her shoes off.

David switched all but the front lights off and made sure the cigarette display cases were locked. He winced and rubbed his right knee, then lumbered to the front counter where Charlotte was wrapping up.

"You got the register locked, Char?"

"Yeah. You okay?"

"Oh, yeah. Just a little bit past my old football days," he chuckled. "You ready to get the hell out of this place?"

"Oh, boy. Am I ever." She slipped into her favorite green coat and threw a scarf around her neck.

She took out her phone and texted Freddy: *On my way home babes*

A moment later he replied, *Okay be safe sweet cheeks*

"You seeing Freddy tonight?"

"Not tonight. I'm going home and straight to bed."

Dave chuckled and slipped into his winter coat and hat. "Well, I got me a date with a six-pack of Heineken and a tube of Icy-Hot."

"When are you gonna get on OK Cupid, get yourself a date with an actual woman?" She chided.

"After my last two marriages, I think I'll stay single, thank you very much. Besides, you're already spoken for."

"Ha ha, very funny, Dave."

"C'mon, you ready to go or what?"

"Yeah," she scooped up a plastic bag full of groceries and scooted to meet him by the alarm panel.

David entered his password and activated the alarm. They pushed through the front door and she used her key to lock it. December winds hit them and their bodies reflexively tensed.

"Hoo! God damn, it's cold!" David began to close the steel grate, when suddenly Charlotte swore under her breath. "What's wrong?"

"I forgot my purse in the bathroom. Crap."

"Ugh!" David bounced in place, shivering as the icy wind sliced through his clothes. "Well, hurry up and go get it. I'll wait here."

"Oh, no. You go ahead. I'll be fine."

"Don't you want me to walk you to your car?"

"No, it's fine. Go home to your six-pack." She pushed

the steel gate back up and began to unlock the front door again.

"You sure?"

"Yeah yeah, I'll only be a second. See you tomorrow."

"If you say so," he said, turning and shuffling away. "Good night then, Char."

"Night."

She pushed into the dark store, the alarm starting to beep. She went to the control box, entered the code, and disarmed it. The empty space was eerily quiet, and she hated being in there alone with the lights out. She hustled up the center aisle, the shelves and products surrounding her like tombstones in an old cemetery.

She pushed through the back doors and into the stock room, plunging into nearly complete blackness. Holding her hands out like a blind person, she found her way to the bathroom and switched the light on. There was her purse on the counter. She slung it over her head and wasted no time getting out of there.

The walk back through the store was brisk. Christmas Santa toys looked like gargoyles in the dark, perched atop the shelves. Smiling babies printed on toilet paper packaging leered at her, suddenly sinister. Charlotte kept her head down and didn't look. She reached the entrance again, turning to the alarm controls and entering her password. The unit beeped and began its thirty-second countdown to arm itself.

Charlotte pushed outside into the cold, closing and locking the door. She shivered as the icy wind whistled across her exposed skin, closing and locking the sliding gate. She got her car key ready and began the long trek across the parking lot. Her nose started to go numb and her breath billowed from her lungs like steam from a locomotive. Her car was the only one left in the lot. There were no cars on the road and nobody else on the...

Charlotte gasped and stopped in her tracks.

There was a man standing across the street.

He leaned against a tree in the parking lot of the strip mall. He was tall, burly, wearing a heavy coat and hat. Standing in the shadows, he did not move. He was looking right at her.

Charlotte's heart stammered and she forced herself to keep walking, looking away. Her pulse picked up, her feet moved faster. Her white Ford Fiesta was fifty yards away. Keys gripped tight. Teeth chattered. She dared not look again. She dared not look.

She looked.

He was still standing there.

"Shitshitshitshitshit..." she hissed, speeding up more.

She couldn't see his face, but she could feel his eyes on her. The frozen air stung her face. Her heart pounded. She was almost there. Almost there.

She broke into a panicked sprint the last few yards, sliding into her driver's door. Her hand trembled with fear and cold as she desperately tried to unlock the door. She aimed the key for the lock and missed. Missed again.

"Damn it!"

She looked back. The man was gone.

There was no sign of him. She whipped around, scanning the streets, the parking lots. Nothing. He had vanished into the cold darkness.

With frosty wind nearly blowing her hat off, Charlotte turned back to her car, feverishly trying to unlock it. She finally got the key into the lock and flew inside, slamming the door closed behind her. She locked the door and gasped for air. Her head fell back against the head rest and she tried to compose herself. She caught her breath and sat forward, putting her key in the ignition and starting the engine.

Something slapped into her windshield with a wet *thwack* and she shrieked in terror. It was the front page of the local newspaper, soggy and torn, blown in by the wind. The headline stared at her, black and bold —

He's Still Out There. Police Say No New Leads in "Basher" Case.

Charlotte felt a sense of both relief and dread.

With a flick of her hand, she hit the windshield wiper and swept away the ominous message, put her car into drive, and peeled away.

CHAPTER 22
SHOW AND TELL

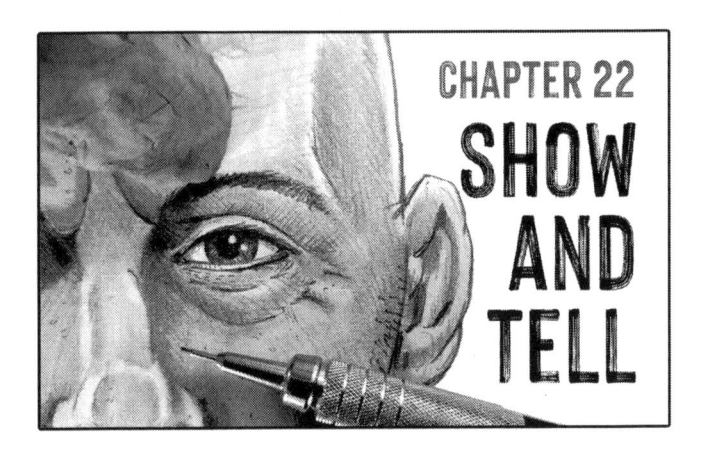

FREDDY WAS ON FIRE.

He held Charlotte tight in his arms as they sat in her living room, with her father, Ben beside them, and Harney and Bagnarol sitting across. It was the next day. The sky was white. The wind whispered. Cold light streamed through the living room window, carving hard shadows across tired faces.

"Go on, Miss Banino," Bagnarol said.

"I-I don't know... He was just standing there across the street. Just watching me. I was so scared... I knew, I just knew... It was him."

"And you couldn't make out his face at all, you say?" John Harney's hands were clasped together. He leaned forward. His blue eyes had clearly not closed for at least a week. Charlotte shook her head, wiping away tears.

"No. I'm sorry. It was too dark."

Freddy rubbed her shoulders and she hugged her knees to her chest. Ben Banino stood up and began to pace. Harney and Bagnarol shared a look, and the junior detective wrote a note in his pad.

"Maybe it was nothing, sweetie," her father grasped. "Maybe he was just a guy standing there..."

"It was *him*, Daddy."

"Guys," Freddy seethed. "What are we gonna do here?"

"We, Freddy? What are *we* gonna do?" Harney looked at him like he was an incredulous punk. "We are gonna investigate this case and catch this fucker. You're gonna stay home and protect your girlfriend and not do anything stupid."

"Guys," Freddy picked his backpack off the floor, unzipping it. "I'm sorry, but I couldn't just sit idly by and not do anything. You asked me for evidence, so I went out and got you some evidence."

"Huh?"

"Okay, what you got for us today, a bag of magic beans?"

"No," Freddy pulled out the baggie with three cigarette butts. "But I did get you James Roy Hiegren's DNA. Owned!" He tossed the bag to Bags and his Italian brother caught it with a look of bewilderment in his eyes.

"Jesus!" Bagnarol shook his head. "How the fuck... What the...? Ugh, what am I gonna do with you, Hollywood?"

"And not only that, I got video of him going out at all hours of the night! I was going to wait till tomorrow to show you all this, but with what just happened, I mean, I gotta show you now! Look!" He dug out his cell phone and turned it on, flipping to the video section. "Look, here it is!"

He pressed play and held the screen up for the two

men to see. It was the amateur surveillance from his stakeout. Bagnarol and Harney watched Hiegren leave his house on the small screen.

"See, here's the guy. He's leaving his house the other night at 12:35. And now here's this other one..." Freddy closed the first video to start the next.

"Y'know, this is all very nice, Freddy," Harney said, "but it's not substantial evidence. And even if this guy were The Basher, we couldn't use any of this stuff in court, 'cause you—"

"Look, look! Here we go!" Freddy started the next video and showed them. "And now there he is coming home at 4:13 a.m. later that night. So tell me, where is this guy going in the middle of the night?"

"To a bar. To get a blowjob." Harney shrugged.

"Gentlemen, *please*..." Ben rubbed his aching Christian temples.

"Look," Freddy dug back into his bag and produced his sketch pad and other assorted papers. "See? This is the original composite I did for you guys," he held it up. "And now here is the same composite, but I traced over it and redrew it without the hair and mustache. And without that little disguise, he looks *just* like James Hiegren!"

Bagnarol leaned in to see better. "Looks kinda like you, Sarge."

"All right, all right, we can run a background check," Harney said. "A DNA test, however, costs money and takes time. And I'd need more than your suspicions to justify that."

"Come on, Harney! Just do it! You have to be sure!"

Freddy was on his feet and shouting, his eyes enraged. Bagnarol stepped up to him with slow, heavy footsteps. He looked down at the young man with intense dark eyes, and held up a finger of warning.

"Hang on a second. You're takin' this shit too far. We're very busy, Freddy. We're working with a multi-bureau task force to find this bastard. We even got the FBI comin' in now. They'll be here later today." Bagnarol shook his head. "We've been analyzing evidence, interviewing suspects, doin' everything we can."

"Oh, like that one guy I saw you talking to at the station? He's a scumbag, sure, but he's not The Basher."

"Why?" Harney snapped. "Because he doesn't look enough like *your* drawing? Let me tell you something, kid. Composites are never one hundred percent accurate. Especially coming from the memories of traumatized victims attacked in the middle of the night!"

Charlotte rocked on the couch, knees tucked to her chest.

"It's not just the drawing," Freddy struggled to find words suitable enough to describe his emotions. "It's just... It's like... It's a *feeling* I have! This Hiegren guy, the first time I saw him, I just knew... He's *evil*. He's just *evil*."

He waited for their response.

Bagnarol shook his head. Harney ran his hands over his shaved head.

"I can't believe this," Freddy snapped. "Aren't you guys supposed to track down every lead, every tip...?"

"We are and we will," Bagnarol said.

"That's right. Go on home now and stay out of this, Freddy."

"How *can* I just stay out of this?" Freddy fought back tears. "What if this maniac is coming after my girl? She's crying, she's terrified, look at her! I'm over here tryin' to tell her everything's gonna be all right! A-And what am I supposed to say? What are we gonna do?"

Harney took a step forward. "You think you know about obsession? You don't think my wife and kids cry in fear? You think I get *any* sleep at night anymore?... Get out of here, Freddy. Just... Go home."

"I-I just wanted—"

"Come on now. Let's go." Harney began to usher Freddy to the door, and Charlotte jumped up and latched on to him, hugging him tight.

"No, I want him to stay!" Charlotte protested.

"Guys, come on. Let's go."

"Well, hold on a minute, we can talk about this," Ben suggested. "Do we need to get a protective detail for Charlotte?"

"We'll talk about that, Mr. Banino," Harney said, pulling Freddy and Charlotte apart, "but first thing's first. Freddy, let's go."

"No, let him stay!"

"Come on, guys!"

"Let's go!"

They bickered and tussled, and didn't even notice Detective Miller run in through the front door. He was out of breath, his cheeks bright red.

"Hey, guys! Guys!" Miller nearly crashed into the

group and demanded their attention. "Guys! We got a dead body reported at Lake Everett! Young female..."

It was like all the air had been sucked from the room.

Harney gritted his teeth.

"Son of a bitch... *God damn it!*" Bagnarol's head dropped.

Freddy and Charlotte held onto each other, speechless.

"Please excuse us, everyone," Bagnarol said as he and the other two detectives stalked their way to the front door. "Go home, Freddy."

"But—"

"Go *home!*"

CHAPTER 23
LAKE EVERETT

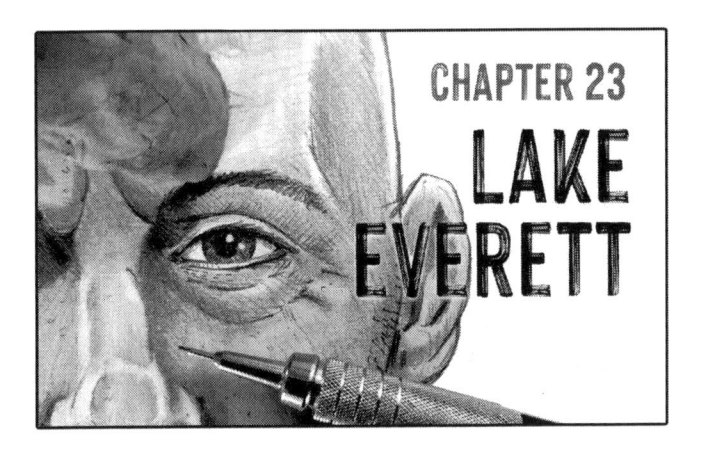

BY THE TIME Freddy arrived on scene there was already a crowd.

A thin layer of snow covered the ground like a wedding dress, pristine and innocent. The lake itself was frozen, surrounded by trees and houses, with a small pier and a playground for the kids. The parking lot was filled with county and state police units, CSI vans, and an ambulance. A border of yellow police tape and several uniformed officers held back the growing mass of onlookers.

Freddy jumped out of his car and ran down a frozen embankment, nearly slipping as he joined the surging crowd. He pushed his way through, desperate to see better. There was panic and fear in the air, whispers and gasps, tears and screams. Freddy fought and shoved his way to the front.

"Excuse me! Excuse me!"

He reached the yellow tape border and stopped, gazing down at the scene ahead. Harney and Bagnarol were there, as were Miller and several other detectives and officers he hadn't seen before. There were CSI's and techs, a photographer and a medical examiner, all circling around a central spot on the ground. From where Freddy was standing, it looked like nothing more than an abstract black shape laying on the ground. A pile of clothes. Red in the snow. It was the body of a young girl.

"Any ID on the victim?" Bagnarol asked a uniformed officer with a note pad.

"Yeah," the officer held out the girl's discarded wallet, pulling out a driver's license and handing it to the detective. "Lisa Carmichael. Seventeen years old."

The detectives studied the body. Poker faces. This was a young girl, one of their own. Full of life. Now she was frozen solid and covered with a layer of ice. A frozen puddle of deep crimson blood. A spatter on her pale white hand. Bare legs, yellow panties hanging from the left ankle. A butterfly hair clip several feet away, strands of blonde hair clinging to it.

Harney observed, "No footprints."

"No, sir," the officer said. "The snow must have fallen after the attack."

"Of course."

The detective sergeant clenched his jaw, containing his rage. His blue eyes scanned the scene. He glanced over at the crowd, studying the faces. His people, his community. People he was responsible for keeping safe. There at the front was Freddy Luccio. Harney made eye contact and shot the young man a disapproving look.

"Make sure no press gets in here this time," Harney pointed a finger at Miller. "And make sure nobody's takin' pictures with their fucking cell phones!"

"You got it."

Harney turned back to regard the CSIs.

"Time of death?"

"Judging from the lividity, I'd say sometime late last night, early this morning."

"No prints, no DNA?"

"Same as always, he's using a condom."

Harney steamed, grinding his teeth.

The sound of screeching tires.

A gray Oldsmobile sedan skidded to a halt in the parking lot and a wild-eyed married couple leapt out. Hysterical, they sprinted for the crime scene.

"Is it her?" the mother screamed. "Is it my *baby?*"

"Lisa! *LISA!!*" the father sobbed.

Freddy watched along with everyone else as the crowd-control officers clustered to block the victim's parents from getting any closer. Overwrought, they fought like crazy to get through.

"Is it her?! IS IT HER?!"

Freddy's heart sank. He watched as Harney rushed to meet them. He couldn't hear the words being spoken, but Harney put his hands on the mother's shoulders, and his head hung low. Then he looked up and spoke softly.

Their faces sank as he told them the news.

"NOOOOOO!!! NOOOOOO!!! NOT MY BABY!!! OH GOD!!! OH MY GOD!!!"

The husband and wife collapsed into each other's embrace, sobbing uncontrollably. Indescribable grief. Three officers helped them back to their feet and held them up, carrying them away. Their cries faded into the distance.

Something deep inside of John Harney snapped.

He looked back to the crowd and his eyes locked right on to Freddy, who watched the scene in wide-eyed amazement. Harney turned and walked toward the crowd, and Freddy knew he was coming right for him. The detective held up the police tape, inviting Freddy to come through.

"C'mon, Freddy. Come with me. Come on."

Freddy could not read the expression in Harney's eyes, and ducked under tentatively. Harney put a hand on Freddy's shoulder and began to lead him towards the body. Freddy looked at him, confused.

"W-What's going on?"

"You wanna see this, don't ya, Freddy? You like playing detective?"

Harney pushed Freddy forward with more force.

"I... Wait—"

Harney shoved Freddy right up to the body, grabbing him by the collar and forcing him to look. Freddy jerked back in horror.

"Fascinating stuff, isn't it?" Harney snarled.

"John, stop it," Bagnarol stepped in. "What the fuck are you doin'?"

"Look at her, Freddy," Harney held him right over the frozen corpse. "He raped her, bludgeoned her to death, then raped her *again*. We haven't told the press that, of course, but oh yeah, that's his favorite thing to do. Take a good look. There's barely anything left of her fuckin' head! *Why don't you draw a picture of that?*"

"Harney, that's *enough!*"

Bagnarol yanked Harney away from the stunned

youth, looking his sergeant in the eyes. He was breaking up inside. Everyone was watching. His eyes were on fire, glazing over with tears. Bagnarol let him go.

Harney stalked away to the water's edge so nobody would see him cry.

"What exactly is going on here?" It was an unfamiliar female voice.

The crime scene workers parted to let three people through. Leading the team was the local police chief, Harley J. Mills. The elder statesman of the department, he shivered in his blue arctic coat, a snow cap over his white hair. Behind him were two suits. Black wool coats. Black shoes. A man and a woman. She was older and clearly in charge.

They wore badges identifying them as federal officers.

Oh shit. This is not good.

"Well?" She pushed.

"No problem, ma'am. Everything is fine." Bagnarol patted Freddy's shoulder and smiled awkwardly.

Chief Mills began, "Fellas, this is—"

"I'm SSA Deborah Jones, this is agent Glenn Crabtree, FBI." Her face was severe and sharp, her hair short and brown and impeccable. The junior agent wore a gray ski-cap and mirrored sunglasses. His generic face betrayed no emotion.

"Um, these are detectives Bagnarol and Miller," the chief pointed them out. "And where the hell is Harney?"

"He's, uh, over by the water."

"And who the hell is this?"

Bagnarol patted Freddy on the back.

"This is Freddy, Chief. He's the one who did the composite of the suspect."

Shit, I was hoping they wouldn't even notice me.

"The sketch artist?" Chief Mills was perplexed. "Okay, so what are you doing here?" All eyes were on Freddy.

"I'm just, I was just..."

The feds watched him squirm.

"Can we get him out of here, please?" Jones ordered.

"I got him," Bagnarol gently touched Freddy on the shoulder, "C'mon, kid." The bigger man led him away in a state of shock. He could hear the senior fed's voice behind him —

"Thank you. We have a crime scene to work here, if you don't mind."

Freddy and Bagnarol walked through the crowd and back to the parking lot. Freddy's legs felt like rubber, his body frozen numb, his head spinning. Bagnarol rolled a cigarette and lit it up.

"Pretty fuckin' cold, y'know?" Bagnarol exhaled a plume of smoke. "Hard to believe it's almost Christmas."

Freddy didn't answer.

"My wife loves this time of year. All the snow, she thinks it's so pretty. She gets all excited about decoratin' the house, y'know? Everything has to be cute, she says." He chuckled and took a drag. "The tree, and the lights, and all her little things she likes to put out... Sure, honey. You go right ahead, make everything look cute if that makes you happy... Like any of that shit matters."

They stood for a moment beside Freddy's car.

"You okay?" Bagnarol tried again.

Him.

Freddy finally spoke. "James Roy Hiegren. Please. Check him out."

Bagnarol shook his head. This kid had balls.

"Fine, I'll look into Hiegren. I'll check for a criminal record, I'll check for alibis, I'll find out how many fuckin' parking tickets the guy's had in his life."

"And the DNA?"

"*And* I'll send the cigarette butts to the lab and check for DNA. But don't come askin' about it every day. This ain't *CSI: Miami* or fuckin' *Criminal Minds*. In real life, DNA testin' actually takes time. So don't come around breakin' my balls. Okay?"

Freddy nodded with a chuckle.

"Okay... Thanks, Bags."

They shook hands.

CHAPTER 24
SPACE MAN

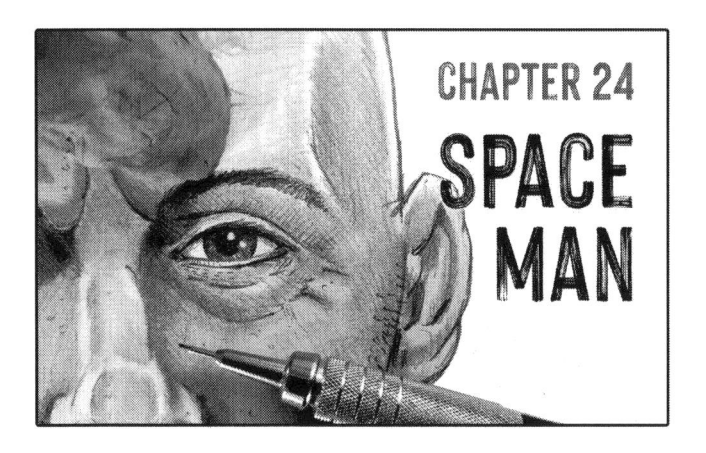

THE COFFEE TABLE was a haphazard collage of notes, drawings, newspapers, and late night snacks. Freddy clinked the bottle of Johnnie Walker into his glass and poured himself another refill. His eyes were red, his hair a mess, his beard coming back in patches. He took a swig of the amber fire and felt it burning in his guts.

He held up his original composite, studying it, then the revised version that looked more like Hiegren. He pored over the newspaper articles again, read through his notes, checked the logs he'd made of Hiegren's comings and goings. There was nothing new or conclusive.

"I gotta be missing something... Gotta be missing something..."

He threw the papers against the wall and pounded the coffee table.

"Fuck." He downed the rest of the bourbon and sat still, staring into nothingness. He felt it coming, tried to stop it. The pressure in his head, the flood pushing against his eyelids. It was far too strong to hold inside.

Freddy broke down and wept.

He slid to the floor, head in his hands.

All the thoughts and emotions pent up over the last several months swirled and surged through him. Failure. Helplessness. Shattered self esteem. That horrible look in the eyes of Lisa Carmichael's parents. That dreadful sight of Lisa's eyes, smashed and splattered on the ground along with chunks of her skull and brain. He could not get that image out of his mind. So many victims, so much pain. And here he was, a failed storyboard artist working the stock room at Clarkson's.

His face was red and drenched with sweat.

A text message came in:

He's comin down to swallow our HEARTS!
He's comin down to tear us APA-A-ART!
He's comin down to INFILTRA-IATE!
He's comin down to SEAL OUR FA-A-ATE!

Freddy laughed, which only made him cry harder. He put the phone down on the floor, not in the mood to play Rick's games. He wiped his eyes and tried to control his breathing, managing to calm himself a bit. His phone chimed again, and he rolled his eyes, picking it up to check the message:

Finish it!!

Freddy began to type a response, but stopped. A text wouldn't do it tonight.

He hit the call button and held the phone to his ear, his eyes bleary and his face red. After two rings, a comfortingly familiar voice came onto the line.

"Mm." The sardonic grunt was how Rick normally answered the phone.

"Hey, dude." Freddy's voice was rough.

"What's up, you okay?"

"...Not really," he cracked up again. "I'm... I'm having a really hard time, man."

"Shit, man... What's going on?" Rick's tone changed.

"I just... It's just... Everything going on over here, y'know? Everybody is so scared, and it's just like, I feel like there's nothing I can do..."

"Dude, you did your part, man. You drew the picture. You're not responsible for this. You can't be so hard on yourself. Fuck, dude, that place is killing you. Seriously, why don't you just move back here?"

"I can't, Rick. I can't afford rent in LA. And where am I gonna stay, on your couch in your little one bedroom with your wife and kid running around?"

"You can always just get into porn. Or sell your ass on the streets."

"Rick, I'm being serious right now!"

"Okay okay, I'm sorry."

"No, man. This is my home now," Freddy looked around his aunt's living room, an episode of *Forensic Justice* muted on the TV. "I can't just up and leave when the going gets tough. This is my community now, and people are dying. I have a girlfriend now, and she's scared to death. I just... I'm having a very hard time."

"Mm," Rick was silent for a moment. "I'm sorry, dude. I'm sure everything will be okay. You'll get through this."

"Thanks, man... So how's Gabe doing?"

"Pfft. He's a little cock blocker. Anyone ever tells you having a kid doesn't take all the joy and spontaneity out of a relationship is fucking *lying!*"

Freddy laughed hard. He needed this.

"How are your parents?"

"Old. Fat and old. You talk to your parents at all?"

Freddy cleared his throat. "Uh, no. Not since I moved here."

"Mm... You're a cunt and a traitor for leaving!"

"Yeah yeah, fuck off."

Rick could hold back no longer, launching into a blasting falsetto, continuing to sing one of their favorite childhood songs they wrote together.

"Oh well oh well I said his claws are like RAZORS! Finish it!"

Freddy chuckled, rolling his eyes. "His eyes are like lasers."

"No! Don't puss out on me! Give it to me hard, fucker! Big dick, baby! *Woo!* Do it right!"

Freddy screamed, *"His eyes are like LASERS!!!"*

They moved into the chorus together, harmonizing perfectly—

"WHOOOAAA!! Talkin' 'bout the SPACE MAN!
Comes from farther than JAPAN!
And soon his silver ship will LAND!
I'm talkin' 'bout the SPACE MAAAAAN!!"

They laughed.

Penny's voice suddenly shouted down from the second floor.

"Freddy? What the hell is going on down there?"

"Oh shit," he gasped, chuckling. "Sorry, Aunt Penny. I'll keep it down."

The two old friends giggled and continued talking into the night.

CHAPTER 25
RED CHRISTMAS

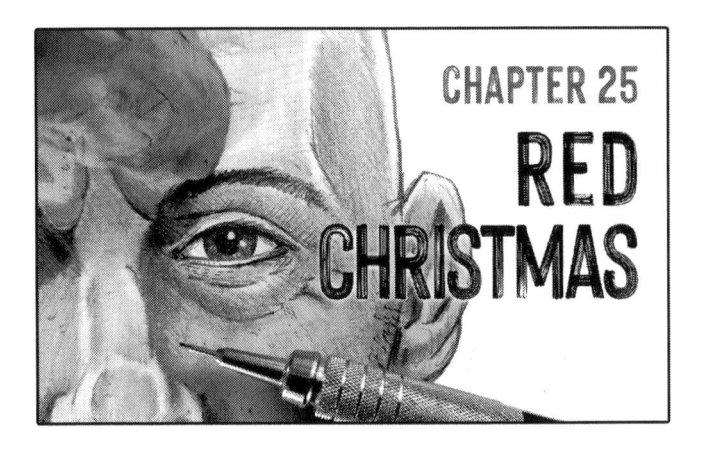

THERE WAS VERY little holiday cheer that year in Everett Falls.

Houses were decorated, but there were no carolers. People bought their loved ones presents, but did not smile at each other in the stores. Those who used to wave at their neighbors now cast sideways glances. Doors were locked. Young women didn't go anywhere alone. Fear lurked just beneath the frosty surface.

Freddy had ceased his surveillance activities. Watching Hiegren's house had not yielded any evidence, and he was tired of freezing his ass off until all hours of the night in his car. He had given the police two sketches, a name, address, DNA, video. Short of breaking into the man's house, there was nothing more he could do.

Just let the professionals do their job.

Bagnarol worked late most nights. He liked being in the office by himself. He rolled cigarettes and stared at the files, the photos, the notes scrolled on white boards. He blew smoke as he reclined in his chair, allowing his eyes to go out of focus and his mind to drift through the silent hallways.

Harney returned home every night where his wife waited for him. He hugged her and kissed her cheek. He ate dinner with his family and forced himself to make small talk. He checked on his five year-old daughter late at night, stroking her hair as she slept. Then he would amble through the house in his pajamas, drinking cans of Miller Highlife and thinking about everything and nothing all at once.

PENNY WAS fast asleep in her favorite armchair.

Charlotte sat on the floor in front of the couch, playing with Stella, while Freddy finished washing the dishes. Wrapped presents and candlelight. Yuletide songs, a screen saver of a fire place, spiked eggnog, presents. It was Christmas Day.

"Such a good girl, yes you are," Charlotte scratched Stella's furry belly.

Freddy came back in, wiping his hands on his pants.

"That dog's gonna give you fleas."

"Oh, stop it, you grouch. Why do you hate dogs so much?"

"I don't hate dogs."

I absolutely fucking hate dogs.

"Hm. Well, you could've fooled me."

"I'm just more of a cat person, that's all."

"Try being nice to her. Pet her a little."

Freddy grunted and reached down to scratch the

mutt's shaggy head. Stella growled and yapped at him. He threw his hands up in defeat.

"See?"

"She knows you don't like her, that's why."

"Whatever, whatever." Freddy went to Penny's chair and gently touched her shoulder. "Aunt Penny. Aunt Penny, wake up." She stirred, grunting as she came to with a yawn. "C'mon, time for bed."

"Mmm, okay, Freddy." She lurched forward, still half asleep, her old joints creaking as she worked to stand up. Freddy went to help her and she waved him away. "I got it, I got it. Come on, Stell. Let's go."

Stella hopped to attention and scurried along to join Penny up the stairs.

"Good night, Aunt Penny."

"Sleep well, Penny. Thanks for a lovely evening." Charlotte smiled.

"Yeeeooooow," Penny yawned, holding on to the railing as she worked her way up the steps. "G'night, kids. Meeerry Christmas. Ho-ho-ho... C'mon, Stell..."

Freddy stepped over the mess of wadded wrapping paper and sat beside Charlotte on the floor, leaning against the couch. He wore his usual pajama pants along with a new sweater, a garish red and green Christmas nightmare of a garment. Charlotte smiled and cuddled up with him.

"What're you thinking, babes?"

Freddy looked out the window and took another sip of eggnog, his eyes focusing on nothing in particular.

"Hello-ooh?" She nudged him.

"Sorry," he cleared his throat. "Nothing. Him. Whoever he is. The fact that he's still out there..."

She rested her head on his shoulder. "You don't think it's Hiegren anymore?"

"Oh, I don't know. I mean, who am I kidding? I jump to conclusions about this one guy just because he looks like my drawing *if* he was in total disguise? That's pretty thin. Oh, and I got a gut feeling about him, *ooh!* That'll really stand up in court."

"Yeah."

"I've taken this thing way too far. It's time to leave it alone and just let the police do their jobs... The real killer's out there somewhere and he's probably someone nobody even suspects yet." Freddy stared into his glass of egg nog, swirling it around. "I just... I don't know. Don't know why I thought I could help. Don't know why I'm here. Don't even know what I'm doing with my life... I used to be a successful artist, now I'm living in my aunt's house, working at a fucking pharmacy, acting like I know something the whole police department and the FBI doesn't... Who the hell do I think I am?"

She pushed away from him and frowned.

"What is it, Char?"

"You realize that working at that 'fucking pharmacy' is how you met *me*, right?"

"Oh, I didn't mean..."

"You have a job and people who love you. There's no shame in that. But you act like... Like it's not good enough. Like I'm not good enough. Well, I'm sorry I'm not some hot Hollywood bimbo, but I'm a real person, and I have feelings."

"Oh, babes..."

"You think I want to be stuck in Clarkson's forever? I want to be a CPA, and I'll get there. But right now I'm here, and that's okay. I'm sorry if you don't want to be here. But I feel like the first chance you get, you're gonna leave. Leave *me*."

"No way, I wouldn't do that to you. I..."

I love her.

"I... I love you."

She turned to him, seeing the sincerity in his eyes.

"I love you, too."

They kissed. He stroked her soft, pink cheeks.

"That's my sweet-cheeks."

She giggled. "So, do you like your sweater?"

Freddy looked down at the gaudy garment he was wearing.

I hate this fucking sweater.

"I love it, babes. How do you like your portrait?"

She smiled and glanced over at a framed pencil portrait of her that Freddy drew on the coffee table. He had captured her eyes, her smile, her essence, perfectly.

"I love it. It's beautiful. Thank you."

"Yeah? You like your pepper spray too?"

"Oh, yeah!" She held up the bottle and pretended to spray him in the eyes. "*Fsssh!* Take that!"

He played along, acting like his eyes were burning. They giggled and fell into each other's arms, kissing again. Their hands began to wander and caress as they eased onto the floor, lost in youthful romance.

Outside, icy winds howled.

. . .

THE BASHER CARESSED what was left of the young woman's head.

Her body was naked and sprawled on the floor in a swamp of blood. He lay beside her, cuddling with the corpse. His meaty fingers stroked her still-warm skin, streaking deep crimson everywhere. He was naked too, hugging her tight to his large, powerful body. He delicately played with her brains and chunks of skull, one of her eyes looking up at him from the puddle of pulp.

Oh yeah, baby. That was good. Mm! Sweet little girl.

The baby was in his bedroom, somehow still sleeping soundly in his crib. Daddy was out of the picture, another deadbeat, leaving poor Mommy alone and defenseless. The screen had been slashed and the window broken. Easy entry. When she got out of the shower, she didn't even know what hit her. Soon they were nude together on the bathroom floor, her unconscious, him rock hard. He'd enjoyed the crack of her skull, savored the warm splash of her blood.

Merry Christmas, little darlin'. Santa came down your chimney tonight, ha!

He sat up, caked in her blood, and pulled the condom off of his penis. He tossed it aside into the plastic baggie he'd brought, along with his usual cleaning supplies. He sat in the drying blood, enjoying the moment.

My turn for a shower now. Look at this mess you made all over me! Don't you go nowhere, honey!

He peeled himself off the floor, husky, hairy, smeared with drying blood and gore. He stretched and yawned. He stepped into the shower and got the hot water going.

He groaned in contentment as he washed himself clean, watching red swirl down the drain.

What a Merry Christmas indeed. Ho-Ho-Ho!

He finished the shower and stepped out, drying himself with a towel he'd brought from home. He put his clothes back on and went about the task of wiping down every surface he might have touched. He used a wet rag to wipe off areas of her skin where he may have left bloody fingerprints. The baby began to cry in the other room. He paid it no mind.

They'll never catch me. I'm too good.

He put on his winter coat and gloves. Stood over the body. Proud of his work.

Peering through the front window, he made sure the coast was clear. There was no one out in the streets late on Christmas Night. He opened the front door and casually strolled out into the dark.

And to all a good night.

CHAPTER 26
JIMBO

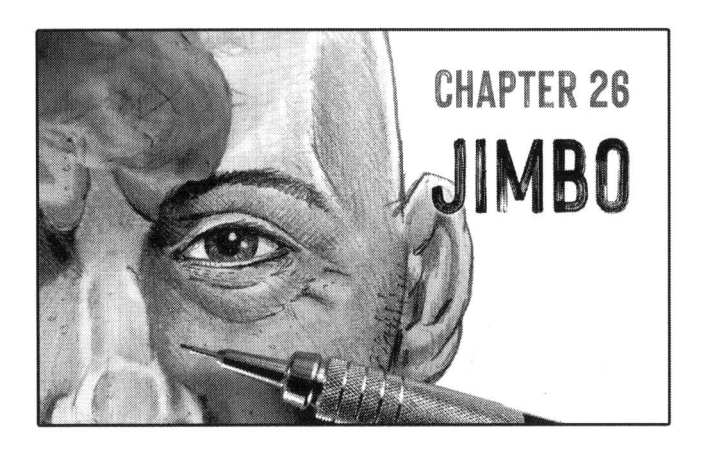

THE SUN WAS bright in the blue sky that morning.

Freddy woke up and rubbed his eyes, looking out the window. Were it not for the snow and ice crystals catching the light, it would look like a summer day. But he knew that one step out the door would bring a sharp chill. He had slept well, no dreams of Little Freddy running from a veiled boogeyman. He stretched and rolled in bed, determined to enjoy another few minutes of soft, warm comfort before heading out into the cold. But he had to pee, so he got up.

He clomped down the stairs ready for work. He contemplated breakfast. *Cook something here? Nah, fuck it, I'll get a couple bacon, egg & cheese croissants at Wendy's on the way.* He heard the news playing in the living room, so he strolled in with a warm smile.

"Morning, Aunt Penny."

Her eyes were bloodshot and fixed on the screen.

She did not answer him. Something was wrong. Freddy crossed in front of the screen to see what was going on, but in his heart he already knew. Ambulances.

Patrol cars. Police. Another crime scene. Freddy's heart sank and his legs went numb, and he had no choice but to sit down. Penny looked over at him, her face streaked with tears.

"Another one last night... On *Christmas!*"

Freddy tried to speak but couldn't find the words. His mind spun as an all-too-familiar story was reported, a photo of a smiling, beautiful young girl superimposed on the screen. Corrina Herman. Twenty-three. Mother of one young child.

Her eyes sparkled with life.

INTERSTATE 22. Driving. Moving. Haze.

Down the slick streets, past the A&P, past the post office, past the police station. The parking lot was abuzz with activity. Freddy sighed and kept driving. He found himself at work, wearing his vest and name tag. There was a mop in his hand. He realized he'd been standing in the same spot for the past two minutes, staring into space. He went about his duties.

The floor was cleaned and trash was taken out. Charlotte was a blur across the room, helping customers at the front register. Freddy saw the newspaper delivery truck drop off the bundle for the day, and he went to collect it. He lifted the stacks of papers by the binding strings and put them by the front display counter. His knife came out with a *click* and he cut through the strings.

"Basher Claims 8th Victim on Christmas Night."

Freddy fumed. He looked up to see Charlotte behind

the register, waiting for him to make eye contact. He forced a reassuring smile as he walked over.

"You okay?" she asked.

"Yeah... You?"

She shrugged. It was hard to find the words.

"David needs me to stay till closing tonight. Could you come meet me to walk me to my car?"

"Of course, babes. I'll be here."

"Corrina was a good person..." Charlotte's chin quivered. "We went to school together senior year. We never hung out or anything, but... I knew her. We were the same age."

Freddy came behind the counter and put his arm around her. She took off her glasses to wipe her eyes. More customers were coming to the counter. Freddy kissed the side of her head and scooted.

"See ya later, sweet-cheeks."

Charlotte put her glasses on, composed herself, and smiled for the next customer. Freddy headed toward the back, mentally counting his list of things to do.

He decided to start with stocking aisle three, passing David on his way to the stock room. He smiled politely.

"How ya doing, David?"

"Living the dream," his manager grumbled.

It was a quick trip to grab a crate of batteries and come back, though he underestimated the weight. He controlled his breathing as his arms bulged and his five-foot-five body strained, carefully placing the heavy box on the floor.

"Hoo!" It was a workout.

Freddy wiped his forehead and began the chore of

putting all the different packs of batteries in their assigned slots. His mind continued to wander. The crime scenes. The blood. *Him.*

His eyes drifted to the front of the store. The doors opened. Freddy's vision came into focus as a large, barrel-chested man walked into the store.

Him.

James Roy Hiegren shook off the cold and removed his hat as he entered the store. Freddy froze. He watched from the corner of his eye as the man picked up a hand basket and began shopping. Freddy reminded himself to breathe and grabbed a few more packs of batteries, trying to look busy.

Hiegren stepped up to the newspaper display and picked up a copy. Freddy watched intently as Hiegren read the headline and began reading the article on the latest murder. He shook his head and cursed under his breath in frustration. He wasn't horrified, he wasn't saddened. He was frustrated.

Freddy noticed more.

Hiegren's knuckles were bruised. His lip was split.

Freddy hissed, "Son... of... a... bitch."

Hiegren put the paper into his basket, shook his head, and continued up the grocery aisle. Freddy noticed that Charlotte didn't see him, dealing with another customer at the register. He backed up, sneaking around to the far right wall. He slinked along to the back of the store, knowing Hiegren would emerge shortly.

Motherfucker! That look in his eye! Who looks at a newspaper article about a murdered girl and makes that face? It's like he was annoyed. And what about the bruises? He's been in a fight! Motherfucker!

Hiegren appeared on the other side of the store, checking prices. He went down the hardware aisle and Freddy followed, nodding to a regular customer and Kevin at the pharmacy. He inched to the edge of the end cap, peeking around. Hiegren continued to shop, unaware he was being watched.

He picked up a few rolls of duct tape, a package of rope, a box of black trash bags. A bottle of Drano. A bottle of bleach. Freddy stood at the end of the aisle, his pulse racing.

Son of a bitch! It's practically a serial killer starter kit! Motherfucker, it's you! It's you it's you, I know it's you! I know it in every fiber of my being. Fuck what everyone says. I'm right. Me. And you, you motherfucker... It's you! You're an evil man! You're a rapist and a killer! You're the fucking Basher!

Hiegren noticed Freddy at the end of the aisle.

Time stood still. Freddy's heart stopped. Hiegren was looking right at him. His face was blank and expressionless. Freddy stammered, thinking quick.

"Um, uh... Help you find anything?"

Hiegren studied him for a moment.

"No, thanks."

You.

Freddy nodded and forced a polite smile, backing away. Hiegren remained planted in place, watching him like a statue. Freddy escaped out of view and took a minute to catch his breath. Between the aisles he could see Hiegren walking towards the front of the store.

I almost gave up on you, Jimbo. But not anymore.
Now I won't stop until I take you down.

Freddy ran into the back to get his coat and hat. David was stuffing a donut into his mouth and nearly spit it out when he saw Freddy throwing on his coat.

"Whoa, what's going on?"

"David, I'm sorry. Something's come up. There's something I gotta do."

"You can't just take off like this, Freddy! I'm short-handed as it is!"

Freddy shrugged and pushed back through the swinging doors.

"Sorry, David. I quit."

Freddy didn't wait around to see the exasperated look on David's face as he hurried back to the front of the store. He peeked around a corner. Hiegren was just then stepping up to the register. Charlotte's face went white.

"Hey there. Miss Charlotte, right?"

"Uh... Hi."

"How you doing today?" He smiled, loading his purchases onto the counter. She trembled, noticing his split lip and bruised knuckles. She forced herself into motion, scanning and bagging the items.

"Uh... Fine." She noticed Freddy across the way.

"You have a nice Christmas?" Hiegren asked.

"Y-Yes, thanks." She couldn't help but look again at his split lip.

"Oh, this?" Hiegren gestured to the injury with a chuckle. "I was setting up the tree, slipped, fell face-first right into the door frame! Ha ha!" He slapped the counter as she finished bagging the items. "But no, otherwise it was a very good Christmas. Had the whole family over. Good times."

Lying motherfucker.

"Uh-um, it's forty-nine fifty-seven."

Hiegren took out a credit card and slid it into the reader. The sale was approved and Charlotte handed him the receipt. He smiled and took the bag.

"Nice to see you again, Charlotte. Have a nice day."

She nodded.

Hiegren strolled out of the store, and Freddy hid behind the end cap of aisle one. He watched as the bald man walked out into the parking lot, then sprang into action.

Freddy flew outside, ducking down and scurrying to the far side of the building. He jumped into his Volvo and started the engine. Hiegren unlocked his Caddy and put his bags in the back, then got in and began backing out.

Freddy shifted into Drive.

It's you, you bastard. It's you.

Hiegren pulled out onto the road and Freddy followed.

Let's go for a ride, Jimbo.

CHAPTER 27
PURSUIT

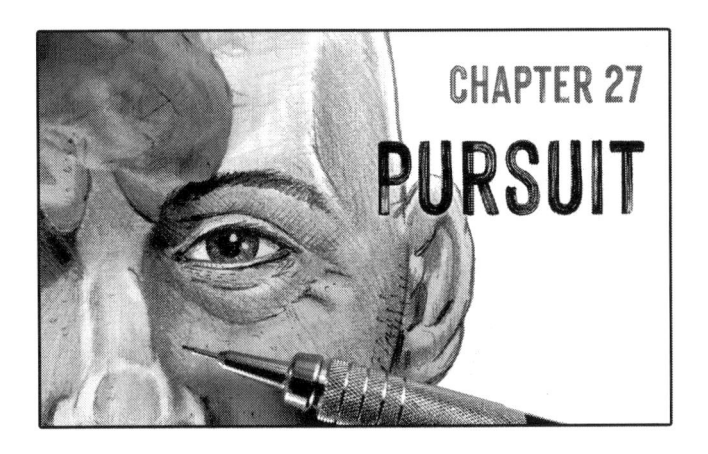

THIS WAS FARTHER UP I-22 than Freddy was used to going.

Hiegren was driving north, flanked on either side by the towering cliffs of granite and their steel netting to protect the road from landslides. Freddy stayed at least four car lengths back, trying to remain invisible as he steered the old Volvo past the border of Everett Falls and into uncharted territory. Hiegren was definitely not going home.

God, I feel like I'm in some 70's cop movie. Something with Gene Hackman or Walter Matthau. All I need is a pair of plaid bell-bottoms and some mutton chops.

Hiegren continued to drive further south on 22, taking the exit towards Mount Vernon and moving west. Freddy checked his dashboard clock—11:33. He'd been following Hiegren for over an hour. The landscape was completely unfamiliar.

"Where the fuck are you *going?*"

Freddy saw signs for the town of Fleetwood. He

slowed down, keeping pace with the Cadillac. A pick-up truck suddenly cut in front of him and a station wagon blocked his view of the target vehicle. Freddy slowed down, changed lanes, slowed down, sped up again.

This shit is a lot harder than it looks in the 70's cop movies.

Hiegren moved into the right lane, getting ready to exit.

Fucker doesn't even use his turn signal. Prick.

Freddy slowed to get off at the exit, losing sight of Hiegren as he went down the other side of a hill. He sped up and reached the top of the hill just in time to see Hiegren turning left up ahead. He cruised down Main Street for some time.

Fleetwood had a different personality than Everett Falls. More brick buildings, less Norman Rockwell. It was closer to Manhattan and had adopted its own city-like aesthetic. The tracks of the Metro North spanned overhead, and city busses and cabs slogged through the slush. There was a younger crowd, fewer families, more professionals. Freddy noticed a cool used book and record shop and made a mental note to check it out some time in the future.

Hiegren cruised onward, past the main drag and into a more residential area. He rolled through a yellow light and Freddy had a split second to decide whether to run it or stop at the red. He stopped, careful not to blow his cover.

"Shit!"

He watched as Hiegren drove three more blocks

down, then made another right, vanishing from sight. He tapped the wheel impatiently, eyes glued to the traffic light.

"Come on, come on..."

Finally the light turned green and Freddy shot forward. He raced three more blocks, turned right, and began scanning the streets. He saw rows of Maple and Elm trees and vast fields. There was a baseball diamond, then a basketball court. It was a community park. Up ahead was a playground and a parking lot.

"Where are you, you fuck?"

Freddy's eyes suddenly locked on a familiar Cadillac parked in the lot near the walking trail and the playground. He silently celebrated and drove on, looking for another way in where he could watch without being seen. He found an entrance on the other side, circled around slowly, and found a spot where he could see Hiegren but also keep his distance.

"Okay, Jimbo. What now?"

Hiegren had cut his engine. He sat in his car, motionless.

There was a bit of foot traffic in the park, but nowhere near what would be in the summer. Three teenage boys were having a snowball fight in the distance. An old couple strolled along the path. A minute later, a woman came along walking her dog. In the playground, a young mother played with her five year-old son.

"Okay..." Freddy tapped the wheel. Hiegren remained still.

What's he fucking doing?

Freddy watched from across the lot, eyes focused on the subject in the car. He could see the back of his bald head and shoulders, and his gloved hands resting on the wheel. He was looking straight ahead. Freddy followed his line of sight.

The playground. The young mother.

She was in her early twenties, bundled up in a red wool coat and a multicolored hat and scarf. She was thin, attractive, vibrant, smiling. *Just his type.*

"Sick fuck."

Hiegren lit a cigarette and continued to watch.

The young mother continued to laugh and play with her little boy. She held him by the waist and helped him climb across the monkey bars. He yelped with joy and ran up the plastic stairs to go on the slide. Hiegren's gaze never wavered.

I never should have doubted my instincts. I knew in my gut the first time I saw you. And now here we are. What are you planning to do, Jimbo? Just jump out of the car and snatch this poor woman away from her kid, bash her fucking brains out? And then what the hell am I gonna do? Shit, I haven't really thought this through. I mean, I have to try and stop him somehow. Right? Fucker's twice my size and I don't have any kind of weapon... Fuck! What the hell do I do?

One thing Freddy could do was tape what he saw. He pulled out his cell with shaking hands and began to record video.

"Okay, it's December 26th, approximately one p.m. I think I'm in... Fleetwood? Um, I've followed the subject, James Roy Hiegren, to a park, where he appears to be watching a young woman. Um... Stand by."

Hiegren continued to smoke.

He looked left and right. Another couple passed by on the trail, walking their poodle. He looked back at the young mother and took a long, savory pull of smoke.

Freddy continued to record, his pulse racing.

Should I call the police now? Should I wait? What would I even tell them? Shit shit shit! Think, Freddy, think!

A young man walked along the path towards the jungle gym carrying two to-go coffees. The woman pointed to him and the child erupted with joy. It was Daddy. The young man walked up to the mother, kissing her on the lips and handing her one of the coffees. The little boy ran to him and hugged him around the waist.

Hiegren smashed out his cigarette and started his car.

Visibly frustrated, he backed out of his parking space and headed for the exit. Freddy fumbled to stop recording and put his phone away, shifting into Drive to continue his pursuit.

"Oh, shit. Okay, here we go..."

Freddy circled around to the far exit as Hiegren pulled down the street. He sped up, seeing the Cadillac disappearing into the distance. He slammed on his brakes to give two passing cars the right of way. Now there were several vehicles between them.

"Come on... Come on..."

Hiegren turned a corner. The cars in front of Freddy were moving too slow. He gnashed his teeth, bounced in his seat, desperate to get past. He got to the corner and turned, following Hiegren's path. He looked left, right, up ahead.

Hiegren was gone.

Freddy punched the steering wheel.

"Fuck me!"

CHAPTER 28
PIZZA DOUGH

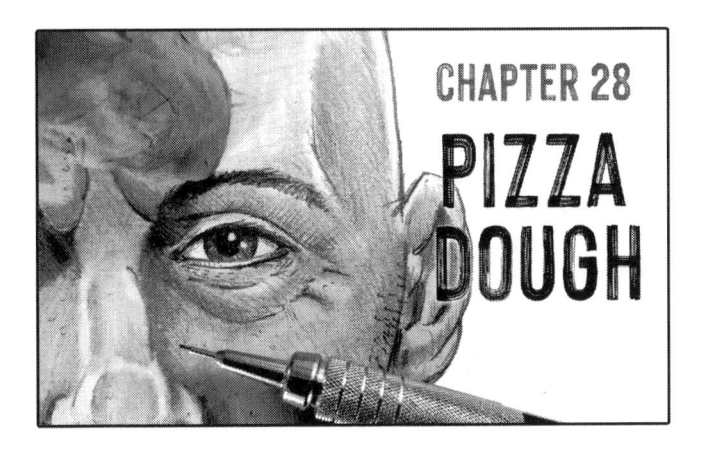

STELLA YAPPED at him as he came home.

Fucking dog.

He went upstairs and crashed into his bed. A groan escaped his body as he melted into the mattress. It was late afternoon and Penny wasn't home. He stared up at the ceiling, seeing through the plaster, into the dry-wall, past the screws and nails, the fiberglass and out the roof. His x-ray eyes were activated. Every three-dimensional object was clear as glass. He could see through everything. Almost.

There was a knock at the front door.

Freddy lifted his head like a turtle, strands of hair hanging into his eyes. He swung his legs off the bed and staggered up, shaking his numb left foot to wake it up. He plodded down the stairs and unlocked the front door, letting in the cold.

Ron Bagnarol stood on his doorstep. In his hand was a six-pack of Peroni, minus two bottles.

"Hey, Hollywood."

"Oh, hey Bags. How you doing?"

"Fine. Hey, can I come in? It's fuckin' freezin' out here!"

"Yeah, sure sure."

Freddy let the hulking detective in and he shook off the cold. They came into the foyer and Bagnarol looked around, smiling pleasantly.

"Nice, place."

"Oh, thanks. It's my aunt's. I'm just staying here a little while."

"It ain't no bachelor pad," he laughed.

"No, sir, haha. So, what's up?"

Bagnarol swung his arms, searching for words.

"Well, I uh, I kinda thought we could settle the dispute of who makes the best pizza in Everett Falls."

Freddy blinked. "What?"

"I mean, you talk a big game. Can you back it up?"

"A-Are you challenging me to a pizza contest?"

"Well, no. I won't be making a pizza. I'll just let *you* make me a pizza."

"Are you serious? I-I mean, I'd love to, really. But I'm really tired and it's been a long day, and," *Tell him about Hiegren going to the park*, "I just don't know..."

"Aw, hey kid, never mind. I just kind of thought... Just kind of sick of fast food, and too lazy to cook myself... Ah, never mind!"

He's acting weird.

"Is everything okay?"

"Yeah! No worries. Thought you might want to throw back a couple brews, have some pizza. But I totally get it, it's all good."

Freddy's face softened. *Looks like you've already had a couple, Bags.*

"Y'know what? Pizza does sound good. And we already have fresh sauce from Christmas, so I only have to make the dough."

"Nice."

FREDDY KNEADED THE DOUGH.

Bagnarol cracked open a bottle of Peroni.

"You ever meet anyone famous out there, workin' in Hollywood?"

"Oh, sure. Met Arnold. Kurt Russell. Paris Hilton. Shit, Salma Hayek gave me a hug once."

Bagnarol's face lit up. "No!"

"I was like 13 and got to meet her on set. She gave me a hug. Super sweet."

"Player player. That's cool."

"So, what's new with the case?" Freddy asked. "Give me all the classified details." The larger man snorted, taking a sip.

"Fuck off."

Freddy laughed and opened his own beer, having a drink. He worked the edges of the dough, stretching it into a pancake, then tossing it into the air, gently at first. Within seconds, he was tossing it high in the air and catching, creating a perfectly thin-stretched New York pizza dough. Bagnarol was impressed.

"Whoa, look at you go!"

Freddy continued, scooping out sweet basil marinara and ladling it onto the dough as he spoke. "Fine, I get it, you can't talk about the case. So what else is going on? What can you talk about? How's your wife doing?"

Bagnarol scoffed and lowered his head. "She's... Well, I guess she's not my wife anymore. I mean, the divorce isn't final or nothin' but, she left."

"Oh, sorry. What happened?"

"We... It was a mutual thing, y'know? We both just felt like, like just goin' our own ways, y'know? It's all right."

His eyes don't look all right. And how empty is his social calendar if he has to resort to hanging out with me? Poor schmuck... Tell him about Hiegren. No, you already tried, you have no evidence. What about the tape? But it's not conclusive!

"Listen, Bags..." Freddy began to sprinkle the shredded mozzarella onto the pizza. "Y'know, I saw some stuff earlier today. Now, I know you don't wanna hear this, I know, but I just have to say, I-I can't just..."

"Spit it out, gavonne."

"I saw him again today. Hiegren."

Bagnarol's head fell back and he closed his eyes.

"Here we go."

"Now listen, I'm cooking you pizza from scratch, you big hairy fuckin' ginny, you! So you're gonna sit there and listen to my crazy theories, you got that?"

Bagnarol burst out laughing, spitting beer across the room.

"You really are a character, Hollywood."

"Listen, I'm serious! I... Look. Okay. He came into Clarkson's this morning, right? And he picked up the morning paper, y'know with the new Basher headline? And he kind of has this look like, I dunno, he was annoyed or something? Oh, and y'know what else? He had bruises on his knuckles and face, like he'd been in a fight!"

"Uh, huh," Bagnarol was listening.

"He bought duct-tape, a rope, bleach, black trash bags. It was practically a Dexter kit! So when he left, I followed him, right?" Bagnarol rolled his eyes. "No, so I followed him, right? He drives to a town called Fleetwood, I think, And he goes to a park, and started spying on this woman while she was with her kid! I mean, come on! ...Um, sausage and meatball good with you?"

"Yeah, that's perfect, thanks. Okay, look. So, we did look into James Hiegren for you, okay? We got the results back a while ago but we didn't tell you 'cause there was nothing to tell."

"Wh-What do you mean...?"

"I mean there's *nothing* to tell. We ran a background check on James Roy Hiegren, like you asked. The guy is clean. No prior arrests. No serious violations. If you're interested, he has been involved in two or three minor traffic accidents in his life, and a failure to appear in court for not coming to a complete stop at a traffic sign. Never married, has a degree in music theory, teaches music, and leads a youth choir."

Freddy stepped back, baffled.

"But... But that doesn't mean... What about his DNA? What about his fingerprints..."

"We don't have Hiegren's prints, and The Basher never leaves his prints anyway. I did send the cigarette butts to the lab, and we're still waiting for the results. Should be any time now."

"So... But... What about what I just told you about him creepin' around, and the bruises, a-and...?"

"Yeah, that's all suspicious. But we checked him out and got balls."

"Come on! I can't believe this! Can't we just—Can't you just get a warrant to search his house? I'm sure you'll find a mountain of evidence..."

"Two words, Freddy. Probable cause."

Freddy steamed, gripping the kitchen counter. "Fuck," he hissed.

Bags is right. They're doing all they can.

"Welcome to my life. Now, are you gonna throw that fuckin' pizza in the oven or am I gonna starve all night?" Freddy laughed, opening the oven and sliding the tray in.

"Yes sir, you royal pain in my *ass*."

It's time for me to end this.

CHAPTER 29
BREAKING AND ENTERING

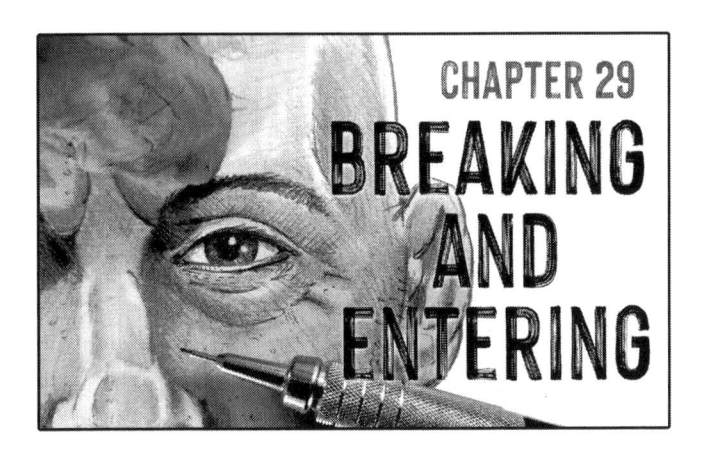

IT'S A THURSDAY NIGHT. Hiegren always goes bowling on Thursdays.

The snow had settled a foot deep and Freddy had found his favorite parking spot to watch Hiegren's house without being seen. He checked the time. 8:57. He scanned the streets. All was quiet and frozen and dark. The lights were on in Hiegren's house, but he was a creature of habit, and Freddy knew he would have at least two hours until he returned.

Headlights.

Freddy scooted down in his seat and looked in the mirror. Another car was parking behind him. *Shit shit shit shit.* Freddy held his breath. The headlights turned off along with the engine, and he heard the driver's door open and close. Footsteps. Someone approaching his window. His body tensed.

Knock! Knock!

A petite, gloved hand rapped against the window.

Charlotte leaned in to see him huddled low.

"What the..." Freddy hopped up and rolled his

window down, shocked to see her there smiling back at him.

"Open the door! I'm freezing!" She scurried around to the passenger door and Freddy let her in. She was carrying her purse, two coffee's in a drink holder, and a box of donuts.

"What are you doing here?"

"I brought Dunkin."

"But... What are you *doing* here? How did you even know I'd be here?"

"Umm, because I know you? And when you send me not-at-all cryptic or worrying texts like 'this all ends tonight,' I don't know, I start to think of the creepy old guy you've been like, stalking and super obsessing about?"

"Look, I'm sorry, but—"

"I know what you're planning to do, Freddy."

"You can't talk me out of it."

"I'm not here to."

Freddy looked at her sideways.

"I mean, I think it's crazy, I think it's incredibly dangerous, and I'd love to talk you out of it. But I understand... You have to be here. So I guess, I have to be here too. Who else is gonna back you up?"

He smiled and caressed her rosy, sweet cheeks.

"That's my lioness... Okay listen, this isn't going to be so bad. He always goes out bowling Thursday nights at nine. Comes back around eleven. All I need is to get some kind of evidence. A glass with his fingerprint, pictures of... whatever the hell I find in there... And get out. No problem."

"And me?"

"I guess you're my lookout. You can just watch the street, text me if he comes home or the police show up or something."

"Okay, I guess. Do you have a weapon, just in case?"

"Just my little knife."

Charlotte nodded and contemplated the situation.

"Want some Dunkin?"

Freddy laughed and nervously ran his fingers through his hair. "Oh man, my heart is beating so fast right now. Coffee, you kidding me?"

"Well, how 'bout a donut?"

"Baby, I need to focus, here. We need—"

Almost on cue, Hiegren's lights turned off and the garage door began to grumble open like the gates of Hades. Red light and swirling smoke.

"Get down," Freddy hissed, and both slid down in their seats.

Hiegren backed his Caddy CT4-V slowly down the drive as they watched.

"Damn, babes," she smirked, "you really have been keeping tabs on this guy. Wish you paid this much attention to *me*."

Freddy ignored the baited comment as he peeked over the window's edge and observed his subject roll onto the street, change gears, and drive on.

Hiegren's taillights vanished down the street on their way to the bowling alley. Freddy looked Charlotte in the eyes and squeezed her hand.

"Okay."

"Okay."

"Freddy, I'm scared."

"Me too..." He pulled out his gloves and began putting them on. "But it'll be fine. If I find anything, I'll be a hero. If not, they'll never even know it was me."

"What could possibly go wrong?"

"Smart ass. Look, everything will be okay." Freddy planted a big kiss on her lips and put on his backpack. "I got about two hours till he comes back, and I plan to be out of there in less than one. You keep your eye on your watch, and the streets. And only text me if it's important. And don't start the engine. Don't draw attention to yourself."

"Fine."

One more kiss. "Sweet-cheeks."

"Hottie."

Freddy popped open his door. Icy air. He zipped up his coat and pulled on his hat. He smiled and gave her a wink. "See you soon."

"Okay."

Freddy slid out into the night and gently closed the door. He looked both ways then strolled up to the house, trying to look as inconspicuous as possible, which only made him look more conspicuous. He crept up the driveway, the only light directly above the front door. He tried the door; locked of course. He crunched through the snow to the front window and tried that as well.

Also locked.

Charlotte sipped her coffee and watched as Freddy crossed around to the side of the house, disappearing from sight. He pushed into the shadows, clicking on his small flashlight. There was a side door and windows.

Locked. He tried to peek in to determine if this was a good entry point. *No, not secluded enough.*

Around to the back.

Every footstep made him cringe, the snow was so loud when it broke under his feet. At least the neighbors were far away and there was good tree coverage back there. Freddy glanced around the back yard. A table and a set of lawn chairs were caked in snow. A sizable back yard led to a fence, then woods and blackness. Beyond that, he heard the low hum of I-22 as it surged like The Nile.

"Freddy, what the fuck are you doing?" he whispered, pointing the flashlight around. "This is so stupid..."

There were two large, steel basement doors protruding from the rear of the house, also covered with a layer of snow. Freddy grabbed the handle and tried to yank it open, but the doors were chained from the inside. He tried the sliding glass back doors and they too were both locked. Freddy cursed.

He continued looking around. There was a stoop and a back porch, where a snowy tarp covered an outdoor grille, a lawnmower, and several landscaping tools. He studied the porch. Above it was a shingled eave and a small ledge where the second floor began. And there it was, a window cracked slightly open.

Freddy shook his head.

"Fuck me."

He snuck over to the porch and walked up the stairs, testing the strength of the hand railing. He looked up; the eave looked sturdy enough. He pocketed his flashlight, then put his boot up on the railing and steadied himself against a side post as he pushed his way up.

He balanced on the railing, reaching up and grabbing the eave. A shelf of snow crumbled and slid off the edge, falling into his face. His grip held and he shook it off, spitting it away. He held strong and lifted his feet up, putting his full weight on the eave. It held. He took two quick breaths and proceeded to do the heaviest pull-up of his life.

Straining from the effort, he threw his left foot up over the eave and pulled himself up onto the ledge. Snow and ice fell beneath him, but it was his private darkness back there. He wobbled up to his feet, found his balance, and took a breath.

There were two windows in front of him, the further being the open one.

Holy shit, I'm out of shape! Can't believe I'm doing this shit...

Inch by inch, he crept across the foot-wide ledge. He looked down and felt much higher than one floor up. *Don't fall, don't fall, don't fall.* He fought to maintain his balance, reaching the window and pulling out his folding knife, slashing through the screen. He put the knife away and reached through the screen, grabbed it and yanked it out of the windowsill.

He tossed the screen behind him where it collided silently with the thick snow cover of the back yard. Now all he had to do was wrap his fingers around the open window and slide it up. His eyes pierced into a black void. He held at the edge, looking into the cavern that was the dragon's lair.

This is it. Don't be a pussy.

Freddy lowered his left foot into the darkness. It touched the floor.

He ducked his head down, ducked it inside. He slid his right leg in.

"Dear God, please protect me..."

CHAPTER 30
LAIR

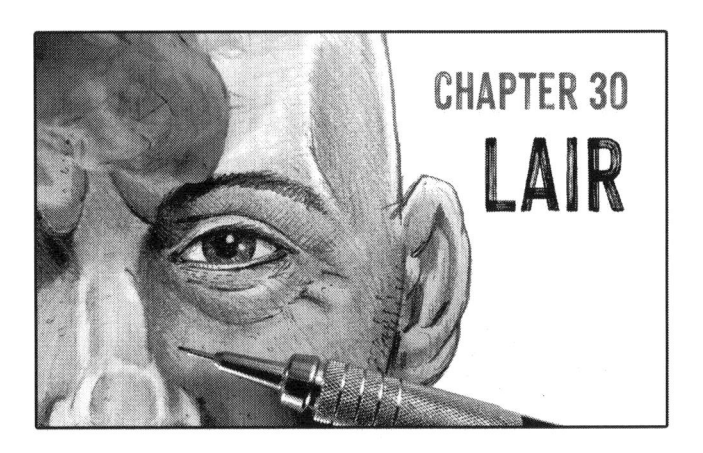

IT WAS A GUEST BATHROOM. Clean and tidy and unused. Freddy closed the window behind him and stepped further into the darkness. His eyes began adjusting. He took out his phone and pulled his right glove off with his teeth.

He texted, *I'm in*

She replied after a moment, *ok luv u*

He pocketed his phone and put his glove back on. The flashlight clicked on and he swung the narrow beam through the dark. The soap in the shower had collected dust. A mop and a bucket were in the corner. Freddy tried to slow his breathing and calm down. He listened to the silence of the house, the whistle of the wind outside. The pounding of his own heart.

He stepped into the hallway, darting the light around as he crept deeper.

Hardwood floors creaked under his wet boots. The bedroom was up ahead. He passed a brass-framed mirror on the wall and a wreath made of branches and dried flowers. His shoulder touched the bedroom door and he smoothly rolled into blackness. The flashlight's beam swept over one detail at a time.

A king-size bed, neatly made with large pillows and an abstract-patterned comforter. A large flatscreen TV with a blu-ray player. There was a CD player and an old record player, and to the right a vast collection of movies and music. The walls offered a few paintings—a vase of flowers, a country landscape, a puppy and kitten playing—but no family photos or anything personal.

It smelled of baby powder and cleaning products. Atop an ornate rosewood stand was a large fish tank, an exotic and eclectic collection of fish inside. Freddy looked closer, fascinated by their beauty. *Hm, pretty cool.* He approached Hiegren's dresser with trepidation. Whether it was finding a bloody murder weapon or dirty men's underwear, he wasn't fond of either prospect. He reached for the handle, slowly gripping it.

His phone chimed and he jumped. He shook his head and yanked the device from his pocket.

"Come on, Char! I said don't text unless..."

It was from Rick: *DIRTY MEATBALL!!!*

Freddy shook his head and put the phone away. "Jesus Christ, dude. Not *now*."

He put the flashlight in his mouth and began going through Hiegren's drawers. The clothes were meticulously folded and put in rows, everything well organized. Socks, underwear, t-shirts, shorts, slacks, belts. No contraband or hidden compartments.

Freddy turned to the closet.

The door creaked open. He turned on the closet light and inspected his surroundings. Neat and organized. An impressive collection of suits hung in a row. Designer shoes and ties. Several boxes stacked on the upper shelf. Many stacked on the floor. He rummaged through the closest box, finding summer clothes. The next held several books of sheet music and music magazines.

The large box on the floor contained several assorted items. The first thing that caught his eye was what looked like a photo album, so he picked that up. He opened the cover and instead of seeing photos, there were plastic sleeves holding collectible coins. Special edition silver dollars, rare quarters, confederate coins, foreign coins, even ancient Roman coins. Freddy was impressed.

"Huh."

He kept looking. In the corner was a large plastic bag. He reached inside and pulled out a small, cheap, generic stuffed teddy bear. The bag was filled with them.

Weird. Why the hell would he have these? In the other corner was a large safe, at least five feet tall. He tried the handle just in case. Locked of course.

He made a face and moved on.

CHARLOTTE REMAINED in Freddy's car.

She twisted her hair around her fingers and tapped her foot. Watching the street was not an exciting job. She shifted in her seat, getting antsy. With the engine off, she was turning into an ice cube. The decision was made and she picked up her phone.

She texted, *Find anything yet?*

. . .

FREDDY TOOK one slow step at a time down the main staircase, descending into a black womb. That familiar John Williams music chirped from his pocket and his entire body spasmed. He cursed and dug out his phone, reading the message.

He replied, *No. But it's creepy AF. Don't text me unless it's important*

He drifted down the stairs.

The first floor of the house was a more open floor plan. He stepped into the foyer, the dining room on the left, living room on the right. Even in the dark, he could tell that everything was pristine and in its place. Large bookshelves were filled with books, alphabetically ordered. Oak chairs circled an oak table, and decorative china was in a glass cabinet. A collection of ornate plates was mounted to the wall next to a stuffed owl.

There were several cardboard boxes in the living room, stacks of newspapers and magazines adjusted so their corners were in a perfect straight line. Freddy pushed one pile over just for spite.

"Jesus."

He tore into the boxes and looked through the drawers, finding nothing but papers and everyday, household items. Board games and children's toys. In one closet was a collection of assorted knives and hunting gear. A large chest was filled with old, used clothes and shoes.

The dining room yielded similarly little.

A bowl of plastic fruit sat at the center of the table. Silk napkins topped with silverware marked each place setting. Still no family photos, just a series of shelves filled with old toys and train sets. Another impressive collection. *Do-de-do-do-doo*. He rolled his eyes and checked his phone. It was Charlotte again:

R u ok? Im scared!

"God!" Freddy bit his glove's finger and pulled it off his hand again. He typed:

Don't text me unless Hiegren comes home or the cops show up! I'm serious!

The clock on his phone read 9:30 p.m. Freddy shook his head in frustration and put it back in his pocket. He slipped his glove back on and continued to scan the darkness with his light. Heavy, ornate curtains hung by the windows. A taxidermied bobcat posed in a fighting stance was perched atop an oak base, its claws flexed, its eyes glassy and lifeless. A good-size home bar was set up in the corner. Freddy contemplated pouring a drink but thought better of it.

He stepped into the kitchen and scanned around.

Nothing of note.

It was clean and orderly. There was a fridge, a dishwasher, a sink, a counter, a trash can, a tile floor. It was a kitchen. On the fridge were over a hundred little magnets, but they held nothing. No family photos, no shopping lists on slips of paper, no greeting cards. Just the magnets, a huge collection of magnets.

Freddy looked closer and saw they were all tourist magnets, each from a different city, town, or attraction. Austin, Texas. Indianapolis, Indiana. Niagra Falls. The Grand Canyon. Nashville, Tennessee. All interesting, but nothing helpful.

He looked in the fridge. No human heads.

"Fuck me, man. Come *on*."

He continued his search, finding a laundry room and space for tools and painting supplies. There was an oak door that appeared to lead to the basement, so Freddy tried the handle. Locked. He pulled harder, jiggled the handle, but the door was solid and strong. He launched a hard front kick and the door wouldn't give. Another couple of kicks, and still nothing.

CHARLOTTE FIDDLED WITH THE RADIO.

She gave up and turned it off, sticking her hands in her pockets and shivering. Looking out the window at the flakes drifting through the air, it occurred to her that maybe she was trapped inside of a snow globe. She smiled, her eyes glancing at the mirror as a light gleamed behind her. A car was coming. It was a Cadillac.

"Oh, shit..."

It was Hiegren.

He wasn't just coming home, he was racing home.

Charlotte slid down in her seat as he drove past her, fumbling her phone as she desperately typed a message to Freddy. She watched helplessly as Hiegren skidded to a halt in his driveway and jumped out of his car.

"Shitshitshitshitshit..."

FREDDY'S PHONE BEEPED. Charlotte again.

"Jesus, baby, Give me a break!"

He didn't bother to check the text, continuing to try and open the cellar door. It would not budge. Frustrated, he stormed back into the dining room, looking around.

Besides that basement, he'd been through every room in the house. He struggled to devise his next move when a sound outside stopped his heart. Footsteps.

He turned to see the front door and heard keys jingling outside.

"Oh, fuck... *Fuck!*"

Hiegren was coming. The deadbolt unlocked. Freddy bolted into the living room, frantically looking for a way out. No time. He would have to hide. He dove into the shadows. The bottom lock opened. Hiegren's massive silhouette filled the doorway.

WITH TREMBLING HANDS, Charlotte dialed 911 and held the phone to her ear, watching as Hiegren cautiously entered his house. She bounced in her seat, waiting for the dispatcher to pick up.

"Everett Falls Police Department."

"Yes, I need to report a burglar! Send the police fast!"

HIEGREN STEPPED INSIDE.

He closed and locked the door. He turned a lamp on. His little eyes darted around the room, suspicious. Things were out of order. His bottom lip trembled with anger. His hands clenched into fists.

"Hello?" Hiegren asked the darkness.

He walked in further, turning on another lamp. The floor was scuffed with muddy boot prints and wet from snow. He growled and ran into the kitchen, turning on the light and immediately checking the basement door.

Freddy pulled aside the curtain.

From where he was hiding, he could see Hiegren standing at the door, checking the handle, the hinges. The man let out a huge sigh of relief and rested his forehead on the door once he'd confirmed it had not been breached. He turned again, stalking back into the main hallway and calling out into the house.

"I know you're here."

Freddy froze behind the curtain, mere feet away. His heart was beating so hard, he was terrified that Hiegren might hear it. He desperately tried to hold his breath, listening to the man's heavy footsteps as he stalked through the house, checking behind doors, looking for hiding places.

Please God, get me out of here!

The front door was closer than the back. All he needed was a window of opportunity to bolt. Hiegren stomped back into the room with a baseball bat. He looked behind the couch, then the love seat. He was less than two feet from where Freddy was standing, hissing curses.

Freddy pulled out his folding knife, hands trembling. All Hiegren would have to do is pull those curtains, and he'd be done for. The threat of death was close enough to taste. Freddy waited for it, his heart pounding in his chest. But Hiegren turned again and stormed upstairs.

It's now or never!

Freddy flung the curtain aside crept as delicately as he could out into the living room, hearing the footsteps of the big bull above him. He tip-toed across the floor, desperate not to make a sound. The front door was twenty feet away. He cringed, taking step by slow step. One more. Then another.

Creeeaaaak!

Freddy stepped on the wrong floorboard. He cringed.

The footsteps upstairs stopped, then Hiegren sprinted for the stairs. Freddy darted for the front door, hearing those heavy feet clomping down behind him. Freddy slid into the door, hands shaking as he tried to open the dead bolt.

"Hey!" Hiegren saw him.

Freddy turned the dead bolt and tried to open the door, but the bottom lock was still in place. Before he could try to open the second lock, a massive hand gripped his shoulder and yanked him back into the hall. Freddy tripped and fell backward, smashing into the floor. Hiegren loomed over him, gripping his baseball bat. Shadows fluttered across his menacing face. A face that Freddy had drawn, thought about, imagined from every angle. Now it was the face of certain death snarling down at him.

"Hey," Hiegren said with a look of recognition. "I know you..."

"L-Look, just stay back. We can work this out..."

"Work it out, huh? We're going to work it out?"

Hiegren stepped forward, squeezing the bat. Freddy scooted back, holding a hand up to hold him back. Freddy tried to stand up, but Hiegren swung the bat, missing him and smashing a display of china on his table. Freddy yelped and fell back again, scurrying away. Out came his folding knife.

"You stay away from me, Hiegren!"

"What? I thought you came here to play?"

Hiegren's voice was disturbingly feminine. He slashed the bat again and nearly hit Freddy, who scrambled back to his feet, brandishing the knife. They circled each other, Freddy trying to get an angle to run for the door, but Hiegren cut him off. He was enjoying this. Murder glinted in his beady eyes and sadistic smile.

Jesus, this guy is really going to kill me!

They circled around a dividing wall, past the stuffed bobcat. Without thinking, Freddy snapped out a kick into the stand, sending the bobcat flying into Hiegren. The large man staggered and fell back.

Freddy had the split second he needed.

He shot for the door, Hiegren right behind him.

He grabbed the handle, unlocked the bottom lock.

Freddy flew outside into the freezing air, Hiegren's baseball bat barely missing behind him. Freddy fell forward onto the front stoop, Hiegren skidding to a halt in the doorway, looking ahead with shocked eyes.

Two police cruisers were in the driveway.

"Get down!"

"Show me your hands!"

CHAPTER 31
NOT A MATCH

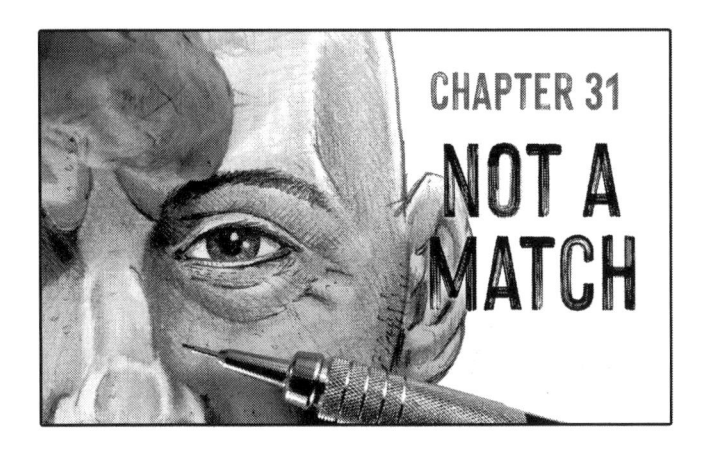

"PUT YOUR HANDS ON YOUR HEAD!"

Freddy did as instructed.

He was on his knees, the snow soaking the jeans halfway up his thighs. Four officers had him circled, stark silhouettes before the headlights and cherries of their cruisers. Their guns were drawn. Their eyes were intense. Freddy was relieved.

Oh, thank God you guys are here!

The look in Hiegren's eyes was pure bewilderment. The baseball ball hung at his side. He blinked as two of the officers approached the young intruder, initiating an arrest. Freddy looked down the street, and could just make out her face through the dark windshield.

He smiled.

Charlotte held her breath. She watched helplessly as handcuffs were slapped onto Freddy's wrists. They hauled him to his feet and led him to the nearest cruiser, stuffing him in the back.

. . .

"OKAY, so as I was saying, I usually go bowling on Thursdays," Hiegren emphatically recounted, "but tonight I got a headache, so I went home early..." The bald man stood at his front door, talking to two of the officers. Freddy sat in the back seat of the cruiser, his forehead leaning against the window.

Way to go, Luccio... God, I really fucked up now.

An unmarked car arrived at the base of the driveway, and four dark figures climbed out. It was Harney, Bagnarol, and federal agents Jones and Crabtree. They were all bundled as much as possible, but a New York winter night is biting cold. They did not look happy.

"Fuck me..." Freddy muttered.

The two detectives looked briefly at Freddy as they walked by. Bagnarol shook his head in disapproval. The Feds didn't bother to look. Harney approached Hiegren, offering his hand.

"Good evening, sir. Detectives Harney and Bagnarol."

"Hello," Hiegren said.

They all shook hands.

"Anything stolen?" Bagnarol asked.

"No, but the little punk messed up my house. Gave me a damn good scare. He swung a knife at me!"

"So you walked in on a burglary in progress?" Harney asked.

"That's right. And I think I know the kid. Works at the supermarket, or the pharmacy or somethin'..." He glared over at Freddy with a sneer.

"Do you have any idea why he would want to break into your house?"

"Nope. No idea at all."

Freddy bounced his forehead against the center divider in the back seat as he listened to the man try to explain. Freddy looked down at his feet, listening to Hiegren talk.

He actually kind of sounds like a woman. Just hearing his voice, if I didn't know better I'd swear he was a woman.

The FBI spoke with Hiegren as the two detectives headed towards Freddy. The young artist sat up with a start as Harney yanked open the door.

"Out."

Freddy sheepishly scooted out of the car, hands cuffed, unable to look them in the eye. Bagnarol stepped up to him, shaking his head.

"What the hell were you *thinkin'*?"

"I-I figured if I broke in and found some evidence... I could give it to you guys... That it could help catch him."

"Mm hm," Harney nodded. "And did you find any evidence?"

Freddy hung his head.

Hiegren suddenly pushed past Jones and Crabtree, furious.

"Okay, evidence of what, huh? What were you looking for in my house, you little punk?"

"Evidence that you're a murderer!" Freddy snarled and tried to lunge forward, but Bagnarol held him back. "And if you hadn't come home when you did, I would've found something!"

"Murder?" Hiegren held his hands up, dumbstruck.

"What the hell's this kid talking about?" His eyes went from Harney to Bagnarol.

"Freddy here thinks you're 'The Everett Falls Basher,'" Bagnarol said. "Won't leave it alone. I'm sorry, Mr. Hiegren."

"Your sketch artist again?" Agent Crabtree asked. Harney nodded.

"He *is* The Basher!" Freddy pushed. "Just search his house, you'll see! I didn't find anything, but his basement door is conveniently locked up like Fort Knox! Tell us, *Jimbo*, what do you keep down in the basement that you have to lock up?"

"Well, that's where my studio is."

"Oh, that's bullshit. You're a fucking murderer, you piece of shit! Let's have a little tour of your basement then, if you got nothing to hide!"

"That's enough, Freddy."

"Come on, Bags! Ask him to show you the basement! If he's innocent, he's got nothing to hide!"

"Fine, you can see the studio," Hiegren shrugged.

"But we don't have to," Agent Jones cut in, her eyes like a cat's. "There's no point."

"Look, he's the man you're looking for right there! *He's The Basher!*"

"No. He. Isn't." Jones stepped right up to him.

"What?"

"Freddy," Bagnarol growled, "if you'd let us do our jobs, we wouldn't have to tell you this way. But earlier today we got the DNA results back from those cigarette butts you took from Mr. Hiegren... They were *not* a match to the DNA left by The Basher."

Freddy staggered a step back, the information hitting him like a punch.

"Wh-What...?"

This can't be...

"Not a match, Freddy," Bagnarol continued. "You want me to spell it out for you?"

Hiegren blinked, trying to catch up. "...What cigarette butts?"

"You've been obsessing over the wrong person for months," Harney growled. "We've been telling you all along it isn't him, but you just wouldn't listen."

Jones added, "You've wasted the time and resources of the local police as well as the FBI, Mr. Luccio. Now you've broken into an innocent man's house, threatened him with a knife, and destroyed his personal property. Now we have to take you to jail. I hope it was worth it."

Freddy could not let it go.

"What about the basement? Ask him to show you the basement!"

Hiegren threw up his hands. "I said I'd show you the basement! You want to see it? Come on!"

"No no, Mr. Hiegren, that won't be neces—"

"No, come on! You want to see?"

The Feds and officers shared a look.

"Why not?" Jones said with a wry smile. "Come on, Mr. Luccio. Now's your chance to prove us all wrong."

"Sure, let's go." Hiegren gestured to the front door.

Harney pushed Freddy forward. The group followed Hiegren as he entered the house, holding the door open for them. Freddy entered last, Harney's hand on his shoulder. The house looked different with the lights on.

Normal, pedestrian. They trailed behind the heavyset bald man as he took out his keys, heading into the kitchen.

"This is the door to my studio." Hiegren unlocked the heavy bolt and swung the door open. Blackness awaited. He flicked on the light switch and began to descend the stairs. "Careful, it's a little steep."

The group entered a clean, well-furnished space, a basement converted into a music studio. The walls were wood paneled and lined with foam sound-proofing material. There was a desk with a computer and mixing board, drum machine, keyboard, and two stand-up microphones. There were bookshelves full of sheet music, a TV and stereo system, an acoustic guitar on a stand, and a small collection of shakers and percussion toys.

"This is where I do my recording and teach lessons."

"Oh, very nice," Jones looked impressed. "What do you teach, sir?"

"Oh, singing, guitar, piano, music theory. I lead the kids' choir at church."

Freddy's eyes scanned every inch of the room. The carpet was gray and clean. There was no possible hiding place for weapons or bodies. A stuffed deer's head was mounted to a plaque on one wall, and a goat's head on the other. A set of stairs at the far end led up to the steel cellar doors, chained from the inside.

"But... But..." Freddy was dumbfounded.

"Are you happy now, young man?" Hiegren asked.

Freddy could find no words.

"You were wrong, Mr. Luccio." Jones seemed to take

pleasure in dishing out the bad news. Without Harney's hand on his shoulder, Freddy may have fallen over.

Agent Crabtree turned to Hiegren. "I presume you will be filing charges, Mr. Hiegren?"

"Damn right, I'm filing charges!"

"Come on, Freddy. Let's go." Harney and Bagnarol turned the dazed young man toward the stairs, guiding him back up. He locked eyes with Hiegren one last time. Those beady eyes, that feeling in his gut.

It can't be...

"Thank you, officers," Hiegren said. "We have to work together to keep deranged criminals like him off the streets, right?"

Harney turned to look at Hiegren. The veneer of his poker face did not crack. He was a seasoned detective, well-traveled down every dark alleyway and stinking crevice of the human psyche. He had seen the best and worst of what human beings had to offer the world. He looked at Hiegren and wondered.

"Have a good night, sir," Harney said. He and Bagnarol led Freddy up the stairs as Jones and Crabtree remained with Hiegren. Freddy found himself floating back out into the cold, feeling the icy sting, yet somehow detached from it.

He found himself in the back seat of a cruiser, and saw the residential street drift past as they drove away. Looking out the window, he caught a glimpse of a pretty blonde girl watching from the passenger seat of a Volvo.

CHAPTER 32
DRAFT

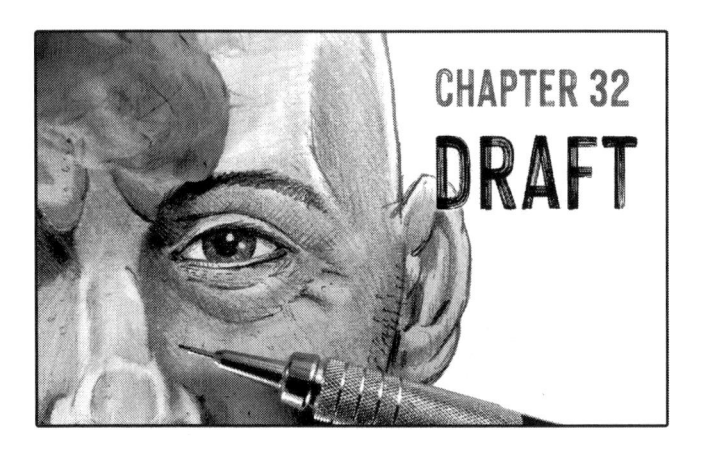

FREDDY WAS ALONE in the cell.

The walls were gray, the floors were gray, and the bars were gray. There was no window and the only lighting came from the hall, casting a cyan hue across his face. He could see his own breath, shivering. It was quiet. Freddy occupied one of the eight holding cells at the station, the only other being a frequent-flyer meth-head who just needed to sleep it off.

He looked up at the ceiling. There were scuff marks, stains, and bathroom stall graffiti everywhere. The mattress felt like a hospital gurney and the pillow felt like a roll of paper towels. Freddy lay in the dark, staring off into space.

Is this really happening? How is this possible? Jesus Christ, Luccio, you really fucked up now. I mean, phew! This is bad, homie. This is bad. I can't believe I'm actually in jail.

The sound of footsteps.

Freddy looked down the hall to see a young officer he'd seen around many times. They were roughly the same age, height, weight, and general description, he and this rookie cop. Freddy's x-ray eyes scanned the officer's face, seeing through it like it was glass. Short, chestnut hair. Brown eyes. Chiseled cheeks and jaw. Classic Roman nose. Angular eyebrows and lips. He looked very much like Freddy.

If I drew a picture of this guy, it would be like a self portrait. If he committed a crime and someone saw the picture, they'd think it was me. The same way I drew a sketch of The Basher and thought it was Hiegren. But I just had to be right, didn't I? What did I think I had to prove? That I'm not a loser? That I could do something important and meaningful? That I'm somebody?

The rookie cop jingled a set of keys and came to Freddy's cell door.

"Luccio."

"Yeah?"

"Time to go. You made bail."

He unlocked the door and it squeaked open.

Freddy sighed, contemplating the option of just staying there and wallowing. The officer gestured for him to come on, and Freddy swung his feet off of the bed. He groaned as he slowly stood, feeling like an old man. He hobbled out of the dark cage and the officer indicated for Freddy to walk ahead of him.

He made his way to the outtake area, where he was given back his coat and belongings. He was escorted past the offices to the main lobby. Leaning in the doorway waiting for him to pass was Bagnarol. They made eye contact and the look on the detective's face was clear disappointment. Freddy looked away, ashamed.

"See you around, Hollywood," Bagnarol said. Freddy didn't answer.

The officer led him to the lobby door and showed him out. At 1:30 a.m., the front desk window where Donna usually sat was dark and unoccupied. Freddy zipped up his coat, put on his beanie, and pushed out into the frigid night.

There were a handful of vehicles in the parking lot and only one of them was idling. Charlotte waited in her white Ford Fiesta, tapping the steering wheel. Her eyes lit up and she pulled forward, stopping with the passenger door facing him. He hustled through the bitter cold and jumped into the car, but he couldn't bring himself to look at her.

"...Thanks for bailing me out."

"Sorry it took so long. Are you okay?"

"Yeah... Where's my car?"

"Still parked by Hiegren's house. You want me to take you to it, or...?"

"No, just take me home."

Freddy stared down at his feet. Charlotte leaned in, putting her hand on his. He clenched his jaw, unable to look her in the eye.

"What happened?"

"...Just take me home."

She decided not to push it, shifted into gear and buzzed away.

BAGNAROL SPRINKLED tobacco into a fresh paper and rolled a cigarette. He reclined in his chair and lit up, watching the smoke swirl into the air. Harney sat across from him, going through the case files again. His intense blue eyes were tired. He was looking for something, anything. Bagnarol shook his head.

"Give it a rest, Sarge."

"Bags, did you read the report from the state crime lab?"

"Yeah," Bagnarol took a pull.

"The whole thing?"

"Well, no. I mean, I didn't get into all the technobabble at the end, but I read the important part where it said Mr. Hiegren was not a match to The Basher's DNA."

Harney stood up and came around the desk with the file, putting it in front of Bagnarol. He tapped his finger into a paragraph underneath a genealogical pie chart.

"It says Mr. Hiegren was not a *positive* match," Harney corrected. "But it does say that he shares many genetic markers. Not enough for a positive match, but close."

"Close, but no cigar. It has to be a one hundred percent match. You know that. Besides, we all share a certain number of genetic markers. That don't mean nothin'."

"Right, but this looks like a lot of common markers, don't you think?"

"What are you gettin' at, boss?"

"We only ordered a general test to determine if James Hiegren was The Basher. We didn't ask for a more thorough genealogical comparison, though."

"So?"

"So, maybe Hiegren isn't The Basher, but maybe he's *related*. Maybe that's why they look so similar. I don't know…"

"You're startin' to sound like Freddy."

"We share what, up to fifty percent of our DNA with our siblings?"

Bagnarol thought for a moment. "…Yeah. Yeah, we do."

CHARLOTTE PULLED into Freddy's driveway.

She shifted into park and they sat in silence. She glanced at him, her eyes pleading, but he still could not look at her. She placed a tender hand on his shoulder.

"Freddy, it's okay. You did your best. And you did what you did because you care… Don't feel ashamed." Freddy stared straight ahead at the house. All the lights were off inside save for the flickering living room TV. The whole street was asleep. "Babes, are you gonna be okay?"

Freddy cracked the passenger door open and stepped his right foot out. "You should get home now," he growled. "Your dad's gonna be worried about you."

She squeezed his shoulder, pulling him back.

"Come on, how could you have known? I mean, everything about this guy looked like he was the guy, right? And—"

"He *wasn't* the guy," Freddy snapped. "And I fucked up, okay? Fucked up big time. And you… You'd better get on home now."

"Freddy, please—"

"Just leave me alone, would you?"

Charlotte pulled back like a scorned puppy. Her eyes began to well with tears and she looked away. Freddy stepped out into the frosty night and slammed the door behind him. He walked up the driveway without looking back.

Charlotte sniffed back the tears and shifted the Fiesta into reverse, pulling back onto the street. Freddy abruptly stopped and turned around to chase after her, but she was gone. He was too late.

Brilliant. Great work again, Luccio. Idiot.

"Shit..."

Freddy huffed and shook his head, ashamed of himself. He put his hands in his pockets and turned back to the house, pulling out his keys. He heard the TV on, saw its light through the front window. He opened the front door and walked into the dark house, locking the door behind him.

He shrugged off his coat and hung it on the rack by the door. It was chilly inside. Either there was a draft or Penny had forgot to turn on the heat. It was quiet, dark, and still. He thought nothing of it and walked past the living room toward the kitchen. Glancing in, he saw his aunt sitting in her favorite chair facing the TV.

"Aunt Penny, you still up?"

No response.

Ah, she's out like a light. Why is it so cold in here?

"Come on, wake up. Time for bed."

Freddy went into the kitchen, popped open the fridge and grabbed himself a beer. He shivered, looking around.

Man, did she leave a window open or something? And why is it so quiet in here? Where is Stella? Every time I come home she barks her head off at me.

The petite mutt was nowhere in sight, and she was not sounding her alarm like she usually did. Freddy cracked open the beer and took a sip.

Weird.

"Come on, Aunt Penny. Wake up. Let me help you get to bed."

Freddy peeked into the living room again. She sat with her back to him in the easy chair, the TV volume low and the latest fashion contest reality show playing on the screen. Penny didn't stir.

Something's off.

"Stella? Where are you, you little feather duster?"

Freddy scanned the darkness. Cold breath whistled against his skin. He shivered and looked around, searching for an answer. He turned on the kitchen light, and nothing seemed out of place. He walked into the laundry room and turned the light on. Everything seemed fine. Freddy reached to turn the light back off, and stopped.

There was broken glass on the floor.

The window pane above the doorknob was broken. It had been smashed in from the outside. Icy air blew in.

Freddy's body tensed.

Oh, no. Oh no oh no oh no...

"Aunt Penny?"

Freddy dropped the beer and raced back to the living room.

Penny remained sitting in the dark. Freddy threw on the lights.

"Aunt Penny, wake up!"

He ran to the easy chair and spun her around.

Then the world dropped out under his feet.

Her face was swollen and deep purple.

A wire had been wrapped around her throat so tightly that her eyes and tongue were popping out of her head. Her hands are feet were also bound, dried blood at the edges of the thin wire as it sliced through layers of flesh.

"AUNT PENNY!!!"

He dropped to her side, feebly trying to help her. The wire was twisted tight and she was long gone. The horrified and confused look in her dead eyes drilled into Freddy's brain and he could feel his heart dropping into his stomach. He wept and pawed at her, his whole body trembling.

No no no no no! Oh sweet God, no!!!

A dark figure melted out of the shadows behind him.

It was a black shape, the figure of a large man. Freddy did not notice his looming presence. A taser gun was in his hand. He pointed the gun, aiming at the center of Freddy's back.

FZZZZZZZZZZZTTZZZZZZ!!!

Two wired prongs carrying fifty-thousand volts of electricity shot through Freddy's shirt and harpooned the flesh of his back. The immense current blazed through his veins and arteries and capillaries and bones, and a searing pain like nothing else took over his whole world. Freddy screamed and spasmed uncontrollably. His body was no longer under his control, collapsing to the floor as he convulsed in all-consuming agony.

Two wet winter boots stepped into his field of vision.

The man was standing over him. Freddy struggled to see him. His eyes traveled from the boots up the brown pants, to a heavy black winter coat, to the taser gun in his gloved hand. Freddy's eyes looked up, up, settling on a face backlit by the living room lights.

The man chuckled. He leaned forward, giving Freddy a good look at his smiling face. He had fleshy cheeks and a bulbous, bald head. He was clean-shaven, wore wire glasses and had lifeless, beady eyes.

James Roy Hiegren leered down at him.

"But... But..."

Before Freddy could say any more, Hiegren loaded up a big fist, dropped down onto his knees and threw all of his momentum into one bone-crunching punch.

Everything went black for Freddy Luccio.

CHAPTER 33
THE COLLECTOR

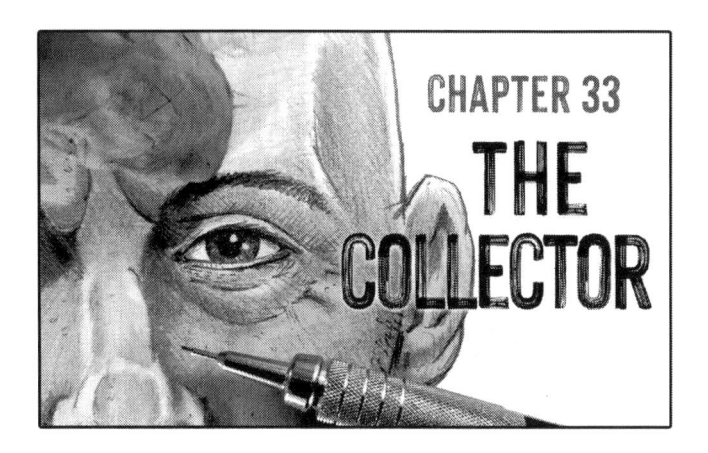

BLACKNESS. Pain. Fog.

Freddy's eyes fluttered open. The world spun around him. Frigid air. Floating outside. Being carried. The squeal of metal hinges. Placed down on a hard surface. A crib for baby to sleep in. A steel coffin. The trunk of a car. The squeal of rusty hinges. The trunk slammed closed and locked.

Blackness.

Movement. Abstract flashes.

Dreams. Pain.

Consciousness crept back for a moment and his eyes opened. Pitch black. Cold. Rocking motion, bumps in the road. Gasoline and rust. Pain. He went out again.

Blackness.

Movement. Floating.

Bing carried. Head throbbing.

No... Stop... Stay awake...

Blackness.

Warmer inside. Hinges creaking. Door closing.

The kitchen looked familiar. The door to the basement. A key slid into the lock. Thumping footsteps and jarring motion. Stairs. Going down.

No... Please... Stay awake... Stay awake...

Blackness.

STAY AWAKE!

Freddy forced his eyes open and willed a surge of adrenaline through his veins. His body jolted with strength, every muscle flexed, every synapse firing. He gasped for air, his mind still spinning, racing to catch up with his surroundings.

It was dark. He was seated. There was a desk, chairs, musical instruments, a microphone. A deer head on one wall, a goat head on the other. Numbing pain at his wrists and ankles. He tried to stand but was stuck in place.

Oh, God... This is bad. This is bad this is bad...

The pain in his skull was nearly overwhelming, a swelling like his head was about to burst. A trickle of blood had run down his cheek and dried in place. A deep bruise had formed where his jaw met his cheek bone. He looked down at his hands to see his wrists had been duct taped to an old wooden chair that he had been seated in. He tried to move his feet but they too were bound to the chair's legs.

"Oh, God..."

Freddy fought, struggled and thrashed. The chair creaked beneath his efforts but held strong. He fought harder, but still nothing. He was trapped, a prisoner, helpless and alone and afraid. No, terrified. Cold terror pumped in his chest and panic descended like a heavy black quilt around his shoulders.

Above his head, floorboards creaked under heavy footsteps. Music was playing in the kitchen. Jazz. It was an uptempo tune, with a French horn and a saxophone and a spicy drum beat. He was upstairs, moving around, opening cabinets, doing something.

Hiegren. The killer. The monster. Pure evil. Images flashed through Freddy's concussed brain. Young women dead in the snow, their heads smashed into pulp, lying in frozen ponds of blood. Aunt Penny's dead eyes, bugging out of her head, begging.

Pure evil.

Panic engulfed him and held him tight, laughing in his face. Dread seized his being as he struggled and strained, the old chair barely moving beneath him. This was the end. The monster would be upon him soon, inching toward him in the darkness with his club, a sadistic smile as he bashed Freddy's head into nothing. Terror overwhelmed him and he wept uncontrollably.

"Oh, God! GODDDD!!! HELP ME!!! GET ME OUT OF HERE!!!"

The door at the top of the stairs creaked open.

Hiegren stood in the doorway.

He descended the stairs and closed the door behind him. He had an open bottle of Armand de Brignac Rose champagne in his hand. Freddy shivered as he approached. The man was like a bald bulldog with savage intent in his eyes. He was unsteady on his feet, the bottle he held less than halfway full. He was definitely feeling the effects of the alcohol. Hiegren stopped, lifted the bottle to his lips and took a swig, his eyes locked on Freddy's.

"HELP ME PLEASE!! SOMEBODY!!!"

Hiegren chuckled, stepping down to the floor.

"Go ahead," he smirked. "Scream all you want. You're in my recording studio. Sound-proofed walls. No one can hear you. *YAAAAAAAAA!!!*" He belted out a chilling laugh, taking another drink and dancing awkwardly to a tune in his head.

"Please, man! Please! I'm sorry! I-I..."

Hiegren stumbled past him, reaching out with his sausage fingers and stroking Freddy's cheek. He approached his computer desk and mixing board, and Freddy noticed his own car keys, wallet and folding knife.

"What do you *want?*"

Hiegren picked up Freddy's wallet and began to rifle through it.

"What I want is to be left alone. But you wouldn't let that happen, would you..." Hiegren pulled out Freddy's driver's license and read aloud, "*Alfredo Luccio?* You trash my house, bring the police here? Give them samples of my *DNA?*"

Hiegren chucked the wallet at Freddy, bouncing it off his chest. The large man was on him in an instant, his right fist shooting into Freddy's mouth, splitting his lower lip. Freddy winced and writhed in his seat as Hiegren circled back around to his bottle of champagne, taking another sip.

"Now here we are, Alfredo... *Alfreeedooooo...*" Hiegren sung in a sweet, feminine voice. "Oh, excuse me.

I should offer you a drink! Here you go." Hiegren stuck the bottle in Freddy's mouth and poured booze down his throat. Freddy hacked and coughed, nearly vomiting all over himself. Hiegren laughed and chugged the rest of the champagne, tossing the bottle behind him with a hoot. Freddy winced as it shattered against the wall.

"I worked so hard to build this life, this home, get everything just right. Fifteen years... Do you have any idea how difficult it is to disappear? And then to start a new life, a new name...? I finally had it all worked out, until you came along... And *he* came back. Now everything's ruined... *Everything* is ruined..."

"So..." Freddy's brain nearly cracked in half. "I was right the whole time! You really *are* The Basher! You raped and murdered all of those women!"

Hiegren snickered, shaking his head.

He walked past Freddy to the wood-paneled wall with the instruments leaning against it. "Tell me something, Mr. Luccio..." He pushed the guitar and keyboard and amp aside. He pressed in a strip of paneling on the wall and located a secret latch, popping it open. A hidden door creaked ajar, and Hiegren pulled it the rest of the way open. Darkness awaited inside. "...Do I look like a man who's got a thing for *women?*"

Hiegren pulled a chain and turned on a hanging light bulb in the secret room. He ducked inside, where there were what appeared to be several small mannequins. With massive hands, he lifted two of the small figures, lifting them like they weighed nothing. Hiegren carried them back out to the main room and delicately placed them in from of Freddy.

What in the absolute... unholy... fuck?

"This here is Thomas, and this is Benji."

Hiegren patted them on the shoulders with pride. He smiled and went back into the hidden room to get more. Freddy's heart stopped. They appeared at first glance to be department store mannequins in the young boys' section, standing on ornately decorated stands. Thomas was six years-old and dressed like a little sailor boy. Benji was twelve and a Cub Scout. They were both smiling. Their eyes were made of glass.

Their flesh was made of flesh.

Oh, my God...

Hiegren came back out with two more.

"This is Brad, and this is Dylan."

The first boy was only a toddler, dressed in PJ's, a diorama of toys part of the base he stood on. The second was ten, frozen in an action pose, wearing a Superman costume. Glass eyes. Leathery skin.

Oh, my God!

Two more boys name Aaron and Billy. Then another two named Johnny and Dakota. Then two more. And two more.

Oh, my God!! They're all real boys! They're all stuffed, taxidermied little boys!!

"This one is Chris, and this is Franky. They're been with me for a while, so they're not looking so great anymore. But I still love you, yes I do! Daddy loves his boys! You're still beautiful!"

Their skin had yellowed and begun to shrivel. Stitched seams ran up the sides of their necks and arms. Glass eyes had been jammed into the orbital sockets, blank and soulless, some of them not looking in the right directions. They were all positioned in front of Freddy, all staring at him with their dead eyes. Hiegren brought out two more, then two more. Flesh flayed from meat and bone, dried and treated with arsenic and borax to preserve it. Stretched around a base of styrofoam, dowels, and wood shavings, the flesh was manipulated to appear as much as possible to what it looked like in life.

"Oh, my God!!" Freddy cried uncontrollably.

Hiegren brought out more, and more, and more.

There was a cowboy spinning a lasso that was frozen in the air. There was a baseball player about to swing his bat. There was a very small boy in a tuxedo and a top hat. One wore nothing but a bathing suit, and his dried flesh was a patchwork of stitches, stretched into a vaguely familiar human shape. Most showed evidence of bruising or scarring over their necks and throats, all likely killed by strangulation.

"OH, MY GOD!!!"

Hiegren brought out his entire collection, setting up the macabre dolls to face their new friend. He adjusted their clothes, fixed their hair. There were at least forty young boys, frozen in time, propped up on their personalized stands like dolls in a store display. Hiegren kissed one on the cheek.

Freddy's mind spun and his stomach twisted into knots.

"JESUS CHRIST!!! OH, FUCK ME, MAN!!!"

"Shut the hell up already!" Hiegren pulled a garrote from his pocket and turned to Freddy. He grabbed the handles on either side of the wire, whipped it over Freddy's head, and tightened the ligature with excessive strength. Freddy felt the wire wrap so tight around his throat, he thought his head might pop off. All blood flow to his brain was instantly cut off, and his eyeballs begin to swell.

I'm dying! He's killing me! This is how Aunt Penny died! Oh God, no!!

Hiegren choked him hard, smiling. The stuffed deer head watched. The stuffed goat head watched. The stuffed young boys watched. Freddy thrashed but could not break his bonds. His left foot had managed to loosen the leg of the chair, but not enough. It was too late. He could feel the lights starting to dim around him.

This is it! This is how I die! He's killing me!

Hiegren suddenly let go of the garrote, carefully timing it so Freddy wouldn't pass out. He smiled and circled back around to the table, letting Freddy choke and sputter for air.

"Oh, you're not getting off that easy, my friend. I'm gonna enjoy this."

Hiegren looked over everything on the table, touching the items with his left hand. With his right, he stroked his penis, his erection showing through his pants. He picked up the newspaper featuring Freddy's original composite sketch, holding it up close for a better look.

"So, you thought this was me, huh? This sloppy idiot? *The Basher?* ...Pssh. You were wrong about me, Mr. Luccio. I'm nothing like him."

"P-Please... Please..."

"No, I'm afraid I don't go after women, okay? And I'm not stupid enough to hunt in my own back yard.

When I'm looking for a new boy, I drive quite a distance to find them. Different towns, different counties... That way it's never traced back to me. I never shit where I eat."

When he's looking for a boy... That day I followed him to the park! He wasn't watching the young mother, he was watching the boy!

"Please... I-I'm sorry..."

Hiegren circled his prisoner, taking a moment to straighten little Maurice's tie, and turned to face Freddy, gripping the garrote handles.

"I've been living here in Everett Falls for fifteen years, and never was I so much as *questioned* by the police about my boys... And now that messy asshole is killing girls again and just leaving them laying around, and *you're* sniffing around, bringing the police to my door! The *FBI!!*"

Hiegren lashed the ligature around Freddy's neck again, pulling him in and looking him in the eye as he squeezed. Freddy gurgled and thrashed, his eyes swelling, tongue bulging from his mouth. His feet kicked, and the left chair leg began to split at its seam.

Hiegren let go again and continued to caress himself.

Freddy sputtered and wept as the blood rushed back to his head, a deep purple welt forming across his throat.

"I-If you...kill me...you'll be the...first one they suspect..."

"Oh, I know," Hiegren stepped back and circled drunkenly, playfully swinging the garrote, "but it's too late for that. I'm on their radar now. I'm going to have to burn my house down and leave all my boys behind, *tonight*. I'll have to hit the road again, kill another poor schmuck, steal his identity, and start all over from scratch. *Again...* All because of you."

Hiegren crossed back to Freddy, toying with the garrote and staring laser beams into the young man's terrified eyes. He leaned in close, fingers stroking Freddy's face and chest, his other hand fondling himself.

Oh God, please don't rape me! Please God, get me out of here!!

"And so, Mr. Luccio," Hiegren pressed his nose into Freddy's, threatening to kiss him, "you are going to suffer tonight more than any other human being has ever suffered. You are going to *know* pain before you die. Starting with the knowledge that your sweet little girlfriend will die first."

The world stopped spinning.

Everything came to a halt.

Freddy lifted his aching eyes up to look at Hiegren.

"Wh-What did you just say...?"

CHAPTER 34
SMASH AND DESTROY

HIEGREN UNROLLED A SPOOLED case of taxidermy tools. There were knives, chisels, scissors, pokers, scrapers, syringes, tubes. He held up a three and a half-inch skinning knife and turned it in the light, savoring the fear in Freddy's eyes.

"Answer me, you son of a bitch!" Freddy raged. *"What did you just say?"*

"Charlotte, right? From Clarkson's?" Hiegren smiled and circled Freddy, stroking his shoulders. "Cute little blondie."

"Don't you go *near* her, you bastard! Don't you fucking touch her!"

Hiegren lit a cigarette and began to smoke.

"Oh, *I'm* not going to touch her, Mr. Luccio. But the man you mistook me for? The man who really killed all those women? That dim-witted, sloppy amateur?" Hiegren sighed, his eyes looking through the wall and into the past. "After all these years... He was the last person I was expecting to see..."

. . .

IT WAS LAST APRIL. No, May. I remember 'cause my bowling team had just lost the league finals. It was a nice, warm night, I had just gone to the alley for a little practice time by myself. Of course, I bowled better that night than I had during the whole tournament, but that's neither here nor there. Anyway, so I'm leaving the alley, it's nice and warm, and I'm walking through the parking lot, right? And then, from behind me I hear this voice.

"Howdy there, Russ," he says.

And I stopped dead in my tracks. That's a voice I'll never forget as long as I live. I thought I'd left him behind, covered my tracks, but there was always something in the back of my mind that knew... He'd find me one day. So I turned around and there he was. That same crooked smile as always, 'cept now with a mustache... You did a pretty good job, *Alfredo*, I have to say. That drawing of yours really did look like him. Not so much like me, but whatever.

So I say, "How did you find me, Bill?"

Pfft. He was all cocky and sarcastic as always. Throwin' up his hands like, "Now, why would you think I been *lookin'* for you? This is just a great big coincidence is all! Me and my family just happened to move here, and who do I bump into... but my very own sweet little brother, Russ."

Asshole. Sure, just a big coincidence.

I told him to keep his damn voice down, and to stop calling me that. There were people around. My name is James Hiegren now. He just laughed, asked me what poor bastard I had to kill to take on that monicker.

And I say, "Some bum I knew no one would miss.

Now what do you *want*, Bill?" Right? So he just smiles with those ugly teeth he never bothered to get fixed, and that bad complexion, and those long, dirty fingernails... And that smell. God, just that smell brought back memories. Back in Chicago, that first time, abandoned house... He let me watch... *Made* me watch. Him and that girl. Cora was her name, I think...

Anyway, so he says, "What makes you think I *want* anything from you?" Always playing mind games, always trying to fuck with me, right? He's like, "What, 'cause you cut a deal with the Chicago DA twenty years ago? Let me do seven years while you skipped town, free as a bird, blah blah blah? Nah, you know I'm over that, Russ. I'm the forgive and forget type!"

And I'm like, "James! My name is James Hiegren now! And this town ain't big enough for the both of us!" And I was right. I have my thing, and he has his. He likes his girls, I like my boys... And he's not exactly subtle. Or smart. What I do is an *art*. It takes skill, talent, patience. I respect my subjects, I love my boys. I keep them beautiful forever. He just wants to rape and smash and destroy like a fucking animal... I knew him being here would just bring the heat down on me. But there was nothing I could do. I mean, I couldn't turn him in or I'd blow my own cover too, y'know?

Anyway, he says, "Oh, blah blah blah, I ain't here to step on your toes or bring any unwanted attention. You still into that *fag* shit, huh? Making your little *dolls*?"

And I'm like, "Fuck you, asshole." Homophobic bastard.

So he just laughed again like he does at everything,

and he's like, "Touchy, touchy. Listen, I just thought this would be a lovely place to raise a family, y'know? Good girls' baseball team..." He started to head back to his own car, laughing like this was all a great big hoot. He's like, "Damn, little Russell Rayburn! What a small world! Guess we're gonna be seeing each other a lot more now! Let's have lunch sometime!" Prick.

HIEGREN TAPPED cigarette ash onto the floor.

Freddy's head spun and throbbed.

An audience of boys watched with glass eyes. Tommy and Benji and Brad. Johnny and Dakota and Chris. Franky and Billy and Aaron and Maurice and all the others, all staring at the young man strapped to the chair.

The name rang in Freddy's head... *Rayburn.*

"Here's another one," Harney had said. *"William Henry Rayburn. Fifty years old. Multiple past convictions, including sexual assault. And the list goes on..."*

Freddy had seen the man. They had passed in the hallway at the station. He was so hung up on Hiegren, he'd barely even looked at Rayburn.

"Well, this guy's stickin' to his story, John," I remember Bagnarol said. *"Unless his wife and kids change their tune, his alibi is tight..."*

Rayburn.

Not my scumbag... Oh, my God.

Hiegren took a puff from his smoke and circled his prisoner as all the pieces began to settle in Freddy's mind.

"Ever since then, he's been a thorn in my side," the

man with the knife continued. "Following me like a shadow, trying to get under my *skin*." He punctuated the word by carving a shallow groove into Freddy's cheek. Freddy hissed and drew back, thrashing as fresh hot blood trickled to his chin. "I knew it was just a matter of time 'fore he started killing... And apparently, while you were busy following me, Bill had taken an interest in *you*... Or more specifically, your girlfriend."

"Oh, please... Please..."

"He finally called to warn me. Said that you two were on to me. That as much as he likes watching me squirm, he knew that if I went down, he'd go down too. He was watching when you broke into my house. Said I'd better hurry on home, so I did. And there you were. And here we are..."

Freddy fought with fury against his bindings. The left leg of the chair was coming looser, but not enough. Sweat beaded on his forehead as his muscles strained and veins bulged. It was no use. Hiegren cut him again.

Freddy jerked and screamed.

"God damn it, you motherfucker! *You motherfucker!*"

Dolls eyes stared at him. Dead boys.

Hiegren laughed. "He even gave me the address where I could find you. Your aunt's house, was it?" Tears burned down Freddy's cheeks. "That's on you, Alfredo. I don't kill women, but she was in the way. Sorry. If it makes any difference, she didn't suffer long. I did it quick. Not like I'm gonna do you, big boy... So big brother actually came through for once. I get you, he gets little Miss Charlotte."

God, please! Please get me out of here! Please don't let him hurt her!!

Hiegren produced a slip of paper from his pocket, then scooped Freddy's cell phone off the table. He looked at the number scribbled on the paper and dialed. He put the phone on speaker, and they both waited while it rang. A voice came on the other end of the line.

"Russ?"

"Bill. Guess who I got with me right now. Wanna say hello? Go ahead, Alfredo. Say hello to Bill." He held the phone out and Freddy jerked back, clenching his jaw closed, still struggling against his constraints. "Say hello." Freddy refused. Hiegren was not having it. "I said *say hello!*"

He slashed down with the skinning knife and sliced a groove across Freddy's forearm. Searing pain shot through and he screamed.

"Ahhh! Fuck you, you piece of shit! Fuck you!!"

William Rayburn laughed through the speaker.

"Hi there, Freddy," the voice on the phone growled. "Just thought you should know that I'm gonna call back in a few minutes. And when I do, your sweet little Charlotte will be with me. Begging for her life. And I'm gonna let you listen while I... Well, you'll see. In the meantime, you get to have some fun with my kid brother. Talk to you soon, slugger."

Click.

WILLIAM RAYBURN HUNG up and slid the phone into his jeans pocket.

He looked into the dirty mirror in his dirty bedroom, smiling. His acne-scarred face demanded attention, so he popped a pimple on his nose and two on his cheeks, wiping the puss on the wall. Rough, leathery hands unscrewed a small jar of Ben Nye flesh foundation #3, and dabbed the makeup over the numerous red spots.

His wife lay on the bed behind him, facing away, the comforter pulled up to her chin. Her eyes were wide open. She dared not turn to look at him or ask where he was going at three in the morning.

She knew.

Rayburn stroked his mustache and pushed the greasy strands of hair out of his eyes. He slipped into a heavy green sweater, and a well-worn ball cap covered the bald spot on the back of his head. He sucked in his gut and checked himself out.

Yeah, I look good. Ready for my big date! You ready for me, Charlotte?

Rayburn sat on the edge of the bed and pulled on a pair of winter boots. His wife shuddered, pretending to be asleep. He threw on a long black rain coat. Out came a pair of black leather gloves, and he stretched them over his hands. He buttoned the coat and looked again in the mirror. There was only one thing missing.

I got a present for you, little girl. It's big, and long, and hard...

He slid open a drawer and pulled out a short baton that looked like a bear had used it as a toothpick. It was an old billy-club with a grooved grip and a hole through the base, a leather lanyard looping through. The numerous nicks and scratches and discolorations told the brutal history of the antique truncheon. Rayburn gripped it in his gloved hand, feeling a surge of power. He slipped the weapon into his coat.

Sweet, sweet little girl.

He tucked his car keys into his pocket and turned off the light. He turned briefly to look at his wife's still form in the bed. He knew she was awake. Didn't care. He turned without saying a word and strode out of the room.

Here I come, baby. Here I come.

CHAPTER 35
FIGHT FOR YOUR LIFE

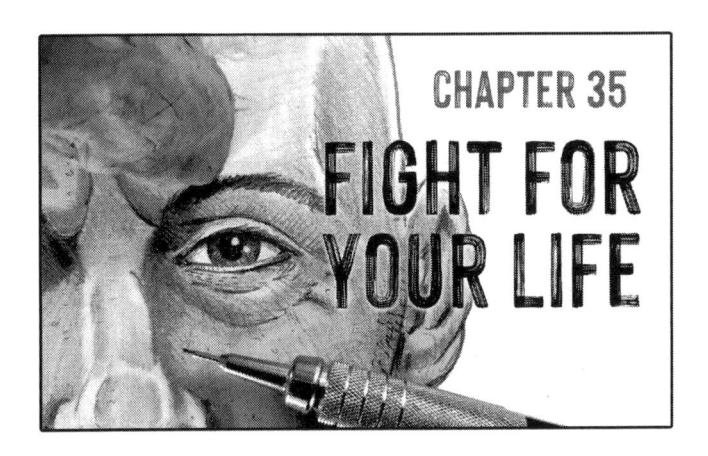

THE LIGHTS BEGAN TO FADE.

Hiegren released his ligature before all went black.

Freddy Luccio gasped and coughed as blood rushed back into his brain. All he knew was pain and panic. The imposing fiend circled him, his shirt stained with sweat over his bulbous gut, a maniacal gleam in his eyes. He gripped his garrote, drops of blood rolling down the wire from where it had begun to break the flesh.

"I had really gotten used to this place," Hiegren mused. "This is my home... *Was* my home. Tonight it all ends. Once I'm done with you, I have to go to the gas station, fill up a couple big cans... Burn it all down." Hiegren glanced over his collection of death dolls, tears brimming in his eyes. "Burn my boys... I'm sorry..."

Sadness flowed back into rage, and the wire was around Freddy's neck again. His body jolted and spasmed, face turning red. The left chair leg cracked further, wobbling as Hiegren dropped his victim back down. He let Freddy catch his breath again, savoring every moment of his delicious agony.

"Don't worry, boy. I won't kill you until I let you say goodbye to your little girlfriend. My brother should be calling back any minute now!"

Please, no more! Plea—

Hiegren whipped the wire over Freddy's head again. Squeezed hard.

Let him go.

He waited a few seconds, then choked him again.

Let him go.

God, I'm sorry... I'm so sorry...

Freddy trembled uncontrollably. Shock was setting in. It was all over. The sick beast leered down at him, taking a last puff from his cigarette and putting it out on Freddy's cheek. He hissed and spasmed. His nose was broken, his cheek slashed, his other cheek burned, the bruise across his throat turning purple-black.

Hiegren tossed the garrote back on his table and returned to the small skinning knife. He crossed back to Freddy, looking down at the blade in contemplation.

"Maybe some more cutting for a bit? What do you think, Alfredo?"

Freddy couldn't answer.

Hiegren caressed his new subject, trying to decide.

"Should I cut your tongue out first? Or maybe your nose? What do you think? Or maybe I should cut off your cock and balls, stick 'em in your mouth?" Hiegren ran his free hand down to Freddy's crotch and squeezed. It was wet with urine. Freddy hadn't even realized that he'd pissed himself. Hiegren laughed and wiped his hand off on Freddy's shirt. "Nah, we'll save that for the end. Then I'll pour gasoline over you, light you up and watch you burn alive. Sound like a good plan, Alfredo?"

"J-Just...as long...as you stop...calling me...Alfredo..."

Hiegren threw his head back and bellowed in laughter.

"You know what? Fair enough! You got it! What is it then, Freddy, right?"

Freddy nodded, tears dripping off his chin.

"Okay then, Freddy. Let's have some more fun, shall we?"

Hiegren put his knee on Freddy's thigh as he leaned in, his massive weight pressing down on the young artist. The chair creaked. Freddy spasmed and trembled. Hiegren grabbed Freddy's right ear, pulling it hard. He flashed the knife and a twisted grin. He aimed the razor edge for Freddy's ear.

Please God no please God no please God no!

Hiegren cut into the helix, right in the sweet spot where the ear connects to the head. Freddy jolted at the stinging pain as the blade sliced downward. Hiegren cut with glee, sawing through layers of flesh and cartilage.

Hot blood.

Fight for your life!

Searing pain.

Screaming.

Fight for your life!!

Chair leg breaking.

Every muscle, every last bit of strength.

FIGHT FOR YOUR LIFE!!!

Freddy kicked and thrashed and the left chair leg finally splintered and gave way. The chair lurched and fell to the left. Hiegren lost his balance, spinning and falling backward. The crown of his bald head cracked into the edge of his desk before his massive weight crashed into the floor, his knife skittering away.

"Hnng!"

Freddy was on his side, all but his left leg still strapped to the chair. He felt a massive burning on the left side of his head, and knew that his ear was barely still attached. The entire auricle of the outer ear hung from the lobule at the base. A dark cranberry puddle was forming under his head. The impact of the fall had further weakened the integrity of the old chair.

Hiegren struggled to sit up.

He touched the top of his head and his fingertips came back coated in blood. The deep gash sliced from the crown to the center of his forehead, and hot red was pumping out like a faucet.

"Son of a *bitch*..."

Hiegren chuckled and shook his head, wiping away the stream of blood running into his eyes. But it just kept running from the jagged head wound. He pressed his hand to the injury, trying to figure out what to do next.

"Well, then," Hiegren hissed, annoyed, "guess I'd better go take care of this, huh? Right, *Freddy?*" He delivered a rib-cracking kick, and Freddy's entire body seized in pain. "Be right back. Don't go anywhere! Ha!"

Hiegren turned and stomped up the stairs, woozy from both drink and blood loss. His footsteps creaked up to the kitchen door, rusty hinges opened and closed, and the door latched closed again.

This is it! If I don't get out of here now, I'm fucking dead! Think!!

Freddy's eyes devoured the space, scanning every inch, every angle.

Roof, walls. Computer desk. Audio mixing board. Guitar. Microphone. Old, gray carpeting. Pool of blood forming. Taxidermy tools dropped on the floor. A crowd of smiling, unblinking, dead boys.

Don't look at them! Don't look!

Footsteps overhead. Hiegren rushing to and fro. Water running. Cabinets opening and closing. Freddy knew he'd be back any minute. He fought his restraints, but he could barely loosen them. His left leg thrashed wildly, the only part of his body that could move freely.

He's cleaning his wound. Hope it fucking hurts!

Freddy kept scanning the room. Toolbox in the corner, the lid open. A hammer, a screwdriver. A rake, a hatchet, gardening shears. The padlocked chain holding the storm doors closed. He looked back at the objects on the floor. Scissors, a scooping tool, what looked like a dental pick.

The skinning knife Hiegren had used to cut him.

It wasn't far away. Freddy pounded down onto the carpet with his left foot and pushed. Again. Again. He stomped down and scooted to the right. He was lying on his left side, his bound left hand rubbing against the floor. He had to drag himself in a near complete circle before the knife was aligned with his hand.

Come on, come on...

The pain in his head had become a dull thud. He could feel the weight of his ear pulling down, away from his head, barely still attached. He pushed the thought from his mind, focused on the task at hand. Hiegren's footsteps continued to stomp around above him. Freddy could hear the deranged bastard heading up to the second floor.

He pushed with his foot, pushed again. The knife was inches away.

He strained with his fingertips, almost touching the hilt. *Come on!*

He pushed a little further and found that he had done it. His fingers grasped the handle and dragged the knife closer, finally scooping it up and gripping it tightly. But his wrist was still bound. Carefully, he used his fingers to reverse his grip on the knife, angling the bloody blade toward the duct tape binding.

After two failed attempts, he slipped the point of the blade under the edge of the tape. He worked the cutting edge in a sawing motion, slowly beginning to sever the strong, silvery layers of bindings. He cut through a little more, then a little more.

Freddy's eyes were laser focused, sweat beading on his intense, brutalized face. He cut through two inches of the tape, then began working his wrist into the tear. Back and forth he yanked, ripping it open further. Further.

"*Come on!!*"

The tape tore open as Freddy jerked his hand free.

Relief washed through him like an ocean wave, but the ordeal was far from over. Still, he had one hand free, and that was all he needed. Wielding the knife in his left hand, he made easy work cutting through the tape binding his right. A few more slashes and his right foot came loose. He fell to the floor, his broken rib punishing him as he gasped for air.

No time to celebrate! Have to escape!

Freddy staggered to his feet. He hesitantly reached up to touch his ear. Fire stung through the wound as his fingers grazed the hanging flesh. Wincing in pain, he pushed it back against his head, holding it in place. He looked around, frantic.

Dead boys. Doll's eyes.

Don't look at them! Think! Where's my phone?

He looked at the desktop and did not see his cell there. Hiegren had pocketed it. Freddy cursed and circled the area like a caged tiger, diverting his eyes from the morbid crowd surrounding him. He took his hand away from the nearly severed ear, and it quickly peeled away again, hanging limp like a banana peel off his head.

Fuck!!

Freddy pushed his ear back into place. He feverishly looked for something, anything... He stopped, turned, and forced himself to look at the audience of little boys behind him. His eyes zeroed in.

Little Billy was dressed up as a business man.

Blue suit and a red tie.

The tie!

Freddy cringed as he forced himself to approach the pint-sized Wall Street mogul, a suitcase in one hand, his other hand posed like he was checking his watch. Freddy inched up to the doll, trying not to look at it as he reached out for the tie. He pulled at the knot with his right hand, but it was on tight. He would need both hands.

Oh my God, this is so disgusting...

Freddy let go of his ear and reached his bloody left hand out. He hissed at the sharp pain as his ear flopped down again. Using both hands, he loosened and untied the knot, pulling the garment strip away from its owner.

Little Billy didn't mind. His smile remained stitched and tucked in place.

Freddy pressed his ear back against his head, then held it in place with his shoulder. He quickly lifted the tie and wrapped it around his head, firmly holding his ear in place. He tied it tight, then double-knotted it.

Footsteps overhead. Hiegren was coming back down from the second floor. Freddy knew he didn't have long. He feverishly looked for a way out, or a way to fight. The small knife in his hand wouldn't do it, and he was far too weak and injured to fight anyway. He had to escape.

Where's the key to the padlock, damn it?

He searched the desk, digging feverishly through the drawers. Nothing.

"Fuck!"

He took notice again of his wallet on the table, and scooped it up quickly, sticking it back in his pocket as he continued to look around. The footsteps were getting closer. Hiegren was nearing the basement door. No more time. Freddy's eyes whipped past every item. He had to get through that padlock.

The hammer.

Freddy ran to the toolbox and swiped the pounding tool into his hands.

The cellar door squeaked open. Hiegren began to descend in silhouette.

Fuckfuckfuckfuckfuckfuckfuck!!

Freddy bolted for the steel storm doors, dashing up the short wooden stairs. A large, heavy duty padlock awaited him. He did not wait.

Bash! Bash! Bash!

Freddy swung the hammer. The lock held strong.

Bash! Bash! Bash!

Hiegren was halfway down the stairs.

He held a Remington 870 pump-action 12 gauge in his right hand, a blood-soaked towel held against the head wound with his left.

"Come on, god damn it!!"

Freddy smashed the padlock over and over with all his rage and strength. It finally gave way, popping open, and Freddy rushed to toss it aside and pull the chain away. Hiegren reached the bottom of the stairs. Saw Freddy about to escape.

"Son of a bitch!" Hiegren snarled.

Chk-chk! He took his hand away from the wound and held the front end with the bloody towel, chambering a round. He aimed at the center of Freddy's back. He put his finger on the trigger.

Freddy undid the chain and pushed the heavy steel doors open.

He exploded up through the doorway.

Hiegren pulled the trigger.

The concussive blast echoed in the confined space, and a cluster of buckshot flew through the air. The shot mostly missed, but three of the lead pellets struck home in Freddy's right hamstring. There was a small eruption of blood and a fiery burst of pain, and he staggered forward into the snow.

Ah!! Motherfucker!!

Freddy gripped his bleeding leg and ran forward into the freezing, dark backyard, each step a limping agony. His blood dripped into the snow. He looked past the fence to the dark woods beyond.

Don't stop! Don't stop!

CHAPTER 36
CLIFFHANGER

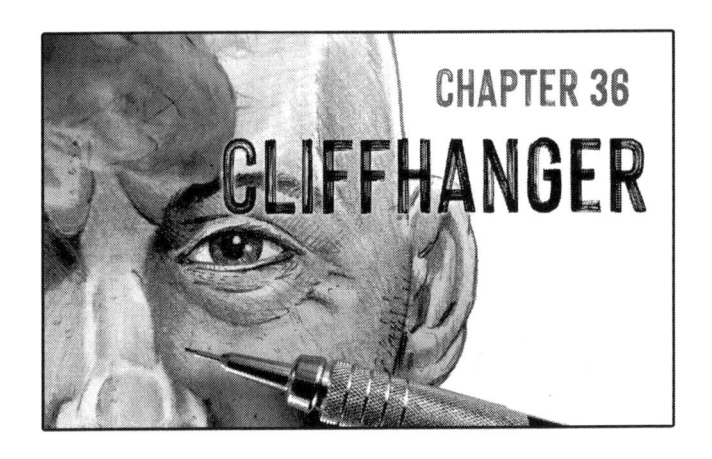

NEW YORK WINTERS are a special kind of cold.

There are other places in the world that do get colder, to be sure. Alaska. The South Pole. Siberia. But New York cold has its own particular attitude. It will freeze you to the bone, but then it will also tell you to go fuck yourself. It's a vicious, cutting cold. It stings and laughs at you. Just when you think it can't get any colder, it sends its friend the wind. It slices through the eyelets in your shoes and the seams in your clothes. It finds your exposed skin and shuts you down. It is overwhelming and cruel.

Freddy limped through the New York cold.

His sneakers crunched in the snow, feet wet and numb. He wore nothing but a blood-drenched button-up over his white t-shirt, and a thin pair of jeans. He may as well have been naked. His leg ached. His ear throbbed, but the tie held it tightly in place. His body seized as the cold began to soak through his skin, sinking down toward his bones and vital organs.

Keep going! Keep...going!

. . .

HIEGREN JOGGED up to the top of the stairs, peering out through the storm doors. His quarry was not far ahead, hobbling towards the dark tree line. Hiegren smiled, taking the towel away from his head wound to once again level the shotgun. But he noticed the lights had come on in his neighbors' houses. They had already been woken up. The bald man cursed, lowering the firearm. He needed both hands to wield it anyway, and his left had to maintain pressure on the wound.

He hurried back down into his basement studio, cursing, putting the gun down and looking for another weapon. Hatchet. He snatched the small axe into his hands, contemplating running back upstairs to grab his coat before going outside. No time. Freddy was getting away. Hiegren snarled, running back up through the storm doors and out into the winter night.

FREDDY REACHED THE FENCE, heaving himself over and crashing down on the other side. He was wet with snow, the bitter cold actually serving to numb the pain. He couldn't feel his feet, couldn't feel his nose, hands were numb aside from the stinging pins and needles.

Oh my God, so cold! So cold! Jesus!

To his left were Hiegren's neighbors. If he circled right around the house, he could be back on the street, surrounded by more neighbors. He could scream and get attention and be saved. But those would be the deductions of a calm, rational mind. All Freddy's brain could process was cold, pain, and fear. His feet moved without thought, driving him forward on instinct alone.

Get away! Get away! Keep going!

He limped forward into the black wood.

"OH, you're not gonna get far going that way," Hiegren growled to himself through a menacing grin. Pressing the bloody towel to his head, he continued after Freddy, clenching the hatchet. He reached the chest-high fence, struggling to heft himself up and throw his massive gut over to the other side. He grunted and tumbled, landing in the snow outside his property. His prey's blood and footprints in the snow pointed him in the right direction.

He stumbled to his feet, blood streaming down into his face again. Pressing the towel back against the gash, he snarled and stalked forward. Biting wind swept through him to the bone, swirling snow into the air.

Little Freddy ran through the trees.

The dark figure with the axe was not far behind.

It was a nightmare come to life. It couldn't be real. Nothing could possibly be this cold. No human being could truly be so evil. He couldn't die like this. Freddy pushed on, his feet frozen solid. He tripped and stumbled back up, then again. Freddy saw Charlotte's face, then Rayburn's. He saw a gloved hand lifting a baton high in the air. Her skull cracking. Crimson streaking her corn-blonde hair. Rayburn's eyes. His yellowed teeth. His pants coming off.

Freddy screamed in rage, fighting off the images in his head.

He screamed again, forcing his adrenaline into action. His fury made his blood boil. He slapped his own face. Screamed again. A primal howl. A challenge. A call to arms, lighting a fire in the glacial night. Spitting in the face of the New York cold and boldly screaming, *"Fuck you too!!"*

This is not the end of me! I will get away! I will save Charlotte! Charlotte!!

He pushed his broken, frozen body harder. His leg wound ached, his lacerations stung with cold, and his head throbbed with blood loss and delirium. His stubborn heart pounded in rebellion. Freddy Luccio felt a new sensation. Strength.

Come get me, motherfucker! Come on, you fat fuck!!

An ambient light glowed ahead beyond the trees. A low hum carried in the wind, a repeating *whoosh*. The light grew brighter. The din became recognizable as the sounds of traffic. Tires speeding across wet pavement. The trees began to thin out, and up ahead was another fence, promising a road on the other side.

Yes! Come on, come on!

Freddy jumped onto the fence, barely able to grip it with his numb fingers, and threw himself over. He looked ahead and saw only light, but no road. Confused, he struggled back to his feet and staggered forward. The land he stood on came to an end. He realized with a sinking dread that the road was not in front of him, but below him. He looked down and confirmed his fears.

The edge of the dynamite-blasted cliff face towered over the always-roaring Interstate 22. One hundred feet below him, cars and trucks raced in both directions on the busy, four-lane highway. Freddy shook his head.

"Oh, you gotta be fucking *kidding me!*"

He looked back. Hiegren was less than fifty yards away, closing in.

There were two choices, go back or go down.

Charlotte!

Freddy gathered his strength, clenched his jaw, and inched his numb feet forward to the edge of the plunging, icy cliff.

CHARLOTTE COULD NOT FALL ASLEEP.

She lay flat on her back in bed, the lights out. Her favorite PJ's, her childhood teddy bear. Her body was exhausted but her mind was racing. She turned onto her side, looking at the red LED readout on her bedside clock. 3:04 a.m. The harder she tried to fall asleep, the less likely it would happen. The image of Freddy in handcuffs flashed in her head. The cold last words he had said to her.

Tears welled up again but she fought them away. She flipped onto her back, still not comfortable, then shifted to lay on her other side. She was facing the window, snowflakes catching the streetlights as they floated past her field of vision. She did not see the van pulling onto her street.

William Rayburn found a spot and parked.

He killed the headlights and cut the engine, sitting in silence and looking at Charlotte's house. All the lights were off inside. All the neighbors' lights were off. He smiled. Slipped his car keys into his pocket.

Opened the door.

Stepped out into the frigid night.

FREDDY LOWERED his feet onto the first rock shelf he could reach.

His toes were so numb, he could barely tell that his shoes had touched down. His frozen hands gripped the rock face, his cheek and stomach pressed tight to the wall. The cliff wasn't a straight ninety degree drop, but it was steep, dark, frozen, icy. Freddy dared to peek behind him.

The drop was certain death. Vehicles whooshed by on the slick road, their voices echoing up the stone channel. Fifty feet down, the net of steel cables began, hugging the cliff to protect against rockslides. Freddy squeezed his eyes closed, tears freezing on his cheeks as he clung to the side helplessly.

I'm gonna die. Oh Jesus Christ, I'm gonna die.

He forced his left hand to reach down. Numb fingers found a snowy edge to grab and gripped hard. Then his right. He lowered his feet, searching around for the next shelf, but couldn't find anything. He slipped, suddenly holding on with nothing but fingertips. He grunted, strained, tried to hold on.

He lost his grip, slipping, falling. He screamed, chest slapping and dragging against the frozen rocks. His feet collided with the next shelf and his fingers found another spot to grip. His eyes bugged and he desperately sucked frigid air into his lungs. Spider-Man, he was not. Inch by trembling, terrified inch, he lowered himself further toward the highway below.

Charlotte!

Hiegren reached the edge of the cliff, struggling to breathe. He was old and fat, and long past the glory of his high school wrestling days. Peeking over the edge, he could see nothing but the road and the cliff facing him on the opposite side. The footprints and blood trail led him to this spot, so he leaned further over the edge and looked straight down. There he was, the little Italian thorn in his side, ten feet below.

"Fuck. Okay..." Hiegren debated his options. The kid might very well fall and be killed. Then again, he'd made it this far, so he just might escape. The killer cursed and paced, kicking the ground. He couldn't let Freddy escape. And he couldn't bear the thought of him simply dropping to his death. He had to be the one to do it.

He stepped back up to the edge, glaring down. Freddy had made it further. Hiegren growled and pulled the towel away from the deep gash across his head. It would not stop bleeding. Hiegren screamed and chucked the towel over the edge in frustration. The bloody rag sailed past him, and Freddy looked up at the raging monster. Hiegren kicked at the edge, sending rocks and snow falling.

Freddy hugged tight to the cliff as the debris sprinkled over him. He kept moving, one hand at a time, one foot after the other. Desperate, Hiegren chucked his hatchet down, and the blade sparked against the stones beside Freddy's head.

Freddy shrieked and slipped again, falling and sliding five more feet down before catching a grip.

"That's fine!" Hiegren bellowed. "You want to go to Hell tonight? Well, I'm coming with you! You hear? *I'm coming with you!*"

Hiegren turned away from the cliff, sliding backwards on his big belly and letting his feet dangle off the edge. He lowered himself down, searching for a foothold. He found it, gripping the rocks with his chubby fingers, and began climbing down.

Freddy looked below. It was another twenty-five feet before he reached the steel netting. He tried to hurry, feeling the presence of death creeping closer. Hiegren had even less grace than his injured victim, slipping and falling and sliding and skidding across the icy rocks. He howled in pain as he slapped into the boulders, but he was far more concerned with reaching Freddy than he was about his own survival.

The brute let go of his grip, sliding down another shelf, aiming for his prey below. Freddy tried to flee, but Hiegren slid from rock to rock, ignoring the pain, intent on colliding and sending both of them over the edge. He practically jumped the last few feet, reaching out to grab the young man and pull him down to Hell.

They collided.

They fell. They slid on ice and snow.

They tumbled through cold and dark.

Flesh and bone met granite.

Freddy screamed, reaching out.

They smashed into the steel net, entangling in the web and dangling high above the roaring traffic. Freddy clung to the net with all his strength. Hiegren growled and gripped at Freddy's shirt, yanking him down. Hiegren punched him in the gut. Freddy kicked Hiegren in the face. They bashed each other into rock and steel and ice before losing grip and hurtling down.

Cold. Swirling. Pain. Ice.

Hiegren gripped the netting and he stopped. Freddy grabbed the beast's shirt to keep from falling to his death. The weight pulled Hiegren off the netting, and his right foot got tangled in a rung of cable. They plunged another six feet down before Hiegren's ankle stopped their fall, taking the entirety of their weight.

Snap! Hiegren's ankle broke like a twig.

"YIIIEEEAAAHHHH!!!"

He bellowed in agony, hanging upside down by the broken limb as Freddy's weight pulled them both down. Freddy reached for the net and grabbed it, jumping away from Hiegren and trying to climb away. Hiegren pulled himself up enough to swivel his foot out, groaning as it pull away from the snare.

Hiegren jumped again at Freddy.

They collided, the bigger man yanking and pulling and punching. Freddy fought back, hanging on with his left hand and socking Hiegren's face with his right.

"Come here, you little bastard!!"

"Fuck you!!"

"GAAA!!! NNGHHH!!!"

Hiegren pressed Freddy's face against the rock, rubbing it against the sharp coils of steel cables. Freddy pushed back, trying to gouge out the beast's eyes. They dropped further down before catching their grip again, hanging just thirty feet above the highway as their battle raged on.

Charlotte!

Those girls! Those boys!

Aunt Penny!!

Rage flooded Freddy's veins and burned his eyes. He lunged forward and head-butted Hiegren, then shattered his nose with a furious fist again and again like a piston. Hiegren's face was a bloody, pulpy mess. His fingertips barely held on to the cable.

Freddy savagely smashed Hiegren's face into the rocks again and again.

"Just... Fucking... *DIE!!*"

Freddy bashed his bald head into the side of the cliff one more time, then with one final yank, sent him hurtling backwards into space. Hiegren collided with a bone-crunching impact against stone and steel cables, somersaulting down the cascade of rocks and pulverizing nearly every bone in his body on the way.

The bloody, broken pulp that used to call itself James Roy Hiegren toppled off the side of the cliff and rolled into a lane of oncoming traffic. He wearily lifted his pitiful head as the horn of a large truck blared. A bright set of headlights blared in his eyes.

A huge, double-tier automobile transport truck sped his way.

Hiegren had just enough time to say, "Huuuuuuh...?"

With a popping *splat*, the giant flatbed truck smashed through Hiegren like a bug, reducing him to a scarlet streak on the frozen face of I-22. The truck skidded and swerved as the driver slammed on the brakes, the luxury cars on top nearly snapping out of their restraints.

Freddy clung to the steel netting above, watching in awe as oncoming traffic beeped their horns and crashed into a multi-car pile-up below. Vehicles screeched to a halt to avoid the mass of carnage. Snow swirled into the air. Motorists climbed out of their cars to assess the damage.

Charlotte.

Freddy forced himself down. There was no time to lose. Rayburn was on his way. Foot by foot he lowered himself, climbing the rest of the way on torn hands and numb feet. He jumped down onto the road, a collection of cuts and breaks and bruises and frostbite and agony. Headlights were in his eyes. Screams coming from all directions. Blood painted the road. A twisted, mangled mess of gore and pedophile guts smeared the road amongst the jumble of crashed cars.

"I was never wrong about you, you piece of shit."

Charlotte!

Freddy's eyes caught sight of something up the road. It was a yellow, highway emergency call box posted on the median. He ran, limping on his wounded leg. Stumbling, gasping, burning every shred of energy in his body.

He reached the phone, falling into it, dragging himself back to his feet as he yanked the receiver off the hook and held it to his good ear. The phone rang, and a moment later a dispatcher came onto the line.

"Roadside assistance. Are you in a safe location?"

"Get me the police right now!! This is an emergency!!!"

CHAPTER 37
VIOLATOR

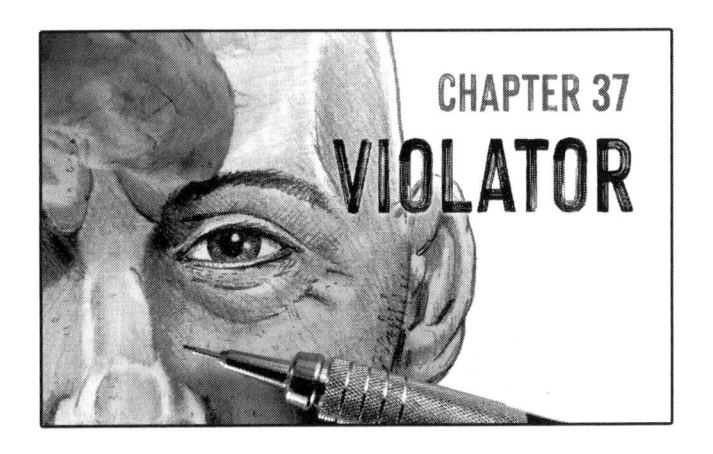

WILLIAM RAYBURN STROLLED up the driveway of the Banino house.

The lights were off. The streets were quiet. The air was frozen and still. He saw his own breath as it wafted through his stained teeth and bristly mustache. The anticipation was getting him hard.

Her window was the one on the second floor, far left. Her father's bedroom was at the far end of the hall, but he had taken to falling asleep on the couch lately. The soft, wan light of the TV coming through the living room window confirmed that habit.

Rayburn smiled.

Oh man, I been waiting for this one. You're special, little Charlotte, yes you are. This whole thing is special. Me and Russ together again. The added fun of having your sweetheart on the phone, making him listen as I do it. Such a cute little voice. Oh, what it'll sound like when you're begging and crying. Using your tight little holes however the fuck I want while I smash your goddamn brains out... Oh, sweet little girl...

The plan was simple. He walked up to the front door. He rang the bell.

BEN BANINO JOLTED awake on the couch.

An infomercial for affordable air-fryers played at a low volume on the TV. It would fry your chicken nice and crispy without all the trans fat. Ben blinked away the bizarre dream he was having, wondering what it was that had awakened him. He sat up, glancing around. The wall clock displayed 3:41 a.m. He grabbed the remote and muted the TV, waiting, his flesh tingling. Silence.

Charlotte came to the top of the stairs.

"Dad?"

Her father held up his hand, indicating for her to be quiet and wait.

He leaned forward, waiting. Listening... Silence. He looked up at his daughter and shrugged. They waited. Darkness lingered...

The doorbell rang again.

A chill shot through Ben's veins and he sprung to his feet. His body trembled. He looked over at the front door with an impending feeling of dread. His hand reached for the drawer beside the couch, sliding it open. He pulled out a stainless steel Taurus 605 snub-nose revolver. Charlotte gripped the railing at the top of the stairs, coiled like a spring.

The doorbell rang again.

"Go to your room and lock the door, baby."

"But..."

"*Go,*" he hissed.

She could not move. Her father snuck barefoot across the carpet, inching towards the front door. The front porch lights were off.

"Wh-Who is it?" Ben Banino took one small step after another. His hands shook, struggling to keep the front sight of the gun pointed ahead. He reached out with his left hand to check the front door. Every lock was in place. The chain was secured. He leaned toward the peep hole. His heart drummed. He leaned closer.

He put his eye up to the peep hole.

The living room window suddenly shattered inward.

Charlotte shrieked.

The Devil himself leapt through the glass in an explosion of slivers and shards. Ben screamed as Rayburn rolled across the floor, then charged him. He squeezed off a shot that missed, and the boogeyman was on him in a second. Rayburn's large gloved hands clasped around Ben's wrist, fighting for the gun.

"Charlotte, call the police!!! Do it now!!! HIDE!!!"

"DADDY!!!" She screamed helplessly from the top of the stairs as the bigger, stronger man threw her father around like a plaything.

"OH MY GOD!!!"

She scrambled back down the dark hallway to her bedroom and grabbed her phone with quivering hands. She slammed and locked the door behind her, dialing 911. Suddenly, she stopped and turned back around, whispering, "Daddy..."

Rayburn used his three hundred pounds to push Ben to the ground, nearly breaking his wrist and shaking the gun loose. Ben fought with every bit of strength he had, and every fiber of his fatherhood. He angled the barrel as well as he could and fired another shot. The .357 round thundered within the confined space, the jacketed hollow-point round grazing across Rayburn's ribs.

Rayburn hissed at the sting, then answered by smashing Ben's gun hand into the floor. After two blows, the bones in Ben's hand were shattered and the gun skittered away under the cabinet. The raging intruder cocked his fat fist and delivered one-two-three-four-five vicious blows to the father's face, knocking him out cold.

He produced his signature weapon, hefting it up high and preparing to reduce the father's head to rubble.

Charlotte ran down the stairs and charged at him, a ceramic lamp in her hands. Her eyes overflowed with tears and fury.

"Get away from my father!!"

She swung the lamp against Rayburn's head, pulverizing the ceramic into shards and knocking him back. He dropped the club, staggered and fell back onto his ass, stunned. Within seconds, he had shaken it off, and looked up at her with a twisted smile.

"Hi, there," he growled, nearly licking his lips.

"No..." Charlotte backed up in horror, realizing she'd provoked the beast. "No..."

Rayburn lurched up to his knees, reaching for his baton. Charlotte yelped and ran back up the stairs, frantically dialing 911. She flew into her room and scrambled to lock the door.

Rayburn found a countertop to hold for balance, hefting himself back up to his feet. He looked back down at the unconscious Ben with a snarl of contempt. *Son of a bitch. Deal with you later. Have to stop little sweetie pie from callin' in the pigs.*

Rayburn groaned to his feet and stalked up the stairs.

"911, what is your emergency?"

"Oh my God! Please! Somebody help us! My Da—"

SMASH.

It took only one kick and the door blasted open. Charlotte knew she must have been screaming, but she heard nothing. Her cell phone flew into the shadows. There was only buzzing. Time moved in slow motion. Splinters and dust floated in the air. She found herself in a corner, curled into a ball.

The man walked through the door.

He was huge. He was disgusting. He was utterly insane. He had stinking teeth and pock-marked skin, and the horror of Hell in his eyes.

He was in her room. In her room.

"NOOOO!!! HEEEEEEELPP!!!"

He unbuttoned his slicker and opened it wide. His erection strained against his pants, and he rubbed it, thumbing the head. He smiled at her, his eyes locked onto hers. The look on his face promised pain. He stepped closer.

"I've been watching you, little Charlotte," Rayburn whispered. "I like you..."

She was cornered, weeping.

"Please, God... *Please, God!* No..."

He gripped the short truncheon. The leather of his gloves creaked as he squeezed the wooden grip. He put his left hand into his mouth, biting into the fingertips of the glove to pull it off. He slipped the glove into his slicker pocket and unbuttoned his pants.

Oh yes, baby. Oh yes.

Charlotte yelped and squealed, trying to scurry away. Rayburn whacked her in the stomach with his billy-club, knocking the air out of her. He flung her across the room and she crashed into her chest of drawers, shattering the mirror on top and knocking her purse onto the floor.

Trinkets and decorations fell around her as she crawled away. Rayburn stepped over her, looking down, enjoying the moment. He took out his phone.

"Time to call your boyfriend, sweetie-pie. I want him to hear every little thing I do. Ohhh, yeah..." He massaged his cock.

"No... Please..."

Rayburn began to dial. He reached for her and she jerked away. The contents of her purse were strewn across the floor. She kicked up at him but he easily deflected the strikes. Her hand found the bottle of pepper spray. His hand found the crown of her head and grabbed a fistful of hair.

She squealed as he pulled her to her feet by her hair, and without thinking, her hand came up with the pepper spray. She pressed the button and sent a geyser of capsaicin into his eyes. He let her go and staggered back, eyes burning in their sockets. He reached for her and swung blindly with the club as she scurried away.

Rayburn grabbed at the back of her oversized t-shirt, but couldn't get a good grip. He tumbled after her through the dark hallways, grabbing for her shirt, swinging his club. She got halfway down the stairs before he fell into her and they spiraled together to the bottom.

"No! NOOOO!!!"

She scampered for the side door, but he was on her like glue, yanking her back down. They crashed through the coffee table in the living room and Charlotte flailed wildly. They battled in a sea of broken glass from when Rayburn first broke in. She kicked and punched and screamed as he bore down, leering at her with burning, bloodshot eyes.

He swung his baton and she kicked it away.

He lashed out again and hit her on the wrist. Then the shoulder. She kicked straight up into his balls and he folded inward, howling in pain. But he held on to her, beating down and getting closer. One strike clipped across her forehead. Once he found his target, it would only take one good blow before there would be no more fighting.

He suddenly stopped when he heard a very familiar sound. Police sirens. He looked out the window to see red and blue lights flashing. *Oh no... Oh, holy shit, no. Can't let them get me. No way!*

Rayburn grunted to his feet, pulling Charlotte up by her hair, trying to formulate a plan. He pulled her back into the central hallway, trying to get to the back door. She thrashed and screamed for help.

The front door burst in.

Two uniformed cops rushed through, guns drawn. Two more followed behind them. Their flashlights flooded Rayburn's eyes. More units arrived on scene, their sirens wailing. The madman knew this was it.

"Drop the weapon!"

"Get on the ground!"

"Drop it, motherfucker!"

Rayburn clenched his billy club.

He pushed Charlotte aside, raised the weapon, and charged.

BOOM! BOOM!

THE SCENE OUTSIDE WAS A SPECTACLE.

It was 4 a.m. and every resident of the block was standing in their doorways, huddled in warm robes and winter coats, or huddled at their windows, watching the madness ensue. The street roared with sound and color as a cacophony of police cruisers, ambulances, and crime scene personnel buzzed around the normally peaceful cul-de-sac. The community was aghast, watching as a large wounded man was rolled out on a gurney, EMT's working to save his life.

In one ambulance, Ben Banino was driven away to St. Francis Hospital, a medic holding an oxygen mask over his face while a nurse took his vitals.

Bagnarol and a female detective were inside the house with Charlotte, sitting in the dining room as uniformed officers and CSI techs processed the scene. Photos were taken. Fingerprints lifted. Blood stains sampled.

The female detective held Charlotte's hand as she sobbed, a blanket thrown over her shoulders. Bagnarol maintained his poker face and wrote down his notes. Miller was outside interviewing the neighbors. An unmarked car arrived on the scene, and agents Jones and Crabtree jumped out to take over.

Detective Harney stood in the driveway, marveling at the scene before him. He watched the medics preparing to lift Rayburn into the next ambulance. Rayburn made eye contact but had to look away. He did not have the strength to have a staring contest with a man like John Harney.

The detective sergeant approached the gurney with slow, deliberate steps.

He looked down at Rayburn, two 9 mm hollow-points in his gut, an oxygen mask on his face, wires hanging out of his arm, and handcuffs locking him to the gurney. The look on Harney's face was unreadable. Too many emotions flowed together as he observed the evil man, reduced to a pathetic nothing on a slab.

"William Henry Rayburn," Harney began, "You are under arrest for murder and attempted murder. You have the right to remain silent..."

The sound of tires skidding squealed through the cul-de-sac as a construction worker's pickup truck hit the brakes. The passenger door flew open.

Freddy Luccio stumbled out.

"Thanks for the ride!"

Streaked with blood and dirt and grease, he was a mess as he staggered forward, limp-running for the house. *Oh my God, I'm too late!* He blew past the other civilian onlookers and shoved away the first deputy who tried to stop him.

"Charlotte!"

"Stop him!" Agent Crabtree commanded.

Law enforcement personnel tried to restrain Freddy, but he pushed past, enraged.

"CHARLOTTE!!!"

She heard his voice outside and turned to see through the front window. There he was fighting to get to her, cops and crime scene techs holding him back. She jumped to her feet, eyes flooding with tears.

"Freddy!"

She sprinted through the front door, desperate to feel his arms around her. Freddy finally saw her, alive and beautiful, and his heart melted. She held open her arms. The police stepped back and let it happen.

They crashed into each other's embrace.

Every endorphin and ounce of reserve energy in his body crashed, and Freddy's legs finally gave out. They collapsed together in a heap, both sobbing uncontrollably. Everyone watched. Bagnarol came outside and stood beside Harney.

Freddy looked up with bleary eyes and saw them standing across the lawn. They nodded to him. He nodded back.

He buried his face into Charlotte's shoulder, squeezed her even tighter, and continued to cry. They held each other and would not let go.

The neighbors watched. Red and blue lights spun.

Snow covered everything and glittered like diamonds. It was a fine American neighborhood. The houses were quaint and average. The people who lived in them had jobs and drove cars. They slept in warm, soft beds, ate hot food and drank cold lemonade. Dogs barked. In one front yard was a snowman built by a father and son.

The sky was black and spattered with stars.

The heavens were clearly visible through the shriveled, leafless trees. Snow settled on every little branch. On the trunk of one tree was an old inscription carved by two smitten lovers. On another was an old piece of paper, stapled there several months earlier, faded and ripped but still clinging to the bark.

It was a wanted poster. A pencil sketch of The Everett Falls Basher. His beady eyes stared straight ahead in an icy, evil glare.

CHAPTER 38

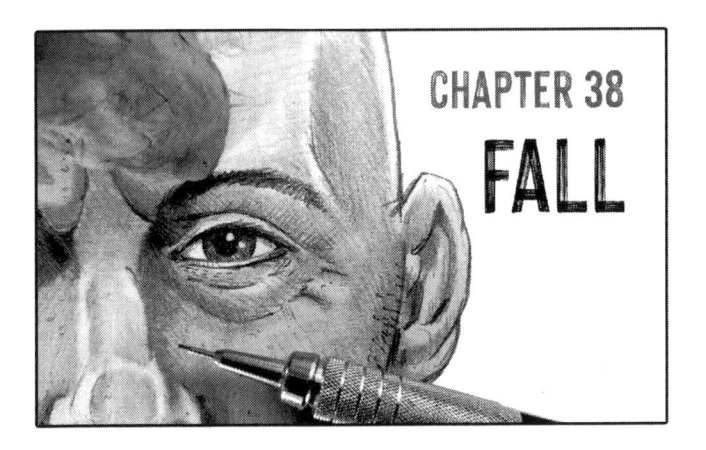

FALL

WHITE PLAINS HAD a different flavor than Everett Falls.

It was bigger, closer to Manhattan on the Metro North line. The streets were wider and the buildings taller, but not by much. There were fewer houses and more apartments. There were hipster bars, skate parks, smoke shops, and bougie coffee shops. Young couples pushed babies in strollers, soccer moms bonded while walking their dogs, and high school sweethearts strolled down sidewalks and licked ice cream cones before it melted down their wrists.

The leaves were changing.

They fluttered orange and yellow as October took its hold. The sun was shining. T-shirts and jeans. Low 70's with a pleasant breeze. The aromas of fresh coffee and pizza in the air. Birds. Laundry hanging out to dry. Children playing stickball in the streets, laughing and shrieking.

Life. The place was alive.

The apartment was modest and comfortable.

Charlotte had been in charge of decorating, placing family photos, plants, mirrors, modern art, and assorted cutesy items in strategic places. A wooden cutting board with the cursive engraving "Freddy and Charlotte" was on display atop the fridge along with photos of them together.

Freddy reclined on the couch, his drawing board across his lap.

He took a sip of seltzer and cranberry, then went back to his drawing. It was whimsical art, cartoony illustrations for an upcoming children's book, *The Turtle and the Butterfly*. The Channel 6 news broadcast played on the TV, and he was only half paying attention. He stretched, wearing his favorite sweats and Judas Priest t-shirt.

A pot of coffee brewed in the kitchen. Charlotte crossed back and forth behind him, slipping into a gray, casual business suit. She hurried into the living room and wrapped her arms around his neck.

"I gotta run, babes," she said, kissing his cheek.

"Mmmm, don't go to work today," he groaned.

"Don't tempt me," she giggled. "How's the book coming?"

Freddy looked down at the cartoonish figures and shrugged. "It's a paying gig," he said, smiling.

Erf! Erf!

The golden retriever puppy was six months old and jumped up on his mommy's leg, vying for attention. She rubbed his head and made kissing noises at him.

"Be nice to Jasper today, okay?"

"Are you kidding?" Freddy balked. "That's my little homie!"

Fucking dogs. She just had to go and get a fucking dog.

"Mm hm, sure," she said. "Well, come here, hottie. Give me some sugar."

Freddy turned and they kissed. She stroked his cheek as she pulled away, tossing her purse over her shoulder.

"Have a good day, sweet cheeks. I love you."

"Love you too."

She smiled and pranced out the door.

Freddy sighed and glanced down at his new canine roommate.

"Just you and me, huh little buddy?" The puppy barked in agreement. Freddy turned back to his drawing when his phone chimed. John Williams, *Close Encounters*. Freddy rolled his eyes and checked the phone. It was a text from Rick:

Did you not get the link I sent you of that one girl on the Deepthroat Addicts website? I want to hear your thoughts! Don't be a CUNT!

Freddy laughed and put the phone down, shaking his head. He continued to draw, but a news bulletin caught his attention. He looked up to see crime scene footage and a local news anchor interviewing witnesses.

"Although a suspect has yet to be identified in the murders of Ryan and Sandy Krysinski, authorities have released a sketch, based on testimony from the couple's ten year-old son..."

Freddy leaned in as a rough composite sketch faded onto the screen. Flat and lifeless, it looked as though it was drawn by a ten year-old. Freddy scoffed.

"God, that's awful," he said.

He ran his hand over his ear, fingers stroking the pink

scar tissue on either side. It was a nervous, involuntary habit. The wounds had all healed, but they'd each left a reminder of pain in their place.

"Police urge anyone with any information to please dial this toll-free tip line. All identities will be kept strictly confidential..."

Freddy read the number aloud as it came on the screen.

"Pfft. 1-800-855-CLUE. Give me a break."

He tried to go back to work, but he stopped. His phone lay right beside him. He could call the tip line. He could volunteer his services, give them a better illustration than the crap they were using. Give them a portrait that actually looked human, with proper facial proportions, lighting and texture. He fought away the urge. None of his business. He scooped up the phone and looked at it in his hands.

He could always text Rick back, or call him.

No.

He scrolled through his contacts. He stopped when he saw one in particular and sighed, looking down at the screen. He hesitated, thought about it. Looked out the window.

It had been over a year now.

They had called him numerous times, but he never called back. Text messages, emails, all unanswered. *I couldn't. Just didn't know what to say.* He couldn't bring himself to go to Penny's funeral either. *Couldn't show my face. Couldn't look them in the eye. This whole thing happened because of me.* But now...

Just do it, jerk-off.

Finally, he tapped on the screen and initiated a call.

He held the phone to his ear and waited.

It rang. There was a click and a woman's voice came on the line.

"Hello?"

"Hi, Mom," Freddy said. "...It's me."

THE END

ALSO BY JESSE D'ANGELO

Lady of the Lake

Skinner

Prey To God

Doomsday Dogs

A Collection of Tails

Jesse D'Angelo is an author and an illustrator, born in New York, raised in California, and currently residing in Tennessee. He is a veteran of the film and television industry and has also worked with law enforcement as a sketch artist on multiple criminal investigations.

He lives with his lovely wife and three cats, writes books, makes pizza and meatballs from scratch, and gets teary-eyed watching cheesy 80's movies.

https://www.jessedangelo.net

Made in the USA
Columbia, SC
23 September 2024